Suspense
A Napoleonic Novel

by

Joseph Conrad

Double9
BOOKS

Suspense
A Napoleonic Novel
by Joseph Conrad

Copyright © 2024

All Rights reserved.

ISBN: 978-93-67142-58-5

Published by

DOUBLE 9 BOOKS

2/13-B, Ansari Road
Daryaganj, New Delhi – 110002
info@double9books.com
www.double9books.com
Tel. 011-40042856

This book is under public domain

ABOUT THE AUTHOR

Joseph Conrad was a Polish-British novelist and short story writer. He is considered as one of the best authors in the English language, despite the fact that he did not speak English effectively until his twenties. He became known as a master prose stylist who introduced a non-English sensibility into English literature. He authored novels and novellas, many of which take place at sea, about crises of human identity in what he perceived as an indifferent, incomprehensible, and amoral world. Conrad is regarded as a literary impressionist by some and an early modernist by others, while his works also incorporate elements of nineteenth-century realism. His storytelling style and anti-heroic characters, such as Lord Jim, impacted a number of authors. Writing near the peak of the British Empire, Conrad drew on his native Poland's national experiences—during nearly all of his life, parcelled out among three occupying empires—as well as his own experiences in the French and British merchant navies, to create short stories and novels that reflect aspects of a European-dominated world, including imperialism and colonialism, and that profoundly explore the human psyche. Apollo took his kid to the Austrian-controlled region of Poland in December 1867, which had enjoyed significant internal freedom and self-government for the previous two years. After seeing Lwow and numerous smaller towns, they relocated to Krakow (Poland's capital until 1596), which is also in Austrian Poland, on February 20, 1869.

CONTENTS

PART I

I

A deep red glow flushed the fronts of marble palaces piled up on the slope of an arid mountain whose barren ridge traced high on the darkening sky a ghostly and glimmering outline. The winter sun was setting over the Gulf of Genoa. Behind the massive shore the sky to the east was like darkening glass. The open water too had a glassy look with a purple sheen in which the evening light lingered as if clinging to the water. The sails of, a few becalmed feluccas looked rosy and cheerful, motionless in the gathering gloom. Their heads were all pointing towards the superb city. Within the long jetty with the squat round tower at the end, the water of the harbour had turned black. A bigger vessel with square sails, issuing from it and arrested by the sudden descent of the calm, faced the red disc of the sun. Her ensign hung down and its colours were not to be made out; but a lank man in a shabby sailor's jacket and wearing a strange cap with a tassel, who lounged with both his arms thrown over the black breech of an enormous piece of ordnance that with three of its monstrous fellows squatted on the platform of the tower, seemed to have no doubt of her nationality; for to the question of a young civilian in a long coat and Hessian boots and with an ingenuous young countenance above the folds of a white neckcloth he answered curtly, taking a short pipe out of his mouth but not turning his head.

"She's Elban."

He replaced his pipe and preserved an unsociable air. The elegant young man with the pleasant countenance, (who was Cosmo, the son of Sir Charles Latham of Latham Hall, Yorkshire), repeated under his breath, "Elban," and remained wrapped up in still contemplation of the becalmed ship with her undistinguishable flag.

It was not till the sun had sunk beneath the waters of the Mediterranean and the undistinguishable flag had been hauled down on board the motionless ship that he stirred and turned his eyes towards the harbour. The nearest prominent object in it was the imposing shape of an English line-of-battle ship moored on the west side not far from the quay. Her tall spars overtopped the roofs of the houses and the English ensign at her flagstaff had been just hauled down and replaced by a lantern that looked strange in the clear twilight. The forms of shipping crowded towards the head of the harbour were merging into one another. Cosmo let his eyes wander over the circular platform of the tower. The man leaning over the gun went on smoking with indifference.

"Are you the guardian of this tower?" asked the young man.

The other gave him a sidelong glance and made answer without changing his attitude and more as if speaking to himself:

"This is now an unguarded spot. The wars are over."

"Do they close the door at the bottom of this tower at night?" enquired Cosmo.

"That is a matter worth consideration especially for those like you, for instance, who have a soft bed to go to for the night."

The young than put his head on one side and looked at his interlocutor with a faint smile.

"You don't seem to care," he said. "So I conclude I need not. As long as you are content to stay here I am safe enough. I followed you up the stairs, you know." The man with the pipe stood up abruptly. "You followed me here? Why did you do that, in the name of all the saints?"

The young man laughed as if at a good joke. "Because you were walking in front of me. There was nobody else in view near the Mole. Suddenly you disappeared. Then I saw that the door at the bottom of the tower was open and I walked up the stairs on to this platform. And I would have been very surprised if I hadn't found you here."

The man in the strange cap ornamented with a tassel had taken his pipe out of his mouth to listen. "That was all?"

"Yes, that was all."

"Nobody but an Englishman would behave like that," commented the other to himself, a slight appearance of apprehension passing over his features. "You are an eccentric people."

"I don't see anything eccentric in what I've done. I simply wanted to walk out of the town. The Mole was as good as any other part. It is very pleasant here."

A slight breeze touched the two men's faces, while they stood silent, looking at each other. "I am but an idle traveller," said Cosmo easily. "I arrived this morning by land. I am glad I had the idea to come out here to behold your town glowing in the sunset and to get a sight of a vessel belonging to Elba. There can't be very many of them. But you, my friend . . ."

"I have as much right to idle away my time here as any English traveller," interrupted the man hastily.

"It is very pleasant here," repeated the young traveller, staring into the dusk which had invaded the platform of the tower.

"Pleasant?" repeated the other. "Yes, perhaps. The last time I was on this platform I was only ten years old. A solid round shot was spinning and rattling all over the stone floor. It made a wondrous disturbance and seemed a living thing full of fury."

"A solid shot!" exclaimed Cosmo, looking all over the smooth flagstones as if expecting to see the traces of that visitation. "Where did it come from?"

"It came from an English brig belonging to Milord Keith's Squadron. She stood in quite close and opened fire on us. . . . Heaven only knows why. The audacity of your people! A single shot from one of those big fellows," he continued, slapping the enormous bulging breech of the gun by his side, "would have been enough to sink her like a stone."

"I can well believe it. But the fearlessness of our seamen has ceased to astonish the world long ago," murmured the young traveller.

"There are plenty of fearless people in the world, but luck is even better than courage. The brig sailed away unscathed. Yes, luck is even better than courage. Surer than wisdom and stronger than justice. Luck is a great thing. It is the only thing worth having on one's side. And you people have always had it. Yes, signore, you belong to a lucky nation or else you would not be standing here on this platform looking across the water in the direction of that crumb of land that is the last refuge of your greatest enemy."

Cosmo leaned over the stone parapet near the embrasure of the gun on the other side of which the man with the short pipe in his hand made a vaguely emphatic gesture: "I wonder what thoughts pass through your head," he went on in a quiet detached tone. "Or perhaps you are too young yet to have many thoughts in your head. Excuse my liberty, but I have always heard that one may be frank in speech with an Englishman; and by your speech there can be no doubt of you being of that nation."

"I can assure you I have no thoughts of hatred. . . . Look, the Elban ship is getting farther away. Or is it only the darkness that makes her seem so?"

"The night air is heavy. There is more wind on the water than up here, where we stand; but I don't think she has moved away. You are interested in that Elban ship, signore."

"There is a fascination now about everything connected with that island," confessed the ingenuous traveller. "You have just said that I was too young to think. You don't seem so very much older than myself. I wonder what thoughts you may have."

"The thoughts of a common man, thoughts that could be of no interest to an English milord," answered the other, in a grimly deprecatory tone.

"Do you think that all Englishmen are lords?" asked Cosmo, with a laugh.

"I didn't think. I went by your appearance. I remember hearing an old man once say that you were a lordly nation."

"Really!" exclaimed the young man and laughed again in a low, pleasant note. "I remember hearing of an old man who called us a nation of traders."

"*Nazione di mercante*," repeated the man slowly. "Well, that may be true too. Different men, different wisdoms."

"This didn't occur to me," said Cosmo, seating himself with a little spring on the stone parapet of the tower. He rested one foot on the massive gun-carriage and fixed his clear eyes on the dark red streak on the western sky left by the retreating sun like a long gash inflicted on the suffering body of the universe. . . . "Different men, different wisdoms," he repeated, musingly. "I suppose it must be. People's lives are so very different. . . . And of what kind was the wisdom of your old man?"

"The wisdom of a great plain as level almost as the sea," said the other gravely. "His voice was as unexpected when I heard it as your own, signore. The evening shadows had closed about me just after I had seen to the west, on the edge of the world as it were, a lion miss his spring on a bounding deer. They went away right into the glow and vanished. It was as though I had dreamed. When I turned round there was the old man behind me no farther away than half the width of this platform. He only smiled at my startled looks. His long silver locks stirred in the breeze. He had been watching me, it seems, from folds of ground and from amongst reed beds for nearly half a day, wondering what I might be at. I had come ashore to wander on the plain. I like to be alone sometimes. My ship was anchored in a bight of this deserted coast a good many miles away, too many to walk back in the dark for a stranger like me. So I spent the night in that old man's ranch, a hut of grass and reeds, near a little piece of water peopled by a multitude of birds. He treated me as if I had been his son. We talked till dawn and when the sun rose I did not go back to my ship. What I had on board of my own was not of much value, and there was certainly no one there to address me as "My son" in that particular tone—you know what I mean, signore."

"I don't know—but I think I can guess," was the answer whose light-hearted yet earnest frankness was particularly boyish and provoked a smile on the part of the older man. In repose his face was grave. His English interlocutor went on after a pause. "You deserted from your ship to join a hermit in a wilderness simply because the tone of his voice appealed to your heart. Is that your meaning?"

"You have guessed it, signorino. Perhaps there was more in it than that. There is no doubt about it that I did desert from my ship."

"And where was that?"

"On the coast of South America," answered the man from the other side of the big gun, with sudden curtness. "And now it is time for us to part."

But neither of them stirred and for some time they remained silent, growing shadowy to each other on the massive tower, which itself, in the advancing night, was but a gray shadow above the dark and motionless sea.

"How long did you stay with that hermit in the desert?" asked Cosmo. "And how did you leave him?"

"Signore, it was he who left me. After I had buried his body I had nothing more to do there. I had learned much during that year."

"What is it you learned, my friend? I should like to know."

"Signore, his wisdom was not like that of other men and it would be too long to explain to you here on this tower and at this late hour of the day. I learned many things. How to be patient, for instance. . . . Don't you think, signore, that your friends or the servants at the inn may become uneasy at your long absence?"

"I tell you I haven't been much more than two hours in this town and I have spoken to nobody in it till I came upon you, except of course to the people at the inn."

"They may start looking for you."

"Why should they trouble their heads? It isn't late yet. Why should they notice my absence?"

"Why? . . . Simply because your supper may be ready by this time," retorted the man impatiently.

"It may be, but I am not hungry yet," said the young man casually. "Let them search for me all over the town if they like." Then in a tone of interest, "Do you think they would think of looking for me here?" he asked.

"No. This is the last spot anybody would think of," muttered the other as if to himself. He raised his voice markedly, "We must part indeed. Good-night, signore."

"Good-night."

The man in the seaman's jacket stared for a moment, then with a brusque movement cocked his cap with the strange tassel more on the side of his head. "I am not going away from this spot," he said.

"I thought you were. Why did you wish me good-night then?"

"Because we must part."

"I suppose we must some time or other," agreed Cosmo in a friendly voice. "I should like to meet you again."

"We must part at once, this moment, on this tower."

"Why?"

"Because I want to be left alone," answered the other after the slightest of pauses.

"Oh, come! Why on earth do you want to be left alone? What is it you could do here?" protested the other with great good humour. Then as if struck by an amusing notion, "Unless indeed you want to practise incantations," he continued lightly, "and perhaps call the Evil One to your side." He paused. "There are people, you know, that think it can be done," he added in a mocking tone.

"They are not far wrong," was the other's ominous reply. "Each man has a devil not very far from his elbow. Don't argue, signore, don't call him up in me! You had better say no more and go in peace from here."

The young traveller did not change his careless attitude. The man in the cap heard him say quietly, almost in a tone of self-communion:

"I prefer to stay in peace here."

It was indeed a wonderful peace. The sound of their quiet voices did not seem to affect it in the least. It had an enormous and overpowering amplitude which seemed rather to the man in the cap to take the part of the Englishman's calm obstinacy against his growing anger. He couldn't repress an impulsively threatening movement in the direction of his inconvenient companion but it died out in perplexity. He pushed his cap still more on one side and simply scratched his head.

"You are one of those people that are accustomed to have their own way. Well, you can't have your way this time. I have asked you quietly to leave me alone on this tower. I asked you as man to man. But if you won't listen to reason I . . ."

Cosmo, putting the palms of his hands against the edge of the parapet, sprang lightly nearly to the middle of the platform and landed without a stagger. His voice was perfectly even.

"Reason is my only guide," he declared. "But your request looks like mere caprice. For what can you possibly have to do here? The sea birds are gone to sleep and I have as much right to the air up here as you. Therefore . . ."

A thought seemed to strike him. "Surely this can't be your trysting place," he commented in a changed tone through which pierced a certain sympathy.

A short scornful laugh from the other checked him and he muttered to himself soberly, "No. Altogether unfit . . . amongst those grim old guns." He raised his voice. "All I can do is to give you all the room." He backed away from the centre of the platform and perched himself this time on the massive breech of a sixty-pounder. "Go on with your incantations," he said then to the tall and dim figure whose immobility appeared helpless for a moment. It broke the short period of silence, saying deliberately:

"I suppose you are aware that at any time since we have begun to talk together it was open to me to fling myself upon you unawares as you sat on the parapet and knock you over to the bottom of this tower?" He waited a moment, then in a deeper tone, "Will you deny it?" he said.

"No, I won't deny it," was the careless answer. "I hadn't thought to be on my guard. But I can swim."

"Don't you know there is a border of big blocks of stone there? It would have been a terrible death. . . . And now, will the signore do what I ask him and return to his inn which is a much safer place than this platform?"

"Safety is not a great inducement; and I don't believe for a moment you ever thought of attacking me in a treacherous manner."

"Well," the tall shadowy figure crowned by the shape of the strange cap admitted reluctantly. "Well, since you put it in those words, signore, I did not."

"You see! I believe you are a fine fellow. But as it is I am under no sort of obligation to listen to you."

"You are crafty," burst out the other violently. "It's in the blood. How is one to deal with people like you?"

"You could try to drive me off," suggested the other.

There was no answer for a time, then the tall figure muttered reflectively to itself.

"After all—he's an Englishman."

"I don't think myself invincible on that account," observed Cosmo calmly.

"I know. I have fought against English soldiers in Buenos Ayres. I was only thinking that, to give the devil his due, men of your nation don't consort with spies or love tyranny either. . . . Tell me, is it true that you have only been two hours in this town?"

"Perfectly true."

"And yet all the tyrants of the world are your allies," the shadowy man pursued his train of thought half aloud.

The no less shadowy traveller remarked quietly into the gathering night:

"You don't know who my friends are."

"I don't, but I think you are not likely to go with a tale to the Austrian spies or consort with the Piedmontese *sbirri*. As to the priests who are poking their noses everywhere, I . . ."

"I don't know a single soul in Italy," interrupted the other.

"But you will soon. People like you make acquaintances everywhere. But it's idle talk with strangers that I fear. Can I trust you as an Englishman not to talk of what you may see?"

"You may. I can't imagine what unlawful thing you are about to commit here. I am dying from curiosity. Can it be that you are really some sort of sorcerer? Go on! Trace your magic circle if that is your business, and call up the spirits of the dead."

A low grunt was the only answer to this speech uttered in a tone between jest and earnest. Cosmo watched from the breech of his gun with intense interest the movements of the man who objected so strongly to his presence but who now seemed to pay no attention to him at all. They were not the movements of a magician in so far that they certainly had nothing to do with the tracing of circles. The figure had stepped over to the seaward face of the tower and seemed to be pulling endless things out of the breast pocket of his jacket. The young Englishman got down from the breech of the gun, without ceasing to peer in a fascinated way, and moved closer step by step till he threw himself back with an exclamation of astonishment. "By heavens! The fellow is going to fish." . . . Cosmo remained mute with surprise for a good many seconds and then burst out loudly:

"Is this what you displayed all this secrecy for? This is the worst hoax I ever . . ."

"Come nearer, signore, but take care not to tangle all my twine with your feet. . . . Do you see this box?"

The heads of the two men had come together confidentially and the young traveller made out a cylindrical object which was in fact a round tin box. His companion thrust it into his hand with the request, "Hold it for me a moment, signore," and then Cosmo had the opportunity to ascertain that the lid of it was hermetically sealed. The man in the strange cap dived into the pocket of his breeches for flint and steel. The Englishman beheld with surprise his lately inimical companion squeeze himself between the massive tube of the piece of ordnance and the wall of stone and wriggle outwards into the depth of, the thick embrasure till nothing of him remained visible but his black stockings and the soles of his heavy shoes. After a time his voice came deadened along the thickness of the wall:

"Will you hand me the box now, signore?"

Cosmo, enlisted in these mysterious proceedings, the nature of which was becoming clear enough to him, obeyed at once, and approaching the embrasure thrust the box in at the full length of his arm till it came in contact with the ready hand of the man who was lying flat on his stomach with his head projecting beyond the wall of the tower. His groping hand found and snatched away the box. The twine was attached to the box and at once its length laid on the platform began to run out till the very end disappeared. Then the man lying prone within the thickness of the gun embrasure lay still as death and the young traveller strained his ears in the absolute silence to catch the slightest sound at the foot of the tower. But all he could hear was the faint sound of some distant clock striking somewhere in the town. He waited a little longer, then in the cautious tone of a willing accomplice murmured within the opening:

"Got a bite yet?"

The answer came hardly audible:

"No. But this is the very hour."

Cosmo felt his interest growing. And yet the facts in themselves were not very exciting, but all this had the complexion and the charm of an unexpected adventure, heightened by its mystery, playing itself out before that old town towering like a carved hill decorated with lights that began to appear quickly on the sombre and colossal mass of that lofty shore. The last gleam had died out in the west. The harbour was dark except for the lantern at the stern of the British ship of the line. The man in the embrasure made a slight movement. Cosmo became more alert but apparently nothing happened. There was no murmur of voices, splash of water, or sign of the slightest stir all round the tower. Suddenly the man in the embrasure began to wriggle back on to the platform and in a very few minutes stood up to his full height facing the unexpected helper.

"She has come and gone," he said. "Did you hear anything, signore?"

"Not a sound. She might have been the ghost of a boat—for you are alluding to a boat, are you not?"

"*Si*. And I hope that if any eye on shore had made her out it had taken her for only a ghost. Of course that English vessel of war rows guard at night. But it isn't to look out for ghosts."

"I should think not. Ghosts are of no account. Could there be anything more futile than the ghost of a boat?"

"You are one of the strong-minded, signore. Ghosts are the concern of the ignorant—yet who knows? But it does sound funny to talk of the ghost of a boat, a thing of brute matter. For wouldn't a ghost be a thing of spirit, a man's soul itself made restless by grief or love, or remorse or anger? Such are the stories that one hears. But the old hermit of the plain, of whom I spoke, assured me that the dead are too glad to be done with life to make trouble on earth."

"You and your hermit!" exclaimed Cosmo in a boyish and marvelling tone. "I suppose it is no use me asking you what I have been just helping you in."

"A little smuggling operation, signore. Surely, signore, England has custom houses and therefore must have smugglers too."

"One has heard of them of course. But I wouldn't mind a bet that there is not one of them that resembles you. Neither do I believe that they deal with packages as small as the one you lowered into that ghostly boat. You saw her of course. There was a boat."

"There was somebody to cut the string, as you see, signore. Look, here is all that twine, all of it but a little piece. It may have been a man swimming in the dark water. A man with a soul, fit to make a ghost of . . . let us call him a ghost, signore." "Oh yes, let us," the other said lightly. "I am sure that when I wake up to-morrow all this will seem to me a dream. Even now I feel inclined to pinch myself."

"What's that for, in Heaven's name?"

"It's a saying we have in our country. Yes, you, your hermit, our talk, and this very tower, all this will be like a dream."

"I would say 'nothing better' if it was not that most people are only too ready to talk about their dreams. No, signore, let all this be to you of less consequence than if it were a tale of ghosts, of mere ghosts in which you do not believe. You forced yourself on me as if you were the lord of this place, but I feel friendly enough to you."

"I didn't ask for your friendship," retorted the young traveller in a clear voice so void of all offence that the other man accepted it for a mere statement of a fact.

"Certainly not. I spoke of my own feelings, and though I am, you may say, a new-comer and a stranger in my own native city, I assure you it is better to have me for a friend than for an enemy. And the best thing of all would be to forget all about me. It would be also the kindest thing you could do."

"Really?" said Cosmo in a tone of sympathy. "How can you expect me to forget the most extraordinary thing that ever happened to me in all my life?"

"In all your life! H'm! You have a long life before you yet, signorino."

"Oh, but this is an adventure."

"That's what I mean. You have so many marvellous adventures before you, signorino, that this one is sure to be forgotten very soon. Then why not at once?"

"No, my friend, you don't seem somehow a person one could easily forget."

"I— — God forbid. . . . Good-night, signore."

No sooner were the words out of his mouth than the man in the cap bounded across the platform, dived into the black square opening on its landward side, and ran down the steps so lightly that not a sound reached the ears of the other. Cosmo went down the winding stair, but cautiously in the profound darkness. The door at the bottom stood open and he stepped out on to the deserted jetty. He could see on it nothing in the shape of a fleeting shadow.

On the very edge of the shore a low little building with three arcades sent a dim gleam of light through its open door. It seemed to be a sort of guardroom, for there was a sentry, an Austrian soldier apparently, in a white coat. His duty, however, seemed to be concerned with the landing-steps in front of the guardhouse, and he let the young traveller pass on as though he had not seen him at all. Dark night had settled upon the long quay. Here and there a dim street lamp threw a feeble light on the uneven stones which the feet of the young traveller with his springy walk seemed hardly to touch. The pleasurable sensation of something extraordinary having happened to him accelerated his movements. He was also feeling very hungry and he was making haste towards his inn to dine first and then to think his adventure over, for there was a strong conviction within him that he certainly had had an adventure of a nature at the same time stimulating and obscure.

II

Cosmo Latham had an inborn faculty of orientation in strange surroundings, most invaluable in a cavalry officer, but of which he had never made much use, not even during the few months when he served as a cornet of horse in the Duke of Wellington's army in the last year of the peninsular campaign. There had been but few occasions to make use of it for a freshly joined subaltern. It stood him in good stead that night, however, while making his way to his inn in a town in which he was a complete stranger, for it allowed him, with but little concern for the direction he took, to think of his home which he loved for itself, every stone and every tree of it—and of the two people he left there, whom he loved too, each in a different way: his father, Sir Charles, and his sister Henrietta.

Latham Hall, a large straggling building showing traces of many styles, flanked by a romantic park and commanding a vast view of the Yorkshire hills, had been the hereditary home of Lathams from the times before the Great Rebellion. That it escaped confiscation then might have been the effect of the worldly prudence of the Latham of the time. He probably took good care not to shock persons of position and influence. That, however, was not the characteristic of the later Lathams down to Sir Charles, Cosmo's father.

Sir Charles's unconventional individuality had never been understood by his country neighbours. Born endowed with a good intellect, a lively imagination, and a capacity for social intercourse, it had been his fate, owing to the idiosyncrasies of his own father, to spend his early youth in the depths of Yorkshire in surroundings not at all congenial to his tastes. Later he served for a time in the Guards; but he very soon left the army to make an extended tour in France and Italy. In those last days before the Revolution *le chevalier* Latham obtained a great social recognition in Paris and Versailles amongst the very best people, not so much by his brilliance as by the depth of his character and the largeness of his ideas. But suddenly he tore himself away from his friendships and successes and proceeded to Italy. There, amongst the members of the English colony in Florence, he met the two Aston girls and, for some reason or other, became a great favourite with their widowed mother. But at the end of some months he suddenly made up his mind to return home. During a long, sleepless night, which he spent pacing up and down in the agony of an internal struggle with himself in the magnificent rooms of his lodgings in Florence, he concluded that he would go home by sea. It was the easiest way of avoiding coming near Paris. He had heard not long before that the best friends he had made in the brilliant society he had frequented in France, the Marquis and the Marquise d'Armand, had a daughter born to them. At Leghorn on the very eve of embarking he had another struggle with himself—but he went by sea. By the time when, after a long sea passage, he put his foot on native soil he had renounced the idea of hurrying on north to shut himself up in his country home. He lingered in London, disdainful and idle, and began reluctantly to fall into the ways of a man about town, when a friend returning from Italy brought him news that Miss Aston was going to marry a Tuscan nobleman of mature years, and, as a piece of queer Florentine gossip, that if the younger sister. Miss Molly Aston, had refused two suitors in quick succession it was because she regarded herself in some way as being engaged to him, Charles Latham.

Whether stung by his conscience or urged by indignation Sir Charles started impulsively for Italy, travelling across the south of France. It was a long road. At first he had been amazed, confounded, and angry; but before he came to the end of his journey he had time to reflect upon what might have easily become an absurd and odious situation. He said to himself that a lot of bother of one sort and another would be saved by his marrying Molly Aston. He did so, to the applause of all right-minded people, and at the end of two years spent abroad came home with his wife to shut himself up in his ancestral hall commanding the view of a wide and romantic landscape, which he thought one of the finest in the world.

Molly Aston had been beautiful enough in her time to inspire several vagrant poets and at least one Italian sculptor; but as Cosmo grew older he began to understand that his mother had been a nonentity in the family life. The greatest piece of self-assertion on her part was his name. She had insisted on calling him Cosmo because the Astons counted, far back in the past, an ancestress of Florentine origin, supposed to have been a connection of the Medici family. Cosmo was fair, and the name was all about him that he had received from his mother. Henrietta was a type of dark beauty. Lady Latham died when both her children were still young. In her life she adorned Latham Hall in the same way as a statue might have adorned it. Her household power was limited to the ordering of the dinner. With habits of meticulous order and a marvellously common-place mind she had a temperament which, if she had not fallen violently in love at the age of eighteen with the same man whom she married, would have made her fond of society, of amusement, and perhaps even of dissipation. But her only amusement and dissipation consisted of writing long letters to innumerable relations and friends all over the world, of whom after her marriage she saw but very little. She never complained. Her hidden fear of all initiative and the secret ardour of her temperament found their fulfilment in an absolute submission to Sir Charles's will. She would never have dreamed of asking for horses for a visit in the neighbourhood, but when her husband remarked, "I think it would be advisable for you, my lady, to call at such and such a house," her face would light up, she would answer with alacrity, "Certainly, Sir Charles," and go off to array herself magnificently indeed (perhaps because of that drop of Medici blood), but also with great taste.

As the years went on Sir Charles aged more than he ought to have done, and even began to grow a little stout, but no one could fail to see that he had been a very handsome man in his time and that his wife's early infatuation for him was justified in a way. In politics he was a partisan of Mr. Pitt rather than a downright Tory. He loved his country, believed in its greatness, in its superior virtue, in its irresistible power. Nothing could shake his fidelity to national prejudices of every sort. He had no great liking for grandees and mere aristocrats, despised the fashionable world, and would have nothing whatever to do with any kind of "upstart." Without being gentle he was naturally kind and hospitable. His native generosity was so well known that no one was surprised when he offered the shelter of his Yorkshire house to a family of French refugees, the Marquis and the Marquise d'Armand and their little daughter Adèle. They had arrived in England in a state of almost complete destitution but with two servants who had shared the dangers and the miseries of their flight from the excesses of the Revolution.

The presence of all these people at Latham Hall which, considered at first as a temporary arrangement, was to last for some years, did not affect in the least Lady Latham's beautifully dressed, idle equanimity. Had not the D'Armands been Sir Charles's intimate friends years ago, in France? But she had no curiosity. She was vaguely impressed by the fact that the Marquise was a god-daughter of the Queen of Naples. For the rest it was only so many people more in the servants' hall, at the dinner table, and in the drawing room where the evenings were spent.

High up on one of the walls a lamp with a shaded reflector concentrated its light on the yellow satin coat on the half-length portrait of a rubicund Latham in a white coburg, which but for the manly and sensitive mouth might have been the portrait of his own coachman. Apart from that spot of beautiful colour the vast room with its windows giving on a terrace (from which Sir Charles was in the habit of viewing sunsets) remained dim with an effect of immensity in which the occupants, and even Sir Charles himself, acquired the appearance of unsubstantial shadows uttering words that had to travel across long, almost unlighted distances.

On one side of the mantelpiece of Italian marbles (a late addition designed by Sir Charles himself) Lady Latham's profuse jewellery sparkled about her splendid and restful person posed placidly on a sofa. Opposite her, the Marquise would be lying down on a deep couch with one of Lady Latham's shawls spread over her feet. The D'Armands in their flight from the Terror had saved very little besides their lives, and the Marquise d'Armand's life had by this time become a very precarious possession.

Sir Charles was perhaps more acutely aware of this than the Marquis her husband. Sir Charles remembered her gentle in her changing moods of gaiety and thought, charming, active, fascinating, and certainly the most intelligent as she was the most beautiful of the women of the French court. Her voice reaching him clear but feeble across the drawing room had a pathetic appeal; and the tone of his answers was tinged with the memory of a great sentiment and with the deference due to great misfortunes. From time to time Lady Latham would make a remark in a matter-of-fact tone which would provoke something resembling curtness in Sir Charles's elaborately polite reply, and the thought that woman would have made the very Lord's Prayer sound prosaic. And then in the long pauses they would pursue their own thoughts as perplexed and full of unrest as the world of seas and continents that began at the edge of the long terrace graced by gorgeous sunsets; the wide world filled with the strife of ideas and the struggle of nations in perhaps the most troubled time of its history.

From the depths of the Italian chimneypiece the firelight of blazing English logs would fall on Adèle d'Armand sitting quietly on a low stool near her mother's couch. Her fair hair, white complexion, and dark blue eyes contrasted strongly with the deeper colour scheme of Henrietta Latham, whose locks were rich chestnut brown and whose eyes had a dark lustre full of intelligence rather than sentiment. Now and then the French child would turn her head to look at Sir Charles, for whom in her silent existence she had developed a filial affection.

In those days Adèle d'Armand did not see much of her own father. Most of the time the Marquis was away. Each of his frequent absences was an act of devotion to his exiled Princes, who appreciated it no doubt but found devotion only natural in a man of that family. The evidence of their regard for the Marquis took the shape mainly of distant and dangerous missions to the courts of north Germany, and northern Italy. In the general disruption of the old order those missions were all futile, because no one ever stopped an avalanche by means of plots and negotiations. But in the

Marquis the perfect comprehension of that profound truth was mingled with the sort of enthusiasm that fabricates the very hopes on which it feeds. He would receive his instructions for those desperate journeys with extreme gravity and depart on them without delay, after a flying visit to the Hall to embrace his ailing wife and his silent child and hold a grave conference with his stately English friend from whom he never concealed a single one of his thoughts or his hopes. And Sir Charles approved of them both; because the thoughts were sober and absolutely free from absurd illusions common to all exiles, thus appealing to Sir Charles's reason and also to his secret disdain of all great aristocracies—and the second, being based on the Marquis's conviction of England's unbroken might and consistency, seemed to Sir Charles the most natural thing in the world.

They paced a damp laurel-bordered walk together for an hour or so: Sir Charles lame and stately like a disabled child of Jupiter himself, the Marquis restraining his stride and stooping with a furrowed brow to talk in measured, level tones. The wisdom of Sir Charles expressed itself in curt sentences in which scorn for men's haphazard activities and shortsighted views was combined with a calm belief in the future.

After the peace of Amiens the Compte d'Artois, the representative of the exiled dynasty in England, having expressed the desire to have the Marquis always by his side, the Marquise and Adèle left Latham Hall for the poverty and the makeshifts of the life of well-nigh penniless exiles in London. It was as great a proof of devotion to his royal cause as any that could be given. They settled down in a grimy house of yellow brick in four rooms up a very narrow and steep staircase. For attendants they had a dark mulatto maid, brought as a child from the West Indies before the Revolution by an aunt of the Marquise, and a man of rather nondescript nationality called Bernard, who had been at one time a hanger-on in the country house of the D'Armands, but following the family in its flight and its wanderings before they had found refuge in England, had displayed unexpected talents as a general factotum. Life at Latham Hall had bored him exceedingly. The sense of complete security was almost too much for his patience. The regularity of the hours and the certitude of abundant meals depressed his spirits at times. The change to London revived him greatly, for there he had something to do and found daily occasion to display his varied gifts. He went marketing in the early morning, dusted the room he called the salon, cooked the meals, inspired and made happy by the large white smile of Mlle. Aglae, the Negress, with whom he was very much in love. At twelve o'clock, after tidying himself a bit, he would go in on the tips of his heavy square shoes and carry the Marquise from her room to the sofa in the salon with elaborate sureness and infinite respect, while Aglae followed with pillow, shawl, and smelling bottle, wearing a forced air of gravity. Bernard was acutely aware of her presence and would be certain—the Marquise once settled on her sofa—to get a flash of a white grin all to himself. Later Mlle. Adèle, white and fair, would go out visiting, followed by Aglae as closely as night follows day; and Bernard would watch them down the depths of the staircase in the hope of catching a sight of a quickly upturned dark brown face with fine rolling eyes. This would leave him happy for the rest of the afternoon. In the evening his function was to announce visitors who had toiled up the stairs: some of the first names in France that had come trudging on foot through the mud or dust of the squalid streets to fill the dimly lighted room which was the salon of the Marquise d'Armand. For those duties Bernard would put on a pair of white stockings, which Miss Aglae washed for him every second day, and encase his wide shoulders in a very tight green shabby jacket with large metal buttons. Miss Aglae always found a minute or two to give him a hasty inspection and a brush-down. Those were delightful instants. Holding his breath and in a state of rigid beatitude he turned about as ordered in gay whispers by his exotic lady-love. Later he would sit on a stool outside the closed door listening to the well-bred soft uproar of conversation; and when the guests began to depart he lighted them downstairs, holding a tallow dip in a small candlestick over the banister of the landing. When his duties for the day were over he made up for himself a bed on the floor of a narrow passage which separated the living rooms from a sort of large cupboard in which Miss Aglae reposed from her daily labours. Bernard, lying under a pair of thin blankets and with the tallow candle burning on the floor, kept slumber off till Miss Aglae stuck out her head tied up in an old red foulard—nothing but her head through the crack of the door—in order to have a little whispered conversation. That was the time when the servants exchanged their views and communicated to each other their ideas and observations. The black maid's were shrewder than the white factotum's. Being a personal attendant of the two ladies she had occasion to see and hear more than her admirer. They commented on the evident decline of the Marquise's health, not dolefully but simply as a significant fact of the situation; on the Marquis's manner of daily life which had become domestic and almost sedentary. He went out every day but now he never went away for weeks and months as he used to before. Those sudden and mysterious missions for which a misanthropic Yorkshire baronet had paid out of his own pocket had come to an end. A Marquis d'Armand could not be sent out as a common spy and there was now no court in Christendom that would dare to receive an emissary, secret or open, of the royal exiles. Bernard, who could read, explained these things shortly to Miss Aglae. All great folk were terrified at that Bonaparte. He made all the generals tremble. On those facts Miss Aglae would have it that he must be a sorcerer. Bernard had another view of Napoleonic greatness. It was nothing but the power of lies. And on one occasion after a slight hesitation he burst out: "Shall I tell you the truth about him. Miss Aglae?" The tied-up black head protruding through the crack of the door nodded assent many times in the dim light of the tallow dip. "Well then," continued Bernard with another desperate effort, "he is of no account."

Miss Aglae repressed with difficulty the loud burst of laughter which was the usual expression of her unsophisticated emotions. She had heard ladies and gentlemen in the salon express a very similar opinion of Bonaparte, but she thought suddenly of Miss Adèle and emitted a sigh.

"He seems to get him paw on the whole world, anyhow. What sort of a fellow is he, Bernard? You have seen him."

Bernard had seen the fellow. He assured Miss Aglae that he was a miserable shrimp of a man in big boots and with lank hair hanging down his yellow cheeks. "I could break him in two like a straw if I could only get him into my hands."

Believing it implicitly, the black maid suggested that Bernard should go and do it.

"I would go at once," said the faithful follower. "But if I went I would never see you again. He has always a hundred thousand men around him."

At this Miss Aglae, who had begun to smile, ended with a sigh of such a deeply sorrowful nature that Bernard assured her that the time would come, yes, some day the time would come when everybody would get back his own. Aglae was ready to believe this prophecy. But meantime there was Miss Adèle. That sweet child was now ready to get married, but everybody was so very poor. Bernard put on a sentimental expression in the dim light of the tallow dip, the flame of which swayed by the side of his straw mattress and made the shadow of his head, protected by a nightcap, dance too, high up the wall of the drafty passage. Timidly he muttered of love. That would get over all the difficulties.

"You very stupid man, Mr. Bernard. Love! What sort of trash you talk? Love don't buy fish for dinner." Then with sudden anxiety she inquired: "Have you got money for marketing to-morrow?" Bernard had the money. Not much, but he had the money. "Then you go out early and buy fish for dinner. This Madame la Marquise orders. Easier than killing an emperor," she continued sarcastically. "And take care fat woman in Billingsgate don't cheat you too much," she added with dignity before drawing her head in and shutting the door of her dark cupboard.

A month later, sitting upon his straw bed and with his eyes fixed on the door of Miss Aglae's cupboard, Bernard had just begun to think that he had done something to offend, and that he would be deprived of his whispered midnight chat, when the door opened, the head of the girl appeared in its usual position. It drooped. Its white eyeballs glistened full of tears. It said nothing for a long time. Bernard was extremely alarmed. He wanted to know in an anxious whisper what was wrong. The maid let him cudgel his brains for a whole minute before she made the statement that oh! she did not like the looks of a certain gentleman visitor in a "too-much-laced coat."

Bernard, relieved but uncomprehending, snatched the candlestick off the floor and raised it to the protruded head of the maid.

"What is there to cry about?" he asked. The tears glistening on the dusky cheek astonished him beyond measure; and as an African face lends itself to the expression of sorrow more than any other type of human countenance, he was profoundly moved, and without knowing the cause, by mere sympathy felt ready to cry himself.

"You don't see! You don't understand anything, Bernard. You stand there at the door like a stick. What is the use of you I can't tell."

Bernard would have felt the injustice to be unbearable if he had not had a strong sense of his own merits. Moreover, it was obvious that Aglae was thoroughly upset. As to the man in the too-much-laced coat, Bernard remembered that he was dressed very splendidly indeed. He had called first in company of a very fine English gentleman, a friend of the family, and he had repeated the call always with that same friend. It was a fact he had never called by himself yet. The family had dined with him only the day before, as Bernard knew very well because he had had to call the hackney coach and had given the address, not to mention the confidential task of carrying the Marquise down the stairs and then up again on their return from that entertainment. There could be nothing wrong with a man with whom the family dined. And the Marquise herself too, she who, so to speak, never went out anywhere!

"What has he done?" he asked without marked excitement. "I have never seen you so distressed. Miss Aglae."

"Me upset? I should think me upset. I fear him wants carry off Mlle. Adèle—poor child."

This staggered the faithful Bernard. "I should like him to try," he said pugnaciously. "I keep a cudgel there in this passage." A scornful exclamation from the maid made him pause. "Oh!" he said in a changed tone, "carry her off for a wife? Well, what's wrong in that?"

"Oh! you silly!" whimpered Aglae. "Can't you see him twice, twice and a half, the age of Miss Adèle?"

Bernard remained silent a minute. "Fine-looking man," he remarked at last. "Do you know anything else about him?"

"Him got plenty of money," sobbed out Aglae.

"I suppose the parents will have something to say about that," said Bernard, after a short meditation. "And if Mlle. Adèle herself . . ."

But Aglae wailed under her breath, as it were. "It's done, Bernard, it's done!"

Bernard, fascinated, stared upwards at the maid. A mental reference to abundance of money for marketing flashed through his mind.

"I suppose Mlle. Adèle can love a man like that. Why not?"

"Him got very fine clothes certainly," hissed Aglae furiously. Then she broke down and became full of desolation. "Oh, Bernard, them poor people, you should have seen their faces this morning when I served the breakfast. I feel as if I must make a big howl while I give plate to M. le Marquis. I hardly dare to look at anybody."

"And Mademoiselle?" asked Bernard in an anxious whisper.

"I don't like to look at her either," went on Aglae in a tone of anguish. "She got quite a flush on her face. She think it very great and fine, make everybody rich. I ready to die with sorrow, Bernard. She don't know. She too young. Why don't you cry with me?—you great stupid man."

III

The marriage, the prospect of which failed to commend itself to the coloured maid, took place in due course. The contract which expressed the business side of that alliance was graced by the signature of a Prince of the blood and by two other signatures of a most aristocratic complexion. The French colony in London refrained from audible comments. The gracious behaviour of H.R.H. the Duc de Berry to the bridegroom killed all criticism in the very highest circles of the emigration. In less exalted circles there were slight shrugs and meaning glances, but very little else besides, except now and then a veiled sarcasm which could be ascribed to envy as much as to any other sentiment. Amongst the daughters of the emigration there must have been more than one who in her heart of hearts thought Adèle d'Armand a very lucky girl. The splendour of the entertainments which were given to the London society by the newly wedded couple after their return from the honeymoon put it beyond all doubt that the man whom Aglae described as wearing a "too-much-laced coat" was very rich. It began also to be whispered that he was a man of fantastic humours and of eccentric whims of the sort that do not pass current in the best society; especially in the case of a man whose rank was dubious and whose wealth was but recently acquired. But the embittered and irreconcilable remnant of the exiled aristocracy gave but little of its sympathy to Adèle d'Armand. She ought to have waited till the King was restored, and either married suitably—or else entered a convent for ladies of rank. For these too would soon be restored.

The Marquis, before the engagement of his daughter had become public, had written to his friend Sir Charles of the impending marriage in carefully selected terms which demanded nothing but a few words of formal congratulation. Of his son-in-law he mentioned little more than the name. It was, he said, that of a long-impoverished Piedmontese family with good French connections formed in the days before it had fallen into comparative obscurity but, the Marquis insisted, fully recognized by the parties concerned. It was the family De Montevesso. The world had heard nothing of it for more than a century, the Marquis admitted parenthetically. His daughter's intended husband's name was Helion—Count Helion de Montevesso. The title had been given to him by the King of Sardinia just before that unfortunate monarch was driven out of his dominions by the armies of republican France. It was the reward of services rendered at a critical time and none the less meritorious because, the Marquis admitted, they were of a financial nature. Count Helion, who went away very young from his native country and wandered in many lands, had amassed a large personal fortune, the Marquis went on to say, which luckily was invested in a manner that made it safe from political revolutions and social disasters overwhelming both France and Italy. That fortune, as a matter of fact, had not been made in Europe, but somewhere beyond the seas. The Marquis's letter reached Latham Hall in the evening of an autumn day.

The very young Miss Latham, seated before an embroidery frame, watched across the drawing room her father reading the letter under the glare of the reflector lamp and at the feet, as it were, of the Latham in the yellow satin coat. Sir Charles raised his eyebrows, which with passing years had become bushy and spoiled a little the expression of his handsome face. Miss Latham was made very anxious by his play of physiognomy. She had already been told after the first rustle of unfolded paper that her big friend Adèle d'Armand (Miss Latham was four years younger) was going to be married, and had become suddenly, but inwardly, excited. Every moment she expected her father to tell her something more. She was dying from impatience; but there was nothing further except the rustle of paper—and now this movement of the eyebrows. Then Sir Charles lowered his hands slowly. She could contain herself no longer.

"Who is it, Papa?" she asked with animation.

Henrietta Latham was fifteen then. Her dark eyes had remained as large as ever. The purity of her complexion, which was not of the milk-white kind, was admirable and the rich shade of the brown curls clustering on each side of her faintly glowing cheeks made a rich and harmonious combination. Sir Charles gazed at his daughter's loveliness with an air of shocked abstraction. But he too could not contain himself. He departed from his stateliness so far as to growl out scathingly:

"An upstart of some kind."

Miss Latham was, for all her lively manner, not given to outward manifestations of emotions. This intelligence was too shocking for a gasp or an exclamation. She only flushed slowly to the roots of her pretty hair. An upstart simply meant to her everything that was bad in the way of a human being, but the scathing tone of Sir Charles's outburst also augmented her profound emotion, for it seemed to extend to Adèle d'Armand herself. It shocked her tender loyalty towards the French girl, which had not been diminished by a separation of more than three years. She said quietly:

"Adèle . . . Impossible!"

The flush ebbed out of her healthy cheeks and left them pale, with the eyes darker than Sir Charles had ever seen them before. Those evidences of his daughter's emotion recalled Sir Charles to himself. After looking at his daughter fixedly for a moment he murmured the word "impossible" without any particular accent and again raised the letter to his eyes.

He did not find it in anything to modify his first impression of the man whom Adèle d'Armand was about to marry. Once more in his vaguely explanatory message the Marquis alluded to the wealth of his prospective son-in-law. It gave him a standing in the best society which his personal merits could not perhaps have secured for him so completely. Then the Marquis talked about his wife's health. The Marquise required many comforts, constant care, and cheerful surroundings. He had been enabled to leave the disagreeable lodgings in a squalid street for a little house in Chiswick very near London. He complained to his old friend that the uncompromising royalists reproached him bitterly for having signed a three-years' lease. It seemed to them an abominable apostasy from the faith in a triumphal return of the old order of things in a month or two. "I have caused quite a scandal by acting in this sensible manner," he wrote. "I am very much abused, but I have no doubt that even those who judge me most severely will be glad enough to come to Adèle's wedding."

Then, as if unable to resist the need to open his heart, he began the next line with the words:

> I need not tell you that all this is my daughter's own doing. The demand for her hand was made to us regularly through Lord G., who is a good friend of mine, though he belongs to the faction of Mr. Fox in which the Count of Montevesso numbers most of his English friends. But directly we had imparted the proposal to Adèle she took a step you may think incredible, and which from a certain point of view might even be called undutiful, if such a word could ever be applied to the sweet and devoted child our Adèle has always been to us. At her personal request, made without consulting either her mother or myself. Lord G. had the weakness to arrange a meeting between her and the Count at his own house. What those two could have said to each other I really cannot imagine. When we heard of it, the matter was so far settled that there was nothing left for us but to accept the inevitable . . .

Again Sir Charles let his big white aristocratic hands descend on his knees. His daughter's dark head drooped over the frame, and he had a vision of another head, very different and very fair, by its side. It had been a part of his retired life and had had a large share of his affection. How large it was he discovered only now, at this moment, when he felt that it was in a sense lost to him for ever. "Inevitable," he muttered to himself with a half-scornful, half-pained intonation. Sir Charles could understand the sufferings, the difficulties, the humiliations of poverty. But the Marquis might have known that, far or near, he could have counted on the assistance of his friend. For some years past he had never hesitated to dip into his purse. But that was for those mysterious journeys and those secret and important missions his Princes had never hesitated to entrust him with without ever troubling their heads about the means. Such was the nature of Princes, Sir Charles reflected with complete bitterness. And now came this . . . A whole young life thrown away perhaps, in its innocence, in its ignorance. . . . How old could Adèle be now? Eighteen or nineteen. Not so very much younger than her mother was when he used to see so much of her in Paris and Versailles, when she had managed to put such an impress on his heart that later he did not care whom he married or where he lived. . . . Inevitable! . . . Sir Charles could not be angry with the Marquise, now a mere languid shadow of that invincible charm that his heart had not been able to resist. She and her husband must have given up all their hopes, all their loyal royalist hopes before they could bow like this to the Inevitable. It had not been difficult for him to learn to love that fascinating French child as though she had been another daughter of his own. For a moment he experienced an anguish so acute that it made him move slightly in his chair. Half aloud he muttered the thought that came into his mind:

"Austerlitz has done it."

Miss Latham raised her lustrous dark eyes with an enquiring expression and murmured, "Papa?"

Sir Charles got up and seized his stick. "Nothing, my dear, nothing." He wanted to be alone. But on going out of the room he stopped by the embroidery frame and, bending down, kissed the forehead of his daughter—his English daughter. No issue of a great battle could affect her future. As to the other girl, she was lost to him and it couldn't be helped. A battle had destroyed the fairness of her life. This was the disadvantage of having been born French or indeed belonging to any other nation of the continent. There were forces there that pushed people to rash or unseemly actions; actions that seemed dictated by despair and therefore wore an immoral aspect. Sir Charles understood Adèle d'Armand even better than he understood his own daughter, or at least he understood her with greater sympathy. She had a generous nature. She was too young, too inexperienced to know what she was doing when she took in hand the disposal of her own person in favour of that apparently Piedmontese upstart with his obscure name and his mysteriously acquired fortune. "I only hope the fortune is there," thought Sir Charles with grim scepticism. But as to that there could be no doubt, judging from the further letters he received from his old friend. After a short but brilliant period of London life the upstart had carried Adèle off to France. He had bought an estate in Piedmont, which was his native country, and another with a splendid house, near Paris. Sir Charles was not surprised to hear a little later that the Marquise and the Marquis had also returned to France. The time of persecution was over; most of the great royalist families were returning, unreconciled in sentiment if wavering in their purposes. That his old friend should ever be dazzled by imperial grandeurs Sir Charles could not believe. Though he had abandoned his daughter to an upstart, he was too good a royalist to abandon his principles, for which certainly he would have died if that had been of any use. But he had returned to France. Most of his exiled friends had returned too, and Sir Charles understood very well that the Marquis and his wife wanted to be somewhere near their daughter. This departure closed a long chapter in his life, and afterwards Sir Charles hardly ever mentioned his French friends. The only positive thing which Henrietta knew was that Adèle d'Armand had married an upstart and had returned to France. She had communicated that knowledge to her brother, who had stared with evident surprise but had made no comment. Living away from home at school and afterwards in Cambridge, his father's French friends had remained for him as shadowy figures on the shifting background of a very poignant, very real, and intense drama of contemporary history, dominated by one enormously vital and in its greatness immensely mysterious individuality—the only man of his time.

Cosmo Latham at the threshold of life had adopted neither of the contrasted views of Napoleon Emperor entertained by his contemporaries. For him as for his father before him, the world offered a scene of conflicting emotions in which facts appraised by reason preserved a mysterious complexity and a dual character. One evening during an artless discussion with young men of his own age, it had occurred to him to say that Bonaparte seemed to be the only man amongst a lot of old scarecrows. "Look how he knocks them over," he had explained. A moment of silence followed. Then a voice objected:

"Then perhaps he is not so great as some of you try to make him out."

"I didn't mean that exactly," said Cosmo in a sobered tone. "Nobody can admire that man more than I do. Perhaps the world may be none the worse for a scarecrow here and there left on the borders of what is right or just. I only wished to express my sense of the moving force in his genius."

"What does he stand for?" asked the same voice.

Cosmo shook his head. "Many things, and some of them too obvious to mention. But I can't help thinking that there are some which we cannot see yet."

"And some of them that are dead already," retorted his interlocutor. "They died in his very hands. But there is one thing for which he stands and that will never die. You seem to have forgotten it. It is the spirit of hostility to this nation; to what we in this room, with our different views and opinions, stand for in the last instance."

"Oh, that!" said Cosmo confidently. "What we stand for isn't an old scarecrow. Great as he is he will never knock that over. His arm is not long enough, however far his thoughts may go. He has got to work with common men."

"I don't know what you mean. What else are we? I believe you admire him."

"I do," confessed Cosmo sturdily.

This did not prevent him from joining the army in Spain before the year was out, and that without asking for Sir Charles's approval. Sir Charles condemned severely the policy of using the forces of the Crown in the Peninsula. He did not like the ministry of the day and he had a strong prejudice against all the Wellesleys to whose aggrandizement this whole policy seemed effected. But when at the end of a year and a half, after the final victory of Toulouse, his son appeared in Yorkshire, the two made up for the past coolness by shaking hands warmly for nearly a whole minute. Cosmo really had done very little campaigning and soon declared to his father the wish to leave the army. There would be no more fighting for years and years, he argued, and though he did not dislike fighting in a good cause, he had no taste for mere soldiering. He wanted to see something of the world which had been closed to us for so long. Sir Charles, ageing and dignified, leaned on his stick on the long terrace.

"All the world was never closed to us," he said.

"I wasn't thinking of the East, sir," explained Cosmo. "I heard some people talk about its mystery, but I think Europe is mysterious enough just now, and even more interesting."

Sir Charles nodded his bare gray head in the chill evening breeze.

"France, Germany," he murmured.

Cosmo thought that he would prefer to see something of Italy first. He would go north afterwards.

"Through Vienna, I suppose," suggested Sir Charles with an impassive face.

"I don't think so, sir," said Cosmo frankly. "I don't care much for the work which is going on there and perhaps still less for the men who are putting their hands to it."

This time Sir Charles's slow nod expressed complete agreement. He too had no liking for the work that was about to begin there. But no objection could be raised against Italy. He had known Italy well thirty or more years ago, but it must have been changed out of his knowledge. He remained silent, gazing at the wide landscape of blue wooded rises and dark hollows under the gorgeous colours of the sunset. They began to die out.

"You may travel far before you see anything like this," he observed to his son. "And don't be in a hurry to leave us. You have only just come home. Remember I am well over sixty."

Cosmo was quite ready to surrender himself to the peace of his Yorkshire home, so different from the strenuous atmosphere of the last campaign in the South of France. Autumn was well advanced before he fixed the day for his departure. On his last day at home Sir Charles addressed him with perfect calmness.

"When you pass into Italy you must not fail to see my old friend the Marquis d'Armand. The French King has appointed him as ambassador in Turin. It's a sign of high favour, I believe. He will be either in Turin or Genoa. . . ." Sir Charles paused, then after a perfectly audible sigh added with an effort: "The Marquise is dead. I knew her in her youth. She was a marvellous woman. . . ." Sir Charles checked himself, and then with another effort, "But the daughter of my old friend is I believe with her father now, a married daughter, the Countess of Montevesso."

"You mean little Adèle, sir," said Cosmo, with interest, but on Sir Charles's face there passed a distinct shade of distress.

"Oh, you remember the child," he said, and his tone was tender but it changed to contempt as he went on. "I don't know whether the fellow, I mean the man she married, is staying with them or whether they are living with him, or whether . . . I know nothing!"

The word "upstart," heard many years ago from his sister Henrietta, crossed Cosmo's mind. He thought to himself, "There is something wrong there," and to his father he said, "I will be able to tell you all about it."

"I don't want to know," Sir Charles replied with a surprising solemnity of tone and manner which hid some deeper feeling. "But give the Marquis my love and tell him that when he gets tired of all his grandeurs he may remember that there is a large place for him in this house as long as I live."

Late that evening Cosmo, saying good-bye to his sister, took her in his arms, kissed her forehead, and holding her out at arm's length said:

"You have grown into a charming girl, Henrietta."

"I am glad you think so," she said. "Alas, I am too dark. I can never be as charming as Adèle must have been at my age. You seem to have forgotten her."

"Oh no," protested Cosmo carelessly. "A marvel of fairness, wasn't she? I remember you telling me years ago that she married an upstart."

"That was Father's expression. You know what that means, Cosmo."

"I do know what it means, exactly," he said, laughing. "But from what Father said this afternoon it seems as if he were a rather nasty upstart. What made Adèle do it?"

"I am awed," confessed Henrietta. "I don't know what made her do it. I was never told. Father never talked much about the D'Armands afterwards. I was with him in the yellow drawing room the evening he got the letter from the Marquis. After he read it he said something very extraordinary. You know it's full nine years ago and I was yet a child, yet I could not have dreamed it. I heard it distinctly. He dropped his hands and said, 'Austerlitz has done it.' What could he have meant?"

"It would be hard to guess the connection," said Cosmo, smiling at his sister's puzzled face. "Father must have been thinking of something else."

"Father was thinking of nothing else for days," affirmed Henrietta positively.

"You must have been a very observant child," remarked her brother. "But I believe you were always a clever girl, Henrietta. Well, I am going to see Adèle."

"Oh yes, you start in the morning to travel ever so far and for ever so long," said Miss Latham enviously. "Oh Cosmo, you are going to write to me—lots?"

He looked at her appreciatively and gave her another brotherly hug.

"Certainly I will write, whole reams," he said.

IV

On his way from the harbour to the upper part of the town where his inn was situated Cosmo Latham met very few people. He had to pass through a sort of covered way; its arch yawned in front of him very black with only a feeble glimmer of a light in its depths. It did not occur to him that it was a place where one could very well be knocked on the head by evil-intentioned men if there were any prowling about in that early part of the evening, for it was early yet, though the last gleams of sunset had gone out completely off the earth and out of the sky. On issuing from the dark passage a maze of narrow streets presented itself to his choice, but he knew that as long as he kept walking uphill he could not fail to reach the middle of the town. Projecting at long intervals from the continuous mass of thick walls, wrought-iron arms held lanterns containing dim gleams of light. The enormous doors of the lofty gateways he passed were closed, and the only sound he could hear was that of his own deliberate footsteps. At a wider spot where several of those lanes met he stopped, and looking about him asked himself whether all those enormous and palatial houses were empty, or whether it was the thickness of walls that killed all the signs of life within; for as to the population being already asleep he could not believe it for a moment. All at once he caught sight of a muffled feminine form. In the heavy shadow she seemed to emerge out of one wall and gliding on seemed to disappear into another. It was undoubtedly a woman. Cosmo was startled by this noiseless apparition and had a momentary feeling of being lost in an enchanted city. Presently the enchanted silence was broken by the increasing sound of an iron-shod stick tapping the flagstones, till there walked out of one of the dark and tortuous lanes a man who by his rolling gait, general outline, and the characteristic shape of the hat, Cosmo could not doubt, was a seaman belonging to the English man-of-war in the harbour. The tapping of his stick ceased suddenly and Cosmo hailed him in English, asking for the way.

The sturdy figure in the tarpaulin hat put its cudgel under its arm and answered him in a deep pleasant voice. Yes, he knew the inn. He was just coming from there. If His Honour followed the street before him he would come to a large open space and His Honour's inn would be across the square. In the deep shadows Cosmo could make out of the seaman's face nothing but the bushy whiskers and the gleam of the eyes. He was pleased at meeting the very day he had reached the Mediterranean shore (he had come down to Genoa from Turin) such a fine specimen of a man-of-war's man. He thanked him for the direction and the sailor, touching his hat, went off at his slightly rolling gait. Cosmo observed that he took a turning very near the spot where the muffled woman had a moment before vanished from his sight. It was a very dark and a very narrow passage between two towering buildings. Cosmo, continuing on his way, arrived at a broad thoroughfare badly lighted but full of people. He knew where he was then. In a very few moments he found himself at the door of his inn in a great square which in comparison with the rest of the town might have been said to blaze with lights.

Under an iron lantern swung above a flight of three broad steps, Cosmo recognized his servant gazing into the square with a worried expression which changed at once into one of relief on perceiving his master. He touched his cap and followed Cosmo into a large hall with several doors opening into it and furnished with many wooden chairs and tables. At one of them bearing four candlesticks several British naval officers sat talking and laughing in subdued tones. A compactly built clean-shaven person with slightly sunken cheeks, wearing black breeches and a maroon waistcoat with sleeves, but displaying a very elaborate frill to his white shirt, stood in the middle of the floor, glancing about with vigilance, and bowed hurriedly to his latest client. Cosmo returned the greeting of Signor Cantelucci, who, snatching up the nearest candlestick, began to ascend a broad stone staircase with an air of performing a solemn duty. Cosmo followed him, and Cosmo's servant followed his master. They went up and up. At every flight broad archways gave a view of dark perspective in which nothing but a few drops of dim fire were forlornly visible. At last Signor Cantelucci threw open a door on a landing and bowing again:

"See, milord! There is a fire. I know the customs and habits of the English."

Cosmo stepped into a large and lofty room where in the play of bright flames under a heavy and tall mantelpiece the shadows seemed very much disturbed by his entrance. Cosmo approached the blaze with satisfaction.

"I had enough trouble to get them to light it," remarked the valet in a resentful tone. "If it hadn't been for a jack-tar with big whiskers I found down in the hall it wouldn't be done yet. He came up from the ship with one of these sea officers downstairs. He drove the fellows with the wood in fine style up here for me. He knows the people here. He cursed them each separately by their Christian names, and then had a glass of wine in the kitchen with me."

Meantime Signor Cantelucci, wearing the aspect of a deaf man, had lighted, on two separate tables, two clusters of candles which drove the restless gloom of the large apartment half way up to the ceiling, and retired with noiseless footsteps. He stopped in the doorway to cast a keen glance at the master and the man standing by the fire. Those two turned their heads only at the sound of the closing door.

"I couldn't think what became of you, sir. I was getting quite worried about you. You disappeared without saying anything to me."

"I went for a walk down to the sea," said Cosmo while the man moved off to where several cowhide trunks were ranged against the wall. "I like to take a look round on arriving at a new place."

"Yes, sir; but when it got dark I wondered."

"I tarried on a tower to watch the sunset," murmured Cosmo.

"I have been doing some unpacking," said the servant, "but not knowing how long you mean to stay . . ."

"It may be a long stay."

"Then I will go on, sir; that is if you are going to keep this room."

"Yes. The room will do. Spire. It's big enough."

Spire took up one of the two candelabras and retired into the neighbourhood of a sort of state bed heavily draped at the other end of the room. There, throwing open the trunks and the doors of closets, he busied himself systematically, without noise, till he heard the quiet voice of his young master.

"Spire."

"Yes, sir," he answered, standing still with a pile of shirts on his arm.

"Is this inn very full?"

"Yes, very," said Spire. "The whole town is full of travellers and people from the country. A lot of our nobility and gentry are passing this way."

He deposited the shirts on a shelf in the depths of the wall and turned round again.

"Have you heard any names, Spire?"

Spire stooped over a trunk and lifted up from it carefully a lot of white neckcloths folded neatly one within the other.

"I haven't had much time yet, sir. I heard a few."

He laid down the neckcloths by the side of the shirts while Cosmo, with his elbow on the mantelpiece, asked down the whole length of the room:

"Anybody I know?"

"Not in this place, sir. There is generally a party of officers from the man-of-war staying here. They come and go. I have seen some Italian gentlemen in square-cut coats and powdered hair. Very old-fashioned, sir. There are some Austrians too, I think; but I haven't seen any ladies. . . . I am afraid, sir, this isn't the right sort of inn. There is another about a hundred yards from here on the other side of the square."

"I don't want to meet anybody I know," said Cosmo Latham in a low voice.

Spire thought that this would make his stay in Genoa very dull. At the same time he was convinced that his young master would alter his mind before very long and change to that other inn patronized by travellers of fashion. For himself he was not averse from a little quiet time. Spire was no longer young. Thirty years ago, before the War and before the Revolution, he had travelled with Sir Charles in France and Italy. He was then only eighteen, but being a steady and trustworthy lad was taken abroad to look after the horses. Sir Charles kept four horses in Florence, and Spire had often ridden on Tuscan roads behind Sir Charles and the two Misses Aston, of whom one later became Lady Latham. After the family settled in Yorkshire he passed from the stables to the house, acquired a confidential position, and whenever Lady Latham took a journey he sat in the rumble with a pair of double-barrelled pistols in the pockets of his greatcoat and ordered all things on the road. Later he became intermediary between Sir Charles and the stables, the gardens, and in all out-of-door things about the house. He attended Lady Latham on her very last drive, all the details for that lady's funeral having been left to his management. He was also a very good valet. He had been called one evening into the library where Sir Charles, very gouty that day, leaning with one hand on a thick stick and with the other on the edge of a table, had said to him: "I am lending you to Mr. Cosmo for his travels in France and Italy. You will know your way about. And mind you draw the charges of the pistols in the carriage every morning and load them afresh."

Spire was then requested to help Sir Charles up the stairs and had a few more words said to him when Sir Charles stopped at the door of his bedroom.

"Mr. Cosmo has plenty of sense. You are not to make yourself a nuisance to him."

"No, Sir Charles," said the imperturbable Spire. "I will know how to look after Mr. Cosmo."

And if he had been asked. Spire would have been able to say that during the stay in Paris and all through France and Switzerland on the way to Genoa Mr. Cosmo had given him no trouble at all.

Spire, still busy unpacking, glanced at his young master. He certainly looked very quiet now, leaning on his elbow with the firelight playing from below on his young thoughtful face with its smooth and pale complexion. "Very good-looking indeed," thought Spire. In that thoughtful mood he recalled very much the Sir Charles of thirty or thirty-five years ago. Would he too find his wife abroad? There had been women enough in Paris of every kind and degree, English and French and all sorts. But it was a fact that Mr. Cosmo sought most of his company amongst men, of whom also there had been no lack and of every degree. In that, too, the young man resembled very much his father. Men's company. But were he to get caught he would get caught properly; at any rate for a time, reflected Spire, remembering Sir Charles Latham's rush back to Italy, the inwardness of which had been no more revealed to him than to the rest of the world.

Spire, approaching the candelabra, unfolded partly a very fine coat, then refolded it before putting it away on a convenient shelf. He had a moment of regret for his own young days. He had never married, not because there had been any lack of women to set their caps at him, but from a sort of half-conscious prudence. Moreover, he had a notion somehow or other that Sir Charles would not have liked it. Perhaps it was just as well. Now he was carefree, attending on Mr. Cosmo without troubling his head about who had remained at home.

Spire, arranging the contents of a dressing case on the table, cast another sidelong look at the figure by the fire. Very handsome. Something like Sir Charles and yet not like. There was a touch of something unusual, perhaps foreign, and yet no one with a pair of eyes in his head could mistake Mr. Cosmo for anything but an English gentleman.

Spire's memories of his tour with Sir Charles had been growing dim. But he remembered enough of the old-time atmosphere to have become aware of a feeling of tension, of a suggestion of restlessness which certainly was new to him.

The silence had lasted very long. Cosmo before the fire had not moved. Spire ventured on a remark.

"I notice people are excited about one thing and another hereabouts, sir."

"Excited. I don't wonder at it. In what way?"

"Sort of discontented, sir. They don't like the Austrians, sir. You may have noticed as we came along . . ."

"Did they like us when we held the town?"

"I can hardly say that, sir. I have been sitting for an hour or more in the couriers' room, with all sorts of people coming in and out, and heard very wild sort of talk."

"What can you know about its wildness?"

"To look at their faces was enough. It's a funny place, that room downstairs," went on Spire, rubbing with a piece of silk a travelling looking-glass mounted cunningly in a silver case which when opened made a stand for it. He placed it exactly in the middle of a little table and turned round to look at his master. Seeing that Cosmo seemed disposed to listen he continued: "It is vaulted like a cellar and has a little door giving into a side street. People come in and put as they like. All sorts of low people, sir, *facchini* and carters and boatmen and suchlike. There was an old fellow came in, a gray-headed man, a cobbler, I suppose, as he brought a bagful of mended shoes for the servants of the house. He emptied the lot on the stone floor, sir, and instead of trying to collect his money from the people that were scrambling for them he made them a speech. He spouted, sir, without drawing a breath. The courier-valet of an English doctor staying here, a Swiss I think he is, says to me in his broken English: 'He would cut every Austrian throat in this town.' We were having a glass of wine together and I asked him, 'And what do you think of that?' And he says to me, after thinking a bit, 'I agree with him. . . .' Very dreadful, sir," concluded Spire with a perfectly unmoved face.

Cosmo looked at him in silence for a time. "It was very bold talk if that is what the man really said," he remarked. "Especially as the place is so public as you say it is."

"Absolutely open to the street, sir; and that same Swiss fellow had told me just before that the town was full of spies and what they call *sbirri* that came from Turin with the King. The King is staying at the Palace, sir. They are expecting the Queen of Sardinia to arrive any day. You didn't know, sir? They say she will come in an English man-of-war. That old cobbler was very abusive about the King of Piedmont too. Surely talk like that can't be safe anywhere."

Spire paused suddenly and Cosmo Latham turned his back to the fire.

"Well, and what happened?" he asked with a smile.

"You could have heard a pin drop," said Spire in equable tones, "till that Signor Cantelucci—that's the padrone of this inn, sir . . ."

"The man who lighted me up?" said Cosmo.

"Yes, sir. . . . I didn't know he was in the room till suddenly he spoke behind my back telling one of the scullions that was there to give the man a glass of wine. And what the old fellow must do but raise it above his head and shout a toast to the Destructor of the Austrians before he tossed it down his throat. I was quite astonished, but Signor Cantelucci never turned a hair. He offered his snuffbox to that doctor's courier and myself and shrugged his shoulders. 'It was only Pietro,' he said, 'a little mad'—he tapped his forehead, you know, sir. The doctor's courier sat there grinning. I got suddenly uneasy about you, sir, and went out to the front door to see whether you were coming. It's very different from what it was thirty years ago. There was no talk in Italy of cutting foreigners' throats when Sir Charles and I were here. It was quite a startling experience."

Cosmo nodded. "You seem impressed. Spire. Well, I too had an experience, just as the sun was setting."

"I am sorry to hear that, sir."

"What do you mean? Why should you be sorry?"

"I beg your pardon, sir, I thought it was something unpleasant."

Cosmo had a little laugh. "Unpleasant? No! Not exactly, though I think it was more dangerous than yours, but if there was any madness connected with it, it had a very visible method. It was not all talk either. Yes, Spire, it was exciting."

"I don't know what's come to them all. Everybody seems excited. There was not excitement in Italy thirty years ago when I was with Sir Charles and took four horses with only one helper from this very town to Florence, sir."

Cosmo with fixed eyes did not seem to hear Spire's complaining remark. He exclaimed: "Really it was very extraordinary," so suddenly that Spire gave a perceptible start. He pulled himself together and asked in a purely business tone:

"Are you going to dine in your room, sir? Time is getting on."

Cosmo's mood too seemed to have changed completely.

"I don't know. I am not hungry. I want you to move one of those screens here near the fire and place a table and chair there. I will do some correspondence to-night. Yes, I will have my dinner here, I think."

"I will go down and order it, sir," said Spire. "The cook here is a Frenchman who married a native and . . ."

"Who on earth is swearing like this outside?" exclaimed Cosmo, while Spire's face also expressed astonishment at the loud burst of voices coming along the corridor, one angry, the other argumentative, in a crescendo of scolding and expostulation which, passing the door at its highest, died away into a confused murmur in the distance of the long corridor.

"That was an English voice," said Cosmo. "I mean the angry one."

"I should think it's that English doctor from Tuscany that has been three or four days here already. He has been put on this floor."

"From what I have been able to catch," said Cosmo, "he seems very angry at having a neighbour on it. That must be me. Have you heard his name?"

"It's Marvel or some such name. He seems to be known here; he orders people about as if he were at home. The other was Cantelucci, sir."

"Very likely. Look here. Spire. I will dine in the public room downstairs. I want to see that angry gentleman. Did you see him, Spire?"

"Only his back, sir. Very broad, sir. Tall man. In boots and a riding coat. Are you going down now, sir? The dinner must be on already."

"Yes," said Cosmo, preparing to go out. "And by the by. Spire, if you ever see in the street or in that room downstairs, where everyone comes in and out as you say, a long fellow wearing a peculiar cap with a tassel, just try to find out something about him; or at any rate let me know when you have seen him. . . . You could perhaps follow him for a bit and try to see where he goes."

After saying those words Cosmo left the room before Spire could make any answer. Spire's astonishment expressed itself by a low exclamation, "Well, I never!"

PART II

I

Cosmo descended into a hall now empty and with most of its lights extinguished. A loud murmur of voices guided him to the door of the dining room. He discovered it to be a long apartment with flat pilasters dividing its whitewashed walls, and resembling somewhat a convent's refectory. The resemblance was accentuated by the two narrow tables occupying its middle. One of them had been appropriated by the British naval officers, had lights on it, and bristled with the necks of wine bottles along its whole length. The talk round it was confused and noisy. The other, shorter, table accommodated two rows of people in sombre garments who at first glance struck Cosmo as natives of the town and belonging to a lower station in life. They had less lights, less wine, and almost no animation. Several smaller tables were ranged against the walls at equal intervals, and Cosmo's eye was caught by one of them because of the candles in the sconce on the wall above it having been lighted. Its cloth was dazzlingly white, and Signor Cantelucci with a napkin in his hand stood respectfully at the elbow of its sole occupant, who was seated with his back to the door.

Cosmo was under the impression that his entrance had been unobserved. But before he had walked half the length of the room Signor Cantelucci, whose eyes had never ceased darting here and there while his body preserved its deferential attitude at the elbow of the exclusive client, advanced to meet him with his serious and attentive air. He bowed. Perhaps the signore would not mind sharing the table of his illustrious countryman.

"Yes, if my countryman doesn't object," assented Cosmo readily. He was absolutely certain that this must be the doctor of whom Spire had spoken.

Cantelucci had no doubt that His Excellency's company would be most welcome to his illustrious countryman. Then stepping aside, he added under his breath: "He is a person of great distinction. A most valued patron of mine. . . ." The person thus commended, turning his head ensconced in the high collar of his coat, disclosed to Cosmo a round face with a shaved chin, strongly marked eyebrows, round eyes, and thin lips compressed into a slightly peevish droop which, however, was at once corrected by an attempt at a faint smile. Cosmo, too, produced a faint smile. For an appreciable moment they looked at each other without saying a word while Cantelucci, silent too, executed a profound bow.

"Sit down, sir, sit down," said the elder man (Cosmo judged him to be well over forty), raising his voice above the uproar made by the occupants of the naval table and waving his hand at the empty chair facing his own. It had a high carved back showing some traces of gilding, and the silk which covered it was worn to rags. Cosmo sat down while Cantelucci disappeared and the man across the table positively shouted, "I am glad," and immediately followed that declaration by an energetic "Oh damn!" He bent over the table: "One can't hear oneself speak with that noisy lot. All heroes, no doubt, but not a single gentleman."

He leaned back and waited till the outburst of noisy mirth had died out at the officers' table. The corners of his mouth drooped again and Cosmo came to the conclusion that face in repose was decidedly peevish.

"I don't know what they have got to be so merry about," the other began, with a slight glance at the naval table and leaning forward again towards Cosmo. "Their occupation is gone. Heroes are a thoughtless lot. Yet just look at that elderly lieutenant at the head of the table. Shabby coat. Old epaulette. He doesn't laugh. He will die a lieutenant—on half pay. That's how heroic people end when the heroic times are over."

"I am glad," said Cosmo steadily, "that you recognize at least their heroism."

The other opened his mouth for some time before he laughed, and that gave his face an expression of somewhat hard jollity. But the laugh when it came was by no means loud and had a sort of ingratiating softness.

"No, no. Don't think I am disparaging our sea service. I had the privilege to know the greatest hero of them all. Yes, I had two talks with Lord Nelson. Well, he was certainly not . . ."

He interrupted himself and raising his eyes saw the perfectly still gaze of Cosmo fastened on his face. Then peevishly:

"What I meant to say was that he at least was indubitably a hero. I remember that I was very careful about what I said to him. I had to be mighty careful then about what I said to anybody. Someone might have put it into his head to hang me at some yard-arm or other."

"I envy your experience all the same," said Cosmo amiably. "I suppose your conscience was clear?"

"I have always been most careful not to give my conscience any license to trouble me," retorted the other with a certain curtness of tone which was not offensive; "and I have lived now for some considerable time. I am really much older than I look," he concluded, giving Cosmo such a keen glance that the young man could not I help a smile.

The other went on looking at him steadily for a while, then let his eyes wander to a door in a distant part of the long room as if impatient for the coming of the dinner. Then giving it up:

"A man who has lived actively, actively I say, the last twenty years may well feel as old as Methuselah. Lord Nelson was but a circumstance in my life. I wonder, had he lived, how he would have taken all this."

A slight movement of his hand seemed to carry this allusion outside the confines of the vaulted noisy room, to indicate all the out-of-doors of the world. Cosmo remarked that the hand was muscular, shapely, and extremely well cared for.

"I think there can be no doubt about the nature of his feelings if he were living." Cosmo's voice was exactly non-committal. His interlocutor grunted slightly.

"H'm. He would have done nothing but groan and complain about anything and everything. No, he wouldn't have taken it laughing. Very poor physique. Very. Frightful hypochondriac. . . . I am a doctor, you know."

Cantelucci was going to attend himself on his two guests. He presented to the doctor a smoking soup tureen enveloped in a napkin. The doctor assumed at once a business-like air, and at his invitation Cosmo held out his plate. The doctor helped him carefully.

"Don't forget the wine, my wine, Anzelmo," he said to Cantelucci, who answered by a profound bow. "I saved his life once," he continued after the innkeeper had gone away.

The tone was particularly significant. Cosmo, partly repelled and partly amused by the man, enquired whether the worthy host had been very ill. The doctor swallowed the last spoonful of soup.

"Ill," he said. "He had a gash that long in his side and a set of forty-pound fetters in his legs. I cured both complaints. Not without some risk to myself, as you may imagine. There was an epidemic of hanging and shooting in the South of Italy then."

He noticed Cosmo's steady stare and raised the corners of his mouth with an effect of geniality on his broad rosy face.

"In '99, you know. I wonder I didn't die of it too. I was considerably younger then and my humane instincts, early enthusiasms, and so on had led me into pretty bad company. However, I had also pretty good friends. What with one thing and another I am pretty well known all over Italy. My name is Martel—Doctor Martel. You probably may have heard. . . ."

He threw a searching glance at Cosmo, who bowed non-committally, and went on without a pause: "I am the man who brought vaccine to Italy, first. Cantelucci was trying to tell me your name but really I couldn't make it out."

"Latham is my name," said Cosmo, "and I only set foot in Italy for the first time in my life two days ago."

The doctor jerked his head sideways.

"Latham, eh? Yorkshire?"

"Yes," said Cosmo, smiling.

"To be sure. Sir Charles . . ."

"That's my father."

"Yes, yes. Served in the Guards. I used to know the doctor of his regiment. Married in Italy. I don't remember the lady's name. Oh, those are old times. Might have been a hundred years ago."

"You mean that so much history has been made since."

"Yes, no end of history," assented the doctor, but checked himself. "And yet, tell me, what does it all amount to?"

Cosmo made no answer. Cantelucci having brought the wine while they talked, the doctor-filled two glasses, waited a moment as if to hear Cosmo speak, but as the young man remained silent he said:

"Well, let us drink then to Peace."

He tossed the wine down his throat while Cosmo drank his much more leisurely. As they set down their empty glasses they were startled by a roar of a tremendous voice filling the vaulted room from end to end in order to "let Their Honours know that the boat was at the steps." The doctor made a faint grimace.

"Do you hear the voice of the British lion, Mr. Latham?" he asked peevishly. "Ah, well, we will have some little peace now here."

Those officers at the naval table who had to go on board rose in a body and left the room hastily. Three or four who had a longer leave drew close together and began to talk low with their heads in a bunch. Cosmo glancing down the room seemed to recognize at the door the form of the seaman whom he had met earlier in the evening. He followed the officers out. The other diners, the sombre ones, and a good many of them with powdered heads, were also leaving the room. Cantelucci put another dish on the table, stepped back a pace with a bow, and stood still. A moment of profound silence succeeded the noise.

"First rate," said Doctor Martel to Cosmo, after tasting the dish, and then gave a nod to Cantelucci, who made another bow and retreated backwards, always with a solemn expression on his face.

"Italian cooking, of course, but then I am an old Italian myself. Not that I love them, but I have acquired many of their tastes. Before we have done dining you will have tasted the perfection of their cookery, north and south, but I assure you are sharing my dinner. You don't suppose that the dishes that come to this table are the same the common customers get."

Cosmo made a slight bow. "I am very sensible of the privilege," he said.

"The honour and the pleasure are mine, I assure you," the doctor said in a half-careless tone and looking with distaste towards the small knot of officers with a twenty-four hours' leave who had finished their confabulation and had risen in a body like men who had agreed on some pleasant course of action. Only the elderly lieutenant lagging a little behind cast a glance at his two countrymen at the little table and followed his comrades with less eager movements.

"A quarter of a tough bullock or half a roast sheep are more in their way, and Cantelucci knows it. As to that company that was sitting at the other table, well, I daresay you can tell yourself what they were, small officials or tradesmen of some sort. I should think that emptying all their pockets—and they were how many, say twenty—you couldn't collect the value of one English pound at any given time. And Cantelucci knows that too. Well, of course. Still he does well here, but it's a poor place. I wonder, Mr. Latham, what are you doing here?"

"Well," said Cosmo with a good-humoured smile, "I am just staying here. Just as you yourself are staying here."

"Ah, but you never saved Cantelucci's life, whereas I did and that's the reason why I am staying here: out of mere kindness and to give him an opportunity to show his gratitude. . . . Let me fill your glass. Not bad, this wine."

"Excellent. What is it?"

"God knows. Let us call it Cantelucci's gratitude. Generous stuff, this, to wash down those dishes with. Gluttony is an odious vice, but an ambition to dine well is about the only one which can be indulged at no cost to one's fellow men."

"It didn't strike me," murmured Cosmo absently, for he was just then asking himself why he didn't like this pleasant companion, and had just come to the conclusion that it was because of his indecisive expression wavering between peevishness and jocularity with something else in addition, as it were, in the background of his handsome, neat, and comfortable person. Something that was not aggressive nor yet exactly impudent. He wondered at his mistrust of the personality which certainly was very communicative but apparently not inquisitive. At that moment he heard himself addressed with a direct inquiry.

"You passed, of course, through Paris?"

"Yes, and Switzerland."

"Oh, Paris. I wonder what it looks like now. Full of English people, of course. Let's see, how many years is it since I was last there? Ha, lots of heads rolled off very noble shoulders since. Well, I am trying to make my way there. Curious times. I have found some letters here. Duke of Wellington very much disliked, what? His nod is insupportable, eh?"

"I have just had a sight of the Duke two or three times," said Cosmo. "I can assure you that everybody is treating him with the greatest respect."

"Of course, of course. All the same I bet that all these foreigners are chuckling to themselves at having finished the job without him."

"They needn't be so pleased with themselves," said Cosmo scornfully. "The mere weight of their numbers . . ."

"Yes. It was more like a migration of armed tribes than an army. They will boast of their success all the same. There is no saying what the Duke himself thinks. . . . I wonder if he could have beaten the other in a fair fight. Well, that will never be known now."

Cosmo had a sudden sense of an epical tale with a doubtful conclusion. He made no answer. Cantelucci had come and gone solemnly, self-contained, with the usual two ceremonial bows. As he retreated he put out all the candles on the central table and became lost to view. From the illuminated spot at which he sat, Cosmo's eyes met only the shadows of the long refectory-like room with its lofty windows closely shuttered so that they looked like a row of niches for statues. Yet the murmur of the piazza full of people stole faintly into his ear. Cosmo had the recollection of the vast expanse of flagstones enclosed by the shadowy and palatial masses gleaming with lights here and there under the night sky thick with stars and perfectly cloudless.

"This is a very quiet inn," he observed.

"It has that advantage certainly. The walls are fairly thick, as you can see. It's an unfinished palace, I mean as to its internal decorations, which were going to be very splendid and even more costly than splendid. The owner of it, I mean the man who had it built, died of hunger in that hall out there."

"Died of hunger?" repeated Cosmo.

"No doubt about it. It was during the siege of Genoa. You know the siege, surely?"

Cosmo recollected himself. "I was quite a child at the time," he said.

The venerated client of Cantelucci cracked a walnut and then looked at Cosmo's face.

"I should think you weren't seven years old at the time," he said in a judicial tone. "When I first came into Italy with the vaccine, you know, Sir Charles's marriage was still being talked about in Florence. I remember it perfectly though it seems as if it had all happened in another world. Yes, indubitably he died of hunger like ten thousand other Genoese. He couldn't go out to hunt for garbage with the populace or crawl out at night trying to gather nettles in the ditches outside the forts, and nobody would have known that he was dead for a month if one of the bombs out of a bomb-vessel with Admiral Keith's blockading squadron hadn't burst the door in. They found him at the foot of the stairs, and, they say, with a lot of gold pieces in his pockets. But nobody cared much for that. If it had been a lot of half-gnawed bones there would have been blood spilt, no doubt. For all I know there were or may be even now secret places full of gold in the thickness of these walls. However, the body was thrown into a corpse-cart and the authorities boarded the doorway. It remained boarded for years because the heirs didn't care to have anything to do with that shell of a palace. I fancy that the last of them died in the snows of Russia. Cantelucci came along, and owing to a friendship with some sort of scribe in the Municipality he got permission to use the place for his hostelry. He told me that he found several half ducats in the corners of the hall when he took possession. I suppose they paid for the whitewash, for I can't believe that Cantelucci had much money in his pockets."

"Perhaps he found one of those secret hiding-places of which you spoke," suggested Cosmo.

"What? Cantelucci? He never looked for any gold. He is too much in the clouds; but he has made us dine well in the palace of the starved man, hasn't he? Sixteen years ago in Naples he was a Jacobin and a friend of the French, a rebel, a traitor to his king if you like—but he has a good memory, there is no denying that."

"Is he a Neapolitan, then?" asked Cosmo. "I imagined they were of a different type."

"God only knows. He was there and I didn't ask him. He was a prisoner of the royalists, of the reactionaries. I was much younger then and perhaps more humane. Flesh and blood couldn't stand in the sight of the way in which they were being treated, men of position, of attainments, of intelligence. The Neapolitan Jacobins were no populace. They were men of character and ideas, the pick of all classes. They were properly liberals. Still they were called Jacobins and you may be surprised that I, a professional man and an Englishman . . ."

Cosmo, looking up at the sudden pause, saw the doctor sitting with the dull eyes and the expression of a man suddenly dissatisfied with himself. Cosmo hastened to say that he himself was no friend of reactionaries and in any case not conceited enough to judge the conduct of men older than himself. Without a sign that he had heard a word of that speech the doctor had a faint and peevish smile. He never moved at all till, after a longish interval, Cosmo spoke again.

"Were you expecting somebody that would want to see you this evening?" he asked.

The doctor started.

"See me? No. Why do you ask?"

"Because within the last five minutes somebody has put his head twice through the door; and as I don't expect either a visitor or a messenger, I thought he was looking for you. I don't know a single soul here."

The doctor remained perfectly unmoved. Cosmo, who was looking towards the distant door, saw the head again and this time shouted at it an inquiry. Thereupon the owner of the head entered and had not advanced half the length of the room before Cosmo recognized in him the portly figure of Spire. To his great surprise, however. Spire instead of coming up to the table made a vague gesture and stopped short.

This was strange conduct. The doctor sat completely unconscious, and Cosmo took the course of excusing himself and following Spire, who, directly he had seen his master rise, had retreated rapidly to the door. The doctor did not rouse himself to answer, and Cosmo left him leaning on his elbow in a thoughtful attitude. In the badly lighted hall he found Spire waiting for him between the foot of the stairs and the door which Cosmo presumed was leading to the offices of the hotel. Again Spire made a vague gesture which seemed to convey a warning, and approached his master on tiptoe.

"Well, what is it? What do you mean by flourishing your arm at me like this?" asked Cosmo sharply, and Spire ventured on a warning "Ssh!"

"Why, there is nobody here," said Cosmo, lowering his voice nevertheless.

"I wanted to tell you, sir, I have seen that fellow."

"What fellow? Oh yes. The fellow with the cap. Where did you see him?"

"He is here," said Spire, pointing to the closed door.

"Here? What could a man like that want here? Did you speak to him?"

"No, sir, he has just come in and for all I know he may be already gone away—though I don't think so."

"Oh, you don't think so. Do you know what he has come for?"

Spire made no answer to the question, but after a short silence: "I will go and see, and if you stand where you are, sir, you will be able to look right into the room. He may not be the man."

Without waiting for an answer he moved towards the closed door and threw it wide open. The room, very much like the dining room but smaller, was lighted gloomily by two smoky oil lamps hanging from the ceiling, over a trestle table having a wooden bench on each side. Bad as the light was Cosmo made out at once the peculiar cap. The wearer, sitting on one of the benches, was leaning with both elbows across the table towards the fair head of a girl half-hidden by a lace scarf. They were engaged in earnest conversation so that they never turned their heads at Spire's entrance. Cosmo had just time to discern the fine line of the girl's shoulders, which were half-tinned from him when Spire shut the door.

II

Returning to his bedroom, Cosmo found the fire of logs still playing fitfully upon the drawn curtains, upon the dim shape of the canopied bed of state, and perceived that Spire as directed had prepared the writing table and had placed a screen round the inviting-looking armchair.

He did not sit down to write. He felt more than ever that in a moment of amused expansion he had made a rash promise to his sister. The difficulty in keeping it had confronted him for the first time in Paris. Henrietta would have liked to hear of people he met, of the great world indulging in the new-found freedom of travel, the English, the French, the Poles, the Germans. Certainly he had seen quite a lot of people; but the problem was as to what could be said about them to a young girl, ignorant of the world, brought up in the country, and having really no notion of what mankind was like. He admitted to himself with introspective sincerity that even he did not exactly know what mankind was really like. He was too much of a novice, and she, obviously, was too innocent to be told of his suspicions and of what it was like. Even to describe the world outwardly was not an easy task—to Henrietta. The world was certainly amusing. Oh yes, it was amusing; but even as he thought that, he felt within him a certain distaste. Just before he had left Paris he had been at a rout given by a great lady. There was a fellow there who somehow became suspected of picking pockets. He was extremely ugly and therefore attracted notice. The great lady, asked if she had invited him, denied ever having seen him before, but he assured her that he had spoken to her already that evening. Her Ladyship then declared that if he was really the man he gave himself out to be, she was not aware that he was in Paris. She imagined him to be in Ireland. Altogether a peculiar story. Cosmo never knew how it had ended because his friend Hollis led him away to introduce him to Mrs. R., who was most affable and entertained him with a complete inventory of her daughter's accomplishments, the daughter herself being then in the room, obviously quite lovely and clever, but certainly a little odd; for a little later, on his being introduced, she had discoursed to him for half an hour on things of the heart, charmingly, but in a perfectly cool and detached manner. There was also Lady Jane, very much in evidence, very much run after, with a voice of engaging sweetness, but very free, not to say licentious, in her talk. How could he confide his impressions of her to Henrietta? As a matter of fact his head had been rather full of Lady Jane for some time. She had, so to speak, attended him all the way from Paris up to the morning of his arrival at Cantelucci's inn. But she had now deserted him. Or was it his mind that had dropped her out of a haunting actuality into that region where the jumble of one's experiences is allowed to rest? But was it possible that a shabby fellow in tight breeches and bad boots, with a peculiarly shaped cap on his head, could have got between him and Lady Jane about the time of sunset?

Cosmo thought suddenly that one's personal life was a very bizarre thing. He could write to his sister that before he had been three hours in Genoa he had been involved in passing secret correspondence from Italy to the Island of Elba. Henrietta had solemnly charged him to write everything he could find out, hear, or even guess about Napoleon. He had heard certainly a lot of most extraordinary stories; and if he had not made any guesses he had been associating with persons who actually had been doing nothing else; frightened persons, exulting people, cast-down people, frivolous people, people with airs of mystery or with airs of contempt. But by Jove, now he had been in personal touch and had actually helped a man of the people who was mysteriously corresponding with Elba. He could write something about that but, after all, was it worth while? Finally he concluded he wouldn't write home at all that evening; pushed the table away, and throwing himself into the armchair extended his legs towards the fire. A moody expression settled on his face. His immobility resembled open-eyed sleep with the red spark of the fire in his unwinking eyes, and a perfect insensibility to outward impressions. But he heard distinctly Spire knocking discreetly at the door. Cosmo's first impulse was to shout that he wasn't wanted, but he changed his mind. "Come in."

Spire shut the door carefully, and crossing the room at once put a log on the fire. Then he said:

"Can't get any hot water this evening, sir. Very sorry, sir. I will see that it won't happen again."

At the same time he thought, "Served him right for picking out such an inn to stay at." Cosmo, still silent, stared at the fire, and when he roused himself at last he perceived Spire in the act of putting down in front of his chair a pair of slippers of shiny leather and red heels.

"Take your boots off, sir?" suggested Spire under his breath.

Cosmo let him do it. "Going to bed now, sir?" asked Spire in the same subdued tone.

"No, but you needn't wait. I won't need you any more to-night."

"Thank you, sir." Spire lingered, boots in hand. "The two small pistols are on the bedside table, sir. I have looked to the primings. This town is lull of rabble from all parts just now, so I hear. The lock of your door is fairly poor. I shall be sleeping just outside in the corridor, sir. They are going to put me a pallet there."

"You will be very cold," protested Cosmo.

"It will be all right, sir. I have got the fur rug out of the carriage. I had everything taken out of the carriage. The yard isn't safe, sir. Nothing is properly safe in this house, so far as I can see."

Cosmo nodded absent-mindedly. "Oh, wait a moment, Spire. That man, that fellow in the cap, is he still downstairs?"

Spire thought rapidly that he wouldn't be a party to bringing any of those ragamuffins up to the bedroom. "Gone a long time ago, sir," he said stolidly.

Cosmo had a vivid recollection of the man's pose of being settled for an earnest and absorbing conversation to last half the night.

"He doesn't belong to this house?" he asked.

"No, sir, he only came to talk to a young woman. I left him taking leave of her to come up to you, sir. I suppose he was the man you meant, sir."

"Yes," said Cosmo, "I have no doubt about it. He will probably turn up again."

Spire admitted reluctantly that it was likely. He had been telling a long tale to that young woman. "She is very good-looking, sir."

"Is she a servant here?"

"Oh no, sir. She came in with that old cut-throat cobbler. They seem to be friendly. I don't like the looks of the people in this house."

"I wonder," said Cosmo, "whether you could manage to obtain for me a quiet talk with that man on the next occasion he comes here."

Spire received this overture in profound silence.

"Do you think you could?" insisted Cosmo.

A dispassionate raising of the eyebrows preceded the apparently irrelevant remark. "The worst of this house, sir, is that it seems open to all sorts of rabble."

"I see. Well, try to think of some way. Spire. You may go now."

Spire, carrying the boots, walked as far as the door, where he turned for a moment. "The only way I can think of, sir," he said, "would be to make friends with that young woman." Before Cosmo could recover from the surprise at the positive statement Spire had gone out and had shut the door.

Cosmo slept heavily but fitfully, with moments of complete oblivion interrupted by sudden starts, when he would lie on his back with open eyes, wondering for a moment where he was, and then fall asleep again before he had time to make a movement. In the morning the first thing he did was to scribble a note to the Countess Montevesso to ask her permission to call that very morning. While writing the address he smiled to himself at the idea that it was after all the little Adèle whom he remembered but dimly, mostly as a fair head hovering near his father's armchair in the big drawing room, the windows of which opened on the western terrace. As a schoolboy during his holidays he saw the two girls, Adèle and his sister, mostly in the evening. He had his own out-of-door pursuits while those girls stayed upstairs with their governess. Remembering how he used to catch glimpses of them, the fair and the dark, walking in the Park, he felt a greater curiosity to see the Countess de Montevesso than if he had never seen her before. He found it impossible to represent her to himself grown up, married for years, the daughter of an ambassador.

When the family of D'Armand departed from Latham Hall, it was as if a picture had faded, a picture of faces, attitudes, and colours, leaving untouched the familiar background of his Yorkshire home, on to which he could never recall them distinctly. He would be meeting a complete stranger and he wondered whether that lady, who, young as she still was, had lived through tragic times and had seen so many people, would remember him at all. Him personally. For as to his home he had no doubt she had not forgotten; neither the stones, nor the woods, nor the streams. And as to the people Cosmo had a distinct notion that she was more familiar with his father than he and Henrietta ever had been. His father was not a man whom anybody could forget. And that Countess of Montevesso, more difficult for him to imagine than a complete stranger, would remember his mother better than he could himself. She had seen so much more of her day after day for something like three years; whereas he was at home only at intervals and while there took Lady Latham for granted, a kind, serene presence, beautifully dressed.

He handed the note to Spire with orders to send it off by one of the ragged idlers about the hotel door. There would be an answer. Then, approaching the window, he perceived that he could not see very much out of it. It was too high above the piazza, which furthermore was masked by the jutting balconies. But the sky was blue with a peculiar deep brilliance and the sunlight slanted over the roofs of the houses on the other side of the piazza. When he opened the window the keen pure air roused his vitality. The faint murmur of voices from below reached him very much as it had reached him downstairs the night before through the closed shutters of the dining room, as if the population of the town had never gone to bed.

While Spire was serving his breakfast in his room he wondered what the Countess of Montevesso would look like. The same fair head but higher above the ground and with the hair no longer flowing over the shoulders, but done up no doubt most becomingly and perhaps turned darker with age. It would be the hair of the daughter of an ambassador, able to judge of men and affairs, a woman of position, a very fine lady. Perhaps just a fine lady; but the memory of the child came to him with renewed force, gracious, quiet, with something timid and yet friendly in all its gestures, with his father's hand smoothing the fair hair. . . . No. Not merely a fine lady.

Cosmo had no inborn aptitude for mere society life. Though not exactly shy, he lacked that assurance of manner which his good looks and his social status ought to have given him. He suspected there was too much mockery in the world, and the undoubted friendliness he had met with, especially from women, seemed to him always a little suspect, the effect not of his own merit, of which he had no idea, but of a shallow, good-natured compassion. He imagined himself awkward in company. The very brilliance of the entertainments, of which he had seen already a good many, was apt to depress his spirits. Often during talk with some pretty woman he would feel that he was not meant for that sort of life, and then suddenly he would withdraw into his shell. In that way he had earned for himself the reputation of being a little strange. He was to a certain extent aware of it, but he was not aware that this very thing made him interesting.

A gust of diffidence came over him while he was trying to eat some breakfast. "I really don't want to see that Countess," he thought. Then remembering the intonation in his father's voice when talking of Adèle, he wondered whether perchance he would find an uncommon personality. Cosmo had a profound belief in his father, though he was well aware that he had never understood him thoroughly. . . . But if she is a woman out of the common, he reflected further, then she can't possibly be interested in a rough schoolboy grown into a young man of no particular importance. No doubt she would be amiable enough. . . .

"Clear away all these things. Spire," he said, "and go downstairs to see if the messenger is back."

The messenger was not back yet; and assisted by Spire, Cosmo began to dress himself with extreme care. The tying of his neckcloth was an irritating affair, and so was Spire's perfectly wooden face while he was holding up the glass to him for that operation. Cosmo spoiled two neckcloths and became extremely dissatisfied with the cut and colour of various articles of attire which Spire presented to him one after another. The fashions for men were perfectly absurd. By an effort of mind Cosmo overcame this capricious discontent with familiar things and finished his dressing. Then he sent Spire once more downstairs to inquire if the messenger was back. Obediently, Spire disappeared, but once gone it did not seem as though he meant to return at all. There was no Spire. There was no bell-pull in the room either.

Cosmo stuck his head out through the door. Absolute silence reigned in the well of the stairs. A woman in black, on her knees beside a pail of water and scrubbing the floor of the corridor, looked up at him. Cosmo drew his head in. She was a pitiful hag. . . . He was sure of a gracious reception, of course. He was also sure of meeting a lot of people of all sorts. He wondered what sort of society she received. Everybody, no doubt; Austrians, Italians, French; all the triumphant reactionaries, all the depressed heads bobbing up again after the storm, venomous, revengeful, oppressive, odious. What the devil had become of Spire?

The long window right down to the floor had remained open. Suddenly the sound of a drum reached Cosmo's ears. Stepping out on a balcony, he saw a company of infantry in white coats marching across a distant corner of the piazza. Austrians! Yes, their time had come. A voice behind him said: "The messenger is back, sir." Cosmo stepped in and saw Spire empty-handed. "There's a verbal answer, sir."

"What is it? You haven't spoken with the messenger, have you?"

"I have seen him, sir, but I got the message through the innkeeper. He speaks a little English. The lady would be glad to see you as soon after the fourth hour as possible. They have their own way of reckoning time, but as far as I can understand it, sir, it means something between ten and eleven. At any rate, it's what Cantelucci says, and he can tell the time by an English watch all right."

"Shut the window, Spire. I don't want to hear that drum. Yes, it would mean as soon after ten as possible, but why has the fellow been so long? Is it very far?"

"No, sir, I think it's quite close, really. He was so long because he has been trying to give your note to the lady herself and there was some difficulty about it. That innkeeper tells me that instead of handing it to the porter the fellow got in through the kitchen door and was dodging about a passage for some time."

Cosmo looked fixedly at Spire, whose face expressed no opinion whatever on those proceedings.

"Dodging in a passage," repeated Cosmo. "But did he see the lady herself?"

"Apparently not, sir. Cantelucci slanged him for being so long, but he said he thought he was acting for the best. He would have been there yet if a black woman hadn't come along and snatched the letter out of his hand. It was she too who brought down the message from the lady."

"Oh, yes," said Cosmo. "Don't you remember there was a black maid?"

"Yes, sir, I remember perfectly well, in the house-keeper's room. She learned to talk English very quickly, but she was a little spitfire."

"Was she?"

Spire busied himself in brushing Cosmo's hat while he remarked in an explanatory tone: "She could never understand a joke, sir."

He attended Cosmo into the hall, where Cantelucci with his usual intense gravity and a deep bow asked whether the signore would want a carriage. Cosmo, however, preferred walking; therefore the youth who had taken Cosmo's note was directed to guide the English milord to the Palazzo Brignoli. He had a tousled head of hair and wore a jacket that might have belonged at one time to a hussar's uniform, with all its trimmings and buttons cut off and a ragged hole in each elbow. His cheeks were sunken, his eyes rolled expressively, and his smile discovered a set of very sound teeth.

"*Si, si*, Palazzo Rosso," he said.

Cantelucci explained in his imperturbable and solemn manner that the populace gave that name to the Palace on account of the red granite of which it was built, and the thin-faced lad, bounding forward, preceded Cosmo across the piazza, looking over his shoulder from time to time. Cosmo's doubts and apprehensions disappeared before the inevitable charm and splendour of the town. At the corner of a narrow lane and a small open space with some trees growing in the centre of it the ragged guide stopped and, pointing at a dark and magnificent building, left him alone. Massive and sombre, ornate and heavy, with a dark aspect and enormous carvings, the Palace where little Adèle was living had to Cosmo's eye the air of a sumptuous prison. The portal with its heavy iron-studded doors was reached by a flight of shallow steps, a segment of a wide circle, guarded on each side by an enormous griffin seated, tensely alert with wing and claw, on a high and narrow pedestal. On ascending the steps Cosmo discovered that the heavy door was ajar, just enough to let him slip in; and, at once, from the gloom of the arched passage he saw the inner sunshine on the oleanders of the inner court, flagged with marble, from whence a broad staircase ascended to the colonnaded gallery of the first floor.

Cosmo had seen no porter or other living soul, and there was no sound of any sort, no appearance of movement anywhere. Even the leaves of the oleanders kept perfectly still. In the light of the morning a slanting shadow cut the western wall into two triangles, one dark, the other glowing as with a red fire; and Cosmo remained for a moment spellbound by a strong impression of empty grandeur, magnificence, and solitude.

A voice behind him, issuing from somewhere in the big gateway through which he had passed, cried: "Ascend, signore!" Cosmo began to mount the open staircase, embarrassed as though he had been watched by thousands of eyes. In the gallery he hesitated, for the several doors he could see remained closed, and the only sound that reached his ears was the gentle plashing of the fountain in the court below him.

Before he had made up his mind the door in front of him opened fairly wide, but he could not see the person till he had entered an anteroom with narrow red and gilt settees ranged along its white walls. The door shut behind him and, turning round, he confronted a dark, plump mulatto woman who was staring at him with an expression of intense admiration. She clapped her hands in ecstasy and, opening her mouth, exhibited her white teeth in a low cackling laugh.

"*Bonjour*, Aglae," said Cosmo readily.

The woman laughed again in sheer delight. "You remember my name, Mr. Cosmo! You quite frighten me, you grow so big. I remember you climb tree and throw nice ripe apple to the black girl. . . ." Her eyes gleamed and rolled absurdly.

Cosmo was so strangely touched by this extremely slight reminiscence of his tree-climbing boyhood, that when she added, "That was a good time," he was quite ready to agree, thereby provoking another burst of delightful laughter. But Aglae was controlling herself obviously. Her laughter was subdued. It had not the unbounded freedom of sound that used to reverberate exotically in the dark passages at the back of Latham Hall; though there, too, Aglae tried to subdue it in view of rebukes or sarcastic comments in the servants' hall. It stopped suddenly and Aglae in a tone of sober respect wanted to know how the Seignior was. Cosmo said that his father was very well.

"He a very-great gentleman," commented Aglae. "I always tremble when I see him. You very fine gentleman too, Mr. Cosmo."

She moved to one of the inner doors, but as Cosmo was following her she raised her hand to prevent him and opened the door only a little way, then came back and said in a lower tone, "It's to hear the bell better when it rings. . . . Will you wait a little bit here?" she asked anxiously.

"I will," said Cosmo, "but surely you don't want to tremble before me. What is the matter?"

"Nothing at all is the matter." Aglae tossed her head, tied up in a bandana handkerchief, with something of the spirit of the old days.

Cosmo was amused. "I no tremble before you," she continued. "I always like you very much. I am glad with all my heart to see you here."

All the time she turned her ear to the door she had left the least bit ajar. She had on a high-waisted white calico dress, white stockings, and Genoese slippers on her feet. Her dark brown hands moved uneasily.

"And how is Madame la Comtesse?" asked Cosmo.

"Miss Adèle very well. Anyway she never says anything else. She very great lady now. All the town come here, but she wants to see you alone after all these years."

"It's very kind of her," said Cosmo. "I was wondering whether she remembered me at all."

Now the excitement of seeing him had worn off, he was surprised at the careworn expression of the mulatto's face. For a moment it seemed to him like a tragic mask, then came the flash of white teeth, strangely unlike a smile.

"She remember everything," said Aglae. "She . . . she . . . Mr. Cosmo, you no boy now. I tell you that Miss Adèle had not a moment's peace since she drive away from your big home in the country one very cold day. I remember very well. Little birds fall dead off the tree. I feel ready to fall dead myself."

"I was away at school," said Cosmo. He remembered that on his return the disappearance of those people had not produced a very strong impression on him. In fact, the only thing he had missed was, in the evening, the fair head of the stranger Adèle near the dark head of his sister Henrietta. And the next evening he had not even missed that!

While these thoughts were passing through his head he waited, looking at Aglae with a faint smile of which he was not aware. The mulatto girl seemed to have concentrated all her faculties on listening for the sound of a bell. It came at last. Cosmo heard it, too, very distant, faint and prolonged. A handbell.

"Now," said Aglae under her breath, and Cosmo followed her through a suite of rooms, magnificent but under-furnished, with the full light excluded by half-closed jalousies. The vista was terminated by a white and gold door at which Aglae stopped and looked back at him over her shoulder with an air of curiosity, anxiety, or was it hesitation? But certainly without a smile. As to his own it had stiffened permanently on his lips. Before turning the handle of the door the mulatto listened for a moment. Then she threw it open, disclosing a room full of light indeed but which Cosmo could not see in its full extent because of a screen cutting off the view. His last thought as he crossed the threshold was, "It will be interesting," and then he heard the door shut behind him, leaving him as it were alone with the heavy screen of figured velvet and three windows through which sunshine poured in a way that almost blinded him after his long experience of half lights.

He walked clear of the screen, and he was surprised at the vast size of the room. Here and there were other screens and a quite unexpected quantity of elegant furniture amongst which he felt for a moment as if lost. All this shone and gleamed and glowed with colour in the freshness and brilliance of the sunny morning. "Why, there's nobody here," he thought with a mingled sense of disappointment and relief. To his left above a square of carpet that was like a flower-bed rose a white mantelpiece which in its proportion and sumptuosity was like a low but much carved portal surmounted by an enormous sheet of glass reaching up to the cornice of the ceiling. He stepped on to the flowers, feeling now somewhat vexed, and only then perceived away at the other end of the room, in a corner beyond a fourth window, a lady seated at a writing table with her back to him. Barred by the gilt openwork of the chair-back he saw her dress, the only bit of blue in the room. There was some white lace about her shoulders, her fair head was bent, she was writing rapidly.

Whoever she was she seemed not to be aware of his presence. Cosmo did not know whether to wait in silence or say something, or merely warn her by a slight cough. What a stupid position, he thought. At that moment the lady put the pen down and rose from her chair brusquely, yet there was a perceptible moment before she turned round and advanced towards him. She was tall. But for the manner of his introduction, which could leave no room for doubt, the impression that this could not be the lady he had come to see would have been irresistible. As it was Cosmo felt apologetic, as though he had come to the wrong house. It occurred to him also that the lady had been from the very first aware of his presence. He was struck by the profundity of her eyes, which were fixed on him. The train of her blue robe followed on the floor. Her well-shaped head was a mass of short fair curls, and while she approached him Cosmo saw the colour leave her cheeks, the passing away of an unmistakable blush. She stopped and said in an even voice:

"Don't you recognize me?"

He recovered his power of speech but not exactly the command of his thoughts, which were overwhelmed by a variety of strong and fugitive impulses.

"I have never known you," he said with a tone of the profoundest conviction.

She smiled (Cosmo was perfectly sure that he had never seen that sort of smile or the promise even of anything so enchanting), and sank slowly on to a sofa whose brocaded silk, gray like pure ashes, and the carved frame painted with flowers and picked with gold, acquired an extraordinary value from the colour of her dress and the grace of her attitude. She pointed to an armchair, close by. Cosmo sat down. A very small table of ebony inlaid with silver stood between them, her hand rested on it; and Cosmo looked at it with appreciation, as if it had been an object of art, before he raised his eyes to the expectant face.

"Frankly," he said, "didn't you think that a complete stranger had been brought into the room?"

He said this very seriously, and she answered him in a light tone. "For a moment I was afraid to look round. I sat there with my back to you. It was absurd after having been imprudent enough to let you come in the morning. You kept so still that you might have been already gone. I took fright, I jumped up, but I need not have hesitated. You are still the same boy."

Cosmo paid very little attention to what she said. Without restraint and disguise, in open admiration he was observing her with all his might, saying to himself, "Is it possible—this—Adèle!" He recollected himself, however, sufficiently to murmur that men changed more slowly and perhaps less completely than women. The Countess of Montevesso was not of that opinion, or, at any rate, not in this case.

"It isn't that at all. I know because I used to look at you with that attention worthy of the heir of the Latham name, whereas you never honoured the French girl by anything more than a casual glance. Why should you have done more? You had the dogs, the horses, your first gun.

I remember the gun. You showed it to both of us, to your sister and myself while we were walking in the park. You shouted to us and came across the grass, brandishing your gun, while the governess—I don't remember her name—screamed at you. Oh *mon dieu! N'approaches pas!* You paid not the slightest attention to her. You had a flushed face. Of course her screaming frightened us at first, and just as we were preparing to get very interested in your gun you walked off with a look of contempt."

"Did I behave so badly as that?" said Cosmo, feeling suddenly very much at ease with that lady with whom he had never even exchanged a formal greeting. She had grown more animated. As he was very fond of his sister he answered her numerous questions about Henrietta with interest and pleasure. From that subject the lady on the sofa, who may or may not have been Adèle d'Armand at one time, went on putting a series of questions about the house and all the people in it in a manner that proved a precise and affectionate recollection of those days. The memory of the countryside seemed to have been cherished by her too, and Cosmo's heart warmed to the subject. She remembered certain spots in the park and certain points of view in the neighbourhood as though she had left them but a year before. She seemed not to have forgotten a single servant in the house. She asked after Spire.

"I have got him with me," said Cosmo. "Of course he has grown elderly."

He almost forgot to whom he was speaking. Without associating her very distinctly with the child Adèle, he was taking the Countess de Montevesso for granted. He delighted in seeing her so quiet and so perfectly natural. The first effect of her appearance persisted, with only the added sense of the deep dark blue of her eyes, an impression of living profundity that made his thoughts about her pause. But he was unconsciously grateful to her for the fact that she had never given him a moment of that acute social awkwardness from which he used to suffer so much; though there could not be the slightest doubt that the little Adèle (if there had ever been a little Adèle) was now a very fine lady indeed. But she loved the old place and everything and everybody in it. Of that too there could be no doubt. The few references she made to his mother touched and surprised Cosmo. They seemed to imply some depth in her which he, the son, and Henrietta, the daughter, had failed to penetrate. In contrast with that, Cosmo remarked that after the inquiry after Sir Charles's health, which was one of her first questions, his father was not mentioned again.

"Are you going to make a stay in Genoa?" she asked after a pause.

"A few days," said Cosmo, in an irresolute tone, because he did not know what answer was expected to this inquiry, the first which had nothing to do with Yorkshire. His interest in the rest of Italy was, he perceived, very small. But by the association of ideas he thought suddenly of the passing hours. He raised his eyes to a faintly engraved brass disc with black hands hung on the wall above one of the two doors at that end of the room which he was facing. The black hands pointed to eleven, but what prevented his eyes from returning at once to the delighted contemplation of the Countess of Montevesso was the fact that the door below the clock seemed to have moved slightly.

"I intend to see something of Italy," he said. "My time really is my own, I have nothing special to do. It seems to me that the principal object of my journey has been attained now. I don't think my father would be surprised to hear that I had turned back after leaving Genoa."

The Countess looking up at this, their eyes remained fastened together for a time and Cosmo thought: "What on earth am I saying?" He watched her lips move to form the words which quite frightened him.

"Did Sir Charles give you a message for me?"

He thought he had brought this on himself. It was a painful moment. It lasted long enough to give the Countess the time to assume an expression of indifference, startling after the low tone of her question.

"No," said Cosmo truthfully. "I have only a message for your father." He waited a moment. "But I will tell you one of the last things Henrietta told me. She told me that when you were married my father could think of nothing for days but you."

He did not venture to look at her; then added impulsively, "My father loved you dearly. We children could see it very well. Ad — —"

"Why don't you finish my name?" her seductive voice asked.

Cosmo coloured. "Well, you know, I never heard you really called by any other name. It came naturally since I suppose you must be—Adèle."

Madame de Montevesso, who had been hanging on his lips, was surprised by Cosmo raising his eyes to stare intensely into the part of the room behind her back. Just as he was making his apology he had noticed the door under the clock swing open without any sound at all; and there entered quite noiselessly, too, and with something ambiguous in the very motion, a young girl (nothing could have been more unexpected) in a sort of dishabille of a white skirt and a long pink jacket of some very thin stuff which had a silky shimmer. She made a few steps and stopped. She was rather short, her hair was intensely black and drawn tightly away from her forehead. Cosmo felt sure (though he couldn't see) that it was done in one long plait at the back. Her face was a short oval, her chin blunt, her nose a little too big and her black eyes perfectly round. Cosmo had the time to notice all this because astonishment prevented him from looking away. The girl advanced slowly if with perfect assurance, and stared unwinkingly at Cosmo, who in the extremity of his embarrassment got up from his chair. The young girl then stopped short and for a moment the three persons in the room preserved an absolute immobility. Then the Countess glanced over her shoulder leisurely and addressed Cosmo.

"This is Clelia, a niece of my husband." Cosmo made a deep bow to the possessor of the round black eyes. "I didn't know of her existence till about a fortnight ago," added Madame de Montevesso carelessly. The round-eyed girl still staring hard made a curtsey to Cosmo. "My husband," went on Adèle, "has also two old aunts living here. I have never seen them. This house is very big."

Cosmo resumed his seat and there was a moment of silence. The girl sat down in the chair before the writing table sideways, folded her arms on its back, and rested her chin on her hands. Her round eyes examined Cosmo with a sort of animal frankness. He thought suddenly that it was time to bring his visit to an end. He would have risen at once but for the Countess de Montevesso beginning to speak to him, still in English. She seemed to have guessed what was passing through his mind.

"Don't go yet for a moment," she said, in a perfectly unconcerned voice, then paused. "We were talking about your father."

"As to him," said Cosmo, "I have nothing more to say. I have told you all the truth as far as I am certain of it."

She inclined her head slowly and in the same level voice:

"The Court is here and most of the foreign ambassadors. We are waiting here for the arrival of the Queen of Sardinia, who may or may not come within the next month or so. This is considered a good post of observation, but there is very little to observe just now from the diplomatic point of view. Most of us have exhausted almost all emotions. Life has grown suddenly very dull. We gossip a little about each other; we wait for the end of the Vienna Congress and discuss the latest rumour that floats about. Yes. The play is over, the stage seems empty. If I were you I would stay a little longer here."

"I certainly mean to stay here for some time," declared Cosmo with sudden resolution.

"That's right," she continued in the same indifferent tone. "But wait a few days before you write home. You have awakened old memories in me. Inconceivably distant," she went on in a voice more expressionless than ever, "and the dormant feelings of what seems quite another age."

Cosmo smiled at this. The girl with round eyes was keeping perfectly still with her watchful stare. Madame de Montevesso seemed to read Cosmo's thoughts.

"Yes," she insisted. "I feel very old and everything is very far. I am twenty-six and I have been married very nearly ten years now."

Cosmo, looking at her face, thought that those had been the most agitated ten years of European history. He said, "I have no doubt that Yorkshire must seem very far away to you."

"I suppose you write very often home?" she said.

Cosmo defended himself from being one of those people who write letters about their travels. He had no talent for that; and then what could one write to a young girl like Henrietta and to a man as austere as his father, who had so long retired from the world? Cosmo had found it very difficult. Of course he took care to let them know pretty often that he was safe and sound.

Adèle could see this point of view. She seemed amused by the innocent difficulties of a young man having no one but a father and a sister to write to. She ascertained that he had no intimate friend left behind to whom he could confide his impressions. Cosmo said he had formed none of those intimacies that induce a man to share his innermost thoughts and feelings with somebody else.

"Probably your father was like that too," said Madame de Montevesso. "I fancy he must have been very difficult to please, and still more difficult to conquer."

"Oh, as to that," said Cosmo, "I can safely say I've never been conquered," and he laughed boyishly. He confessed further that he had the habit of thinking contradictorily about most things. "My father was never like that," he concluded.

The gravity with which she listened to him now disconcerted him secretly. At last she nodded and opined that his difficulties had their source in the liveliness of his sympathies. He declared that he suffered most at times from the difficulty of making himself understood by men of his own age.

"And the women?" she asked quietly.

"Oh, the women!" he said, without the slightest levity. "One would not even try." He raised his eyes and, obeying a sudden impulse, added: "I think that perhaps you could understand me."

"That would be because I am so much older," she said. Cosmo discovered in her delicately modelled face, with all its grace and freshness of youth, an interrogative profundity of expression, the impress of the problems of life and the conflicts of the soul. The great light of day had treated her kindly. Bathed in the sunshine entering through the four windows, she appeared to him wonderful in the glow of her complexion, in the harmony of her form and the composed nobility of her attitude. He felt this wonderfulness of her whole person in some sort physically, and thought that he had looked at her too long. He glanced aside and met the dark girl's round unwinking stare of a cat ready to fly at one. She had not moved a hair's breadth, and Cosmo felt reluctant to take his eyes off her exactly as though she had been a fierce cat. He heard the voice of the Countess of Montevesso and had to turn to her.

"Well, wait a few days before you write home about . . . Genoa."

"I had a mind to begin a letter yesterday," he said.

"What? Already! Only a few hours after your arrival!"

"Yes. Henrietta is very anxious to hear everything relating to the Emperor Napoleon."

Madame de Montevesso was genuinely surprised. Her voice lost its equable charm while she asked what on earth could he have had to tell of Napoleon that he could not have written to her from Paris.

"Yes. He is in everybody's thoughts and on everybody's lips there," he said. "Whenever three people come together he is the presence that is with them. But last night . . ."

He was on the point of telling her of his adventure on the tower when she struck in:

"The Congress will put an end to all that presently." It checked Cosmo's expansiveness and he said instead:

"It's very possible. But last night on arriving here I experienced a curious sensation of his nearness. I went down in the evening to look at the Port."

"He isn't certainly very far from here. And what are your feelings about him?"

"Oh," he rejoined lightly, "as about everything else in the world—contradictory."

Madame de Montevesso rose suddenly, saying:

"I won't ask you, then, as to your feelings about myself." Cosmo stood up hastily. He was a little the taller of the two but their faces were nearly on a level. "I should like you to make up your mind about me before you take up your traveller's pen," continued Adèle. "Come again this evening. There will be a few people here; and, as you have said, when a few people come together just now Napoleon is always with them, an unseen presence. But you will see my father. Do you remember him at all?"

Cosmo assured her that he remembered the Marquis d'Armand perfectly. He was on the point of making his parting bow when Madame de Montevesso, with the two words "à l'Anglaise," put out her hand. He took it and forgot himself in the unexpected sensation of this contact. He was in no haste to release it when to his extreme surprise, with a slight movement of her eyes towards the girl at the writing table, Madame de Montevesso said:

"Did you ever see anything like that?"

Cosmo was taken completely aback. He dropped her hand. He did not know what to say, and even if it was proper for him to smile. Madame de Montevesso continued in a voice betraying no sentiment of any kind: "I can never be sure of my privacy now. Do you understand that I am her aunt? She wanders all over this palazzo very much like a domestic animal, only more observant, and she is by no means an idiot. Luckily she knows no language but Italian."

They had been moving slowly towards the other end of the room, but now Madame de Montevesso stopped and returned Cosmo's parting bow with a slight inclination of her head. Before passing round the screen between him and the door Cosmo glanced back. The girl on the chair had not stirred.

He had half a hope that the mulatto maid would be waiting for him. But he saw no one. As he crossed the courtyard he might have thought himself leaving an uninhabited house. But the streets through which he made his way to his inn were thronged with people. The day was quite warm. Already on the edge of the pavements, here and there, there was a display of flowers for sale; and at every turn he saw more people who seemed carefree, and the women with their silken shoes and the lace scarves on their heads appeared to him quite charming. The plaza was a scene of constant movement. Here and there a group stood still, conversing in low voices but with expressive gestures. As he approached his hotel he caught an evanescent sight of the man he had met on the tower. His cap was unmistakable. Cosmo mended his pace but the man had disappeared; and after looking in all directions Cosmo went up the steps of the inn. In his room he found Spire folding methodically some clothes.

"I saw that man," said Cosmo, handing him his hat.

"Was he following you, sir?" asked Spire.

"No, I saw his back quite near this house."

"I shouldn't wonder if he were coming here," opined Spire.

"In any case I wouldn't have spoken to him in the piazza," said Cosmo.

"Much better not, sir," said the servant.

"After all," said Cosmo, "I don't know that I have anything to say to him."

From these words Spire concluded that his master had found something more interesting to occupy his mind. While he went on with his work he talked to Cosmo, who had thrown himself into an armchair, of some repairs needed to the carriage, and also informed him that the English doctor had left a message asking whether Mr. Latham would do him the honour to take his midday meal with him at the same table as last night. After a slight hesitation Cosmo assented, and Spire, saying that he would go and tell them downstairs, left the room.

In the solitude favourable to concentration of thought Cosmo discovered that he could not think connectedly, either of the fair curls of the Countess de Montevesso or of the vague story of her marriage. Strictly speaking he knew nothing of it; and this ignorance interfered with the process of consecutive thinking; but he formed some images and even came to the verge of that state in which one sees visions. The obscurity of her past helped the freedom of his fancies. He had an intuitive conviction that he had seen her in the fullest brilliance of her beauty and of the charm of her mind. A woman like that was a great power, he reflected, and then it occurred to him that, marvellous as she was, she was not her own mistress.

Some church clock striking loudly the hour roused him up, but before he went downstairs he paced the floor to and fro several times. And when he forced himself out of that empty room it was with a profound disgust of all he was going to see and hear, a momentary repulsion towards the claims of the world, like a man tearing himself away from the side of a beloved mistress.

III

Returning that evening to the Palazzo Brignoli, Cosmo found the lantern under the vaulted roof lighted. There was also a porter in gold-laced livery and a cocked hat who saluted him, and in the white anteroom with red benches along the walls two lackeys made ready to divest him of his cloak. But a man in sombre garments detained Cosmo, saying that he was the ambassador's valet, and led him away along a very badly lighted inner corridor. He explained that His Excellency the Ambassador wished to see Monsieur Latham for a few moments in private before Monsieur Latham joined the general company. The ambassador's cabinet into which he introduced Cosmo was lighted by a pair of candelabra. Cosmo was told that His Excellency was finishing dressing, and then the man disappeared. Cosmo noticed that there were several doors besides the one by which he had entered, which was the least conspicuous of them all, and in fact so inconspicuous, corresponding exactly to a painted panel, that it might have been called a secret door. Other doors were framed in costly woods, lining the considerable thicknesses of the walls. One of them opened without noise and Cosmo saw enter a man somewhat taller than he had expected to see, with a white head, in a coat with softly gleaming embroideries and a broad ribbon across his breast. He advanced, opening his arms wide, and Cosmo, who noticed that one of the hands was holding a snuffbox, submitted with good grace to the embrace of the Marquis d'Armand, whose lips touched his cheeks one after another and whose hands then rested at arm's length on his shoulder for a moment.

"Sit down, *mon enfant*," were the first words spoken, and Cosmo obeyed, facing the armchair into which the Marquis had dropped. A white meagre hand set in fine lace moved the candelabra on the table, and Cosmo good-humouredly submitted to being contemplated in silence. This man in a splendid coat, white-headed and with a broad ribbon across his breast, seemed to have no connection whatever with his father's guest, whom as a boy he remembered walking with Sir Charles amongst deep shrubberies or writing busily at one end of the long table in the library of Latham Hall, always with the slightly subdued mien of an exile and an air of being worried by the possession of unspeakable secrets which he preserved even when playing at backgammon with Sir Charles in the great drawing room.

Cosmo, returning the gaze of the tired eyes, remarked that the ambassador looked old but not at all senile.

At last the Marquis declared that he could detect the lineaments of his old friend in the son's face, and in a voice that was low and kindly put a series of questions about Sir Charles, about London and his old friends there; questions which Cosmo, especially as to the latter, was not always able to answer fully.

"I forget! You are still so young," said the ambassador, recollecting himself. This young man sitting here before him with a friendly smile had his friends amongst his own contemporaries, shared the ideas and the views of his own generation which had grown up since the Revolution, to whom the Revolution was only a historical fact and whose enthusiasms had a strange complexion, for the undisciplined hopes of the young make them reckless in words and sometimes in actions. The Marquis's own generation had been different. It had had no inducement to be reckless. It had been born to a settled order of things. Certainly a few philosophers had been indulging for years in subversive sentimentalism, but the foundations of Europe seemed unshakable. He noticed Cosmo's expectant attitude and said:

"I wonder what my dear old friend is thinking of all this."

"It is not very easy to get at my father's thoughts," confessed Cosmo. "After all, you must know my father much better than I do, Monsieur le Marquis."

"In the austerity of his convictions your father was more like a republican of ancient times," said the Marquis seriously. "Does that surprise you, my young friend? . . ." Cosmo shook his head slightly. . . . "Yet we always agreed very well. Your father understood every kind of fidelity. The world had never known him and it will never know him now. But I, who approached him closely, could have nothing but the greatest respect for his character and for his far-seeing wisdom."

"I am very glad to hear you say this," interjected Cosmo.

"He was a scornful man," said the Marquis, then paused and repeated once more: "Yes. *Un grand dédaigneux.* He was that. But one accepted it from him as one would not from another man, because one felt that it was not the result of mean grievances or disappointed hopes. Now the old order is coming back and, whatever my old friend may think of it, he had his share in that work."

Cosmo raised his head. "I had no idea," he murmured.

"Yes," said the Marquis. "Indirectly if you like. All I could offer to my Princes was my life, my toil, the sacrifice of my deepest feelings as husband and father. I don't say this to boast. I could not have acted otherwise. But for my share of the work, risky, often desperate, and continuously hopeless as it seemed to be, I have to thank your father's help, *mon jeune ami*. It came out of that fortune which some day will be yours. The only thing in all the activities the penetrating mind of your father was not scornful of was my fidelity. He understood that it was above the intrigued, the lies, the selfish stupidities of that exiles' life which we all shared with our Princes. They will never know how much they owe to that English gentleman. When parting with my wife and child I was sustained by the thought that his friendship and care were extended over them and would not fail."

"I have heard nothing of all this," said Cosmo. "Of course I was not ignorant of the great friendship that united you to him. This is one of the things that the world does know about my father."

"Have you brought a letter for me?" asked the Marquis. "I haven't heard from him for a long time. After we returned to France, through the influence of my son-in-law, communications were very difficult. Ten years of war, my dear friend, ten years."

"Father very seldom takes a pen in hand now," said Cosmo, "but . . ."

The Marquis interrupted him. "When you write home, my dear friend, tell him that I never gave way to promptings of mean ambition or an unworthy vanity. Tell him that I twice declined the Embassy of Madrid which was pressed on me, and that if I accepted the nomination as a Commissioner for settling the frontiers with the representatives of the Allied Powers it was at the cost of my deepest feelings and only to serve my vanquished country. My secret missions had made me known to many European statesmen. I knew I was liked. I thought I could do some good. The Russians, I must say, were quite charming, and you may tell your father that Sir Charles Stewart clothed his demands in the form of the most perfect politeness; but all those transactions were based after all on the right of the strongest. I had black moments and I suffered as a Frenchman. I suffered . . ."

The Marquis got up, walked away to the other end of the room, then coming back dropped into the armchair again. Cosmo was too startled by this display of feeling to rise. The ambassadorial figure in the laced coat exhaled a deep sigh. "Your father knows that, unlike so many of the other refugees, I have always remained a Frenchman. One would have paid any price almost to avoid this humiliation."

Cosmo was gratified by the anxiety of a king's friend to, as it were, justify himself before his father. He discovered that even this old royalist had been forced, if only for a moment, to regret the days of imperial victories. The Marquis tapped his snuffbox, took a pinch of snuff, and composed himself.

"Of course when this Turin mission was unexpectedly pressed on me I went to the King himself and explained that, having refused a much higher post, I could not think of accepting this one. But the King pointed out that this was an altogether different position. The King of Sardinia was his brother-in-law. There was nothing to say against such an argument. His Majesty was also good enough to say that he was anxious to grant me any favour I might ask. I didn't want any favours but I had to think of something on the spur of the moment and I begged for a special right of entrée on days on which there are no receptions. I couldn't resist so much graciousness," continued the Marquis. "I have managed to keep clear of prejudices that poison and endanger the hopes of this restoration, but I am a royalist, a man of my own time. Remember to tell your father all this, my dear young friend."

"I shall not fail," said Cosmo, wondering within himself at the power of such a strange argument, yet feeling a liking and respect for that old man torn between rejoicing and sorrow at the end of his troubled life.

"I should like him to know, too," the Marquis said in his bland and friendly voice, "that M. de Talleyrand just before he left for Vienna held out to me the prospect of the London Embassy later. That, certainly, I would not refuse, if only to be nearer a man to whom my obligations are immense and only equalled by the affection I had borne towards him through all those unhappy years."

"My father—" began Cosmo—"I ought to have given you his message before—told me to give you his love and to tell you that when you are tired of your grandeurs there is always a large place for you in his house."

Cosmo was surprised at the sudden movement of the Marquis, who leaned over the arm of his chair and put his hand over his eyes. For a time complete silence reigned in the room. Then Cosmo said:

"I think somebody is scratching at the door."

The Marquis sat up and listened, then raising his voice: "You may come in."

The man in black clothes, entering through the hidden door, stopped at some distance in a respectful attitude. The Marquis beckoned him to approach, and the man, bending to his ear, said in a low voice which was, however, audible to Cosmo: "He is here." The Marquis answered in an undertone, "He came rather early. He must wait," at which the man murmured something which Cosmo couldn't hear. He became aware that the Marquis looked at him irresolutely before he said:

"My dear boy, you will have to make your entrance into my daughter's salon together with me. I thought of sending you back the way you came, but as a matter of fact the passage is blocked. . . . Bring him in and let him sit here after we are gone," he directed the man in black, and Cosmo only then recognized Bernard, the servant of proved fidelity in all the misfortunes of the D'Armand family. Bernard withdrew without responding in any way to Cosmo's smile of recognition. "In my position," continued the Marquis, "I have to make use of agents more or less shady. Those men often object to being seen. Their occupation is risky. There is a man of that sort waiting in the corridor."

Cosmo said he was at the Marquis's orders, but the ambassador remained in the armchair, tapping the lid of his snuffbox slightly.

"You saw my daughter this morning, I understand." Cosmo made an assenting bow. Madame de Montevesso had done him the honour to receive him in the morning.

"You speak French very well," said the Marquis. "I don't really know why the English are supposed to be bad linguists. We French are much worse. Did you two speak French together?"

"No," said Cosmo, "we spoke in English. It was Madame de Montevesso's own choice."

"She hasn't quite forgotten it, has she?"

"It struck me," said Cosmo, "that your daughter has forgotten neither the language nor the people, nor the sights of her early life. I was touched by the fidelity of her memory and the warmth of her feelings."

His own tone had warmth enough in it to make the Marquis look up at him. There was a short pause. "None of us are likely to forget those days of noble and infinite kindness. We were but vagrants on a hostile earth. My daughter could not have forgotten! As long as there is anybody of our name left . . ."

The Marquis checked himself abruptly, but almost at once went on in a slightly changed tone: "But I am alone of my name now. I wish I had had a son so that gratitude could have been perpetuated from generation to generation and become a traditional thing between our two families. But this is not to be. Perhaps you didn't know I had a brother. He was much younger than myself and I loved him as though he had been my son.

Directly I had placed my wife and child in safety, your father insisted on giving me the means to return to France secretly in order to try and save that young head. But all my attempts failed. It fell on the scaffold. He was one of the last victims of the sanguinary madness of that time. . . . But let us talk of something else. What are your plans, my young friend?"

Cosmo confessed that he had no plans. He intended to stay in Genoa for some time. Madame de Montevesso had been good enough to encourage him in that idea, and really there was such a feeling of leisure in the European atmosphere that he didn't see why he should make any plans. The world was enjoying its first breathing time. Cosmo corrected himself—well no, perhaps not exactly enjoying. To be strictly truthful he had not noticed much feeling of joy. . . . He hesitated a moment but the whole attitude of the Marquis was so benevolent and encouraging that he continued to take stock of his own sensations and continued in the same strain. There was activity, lots of activity, agitation perhaps, but no real joy. Or at any rate, no enjoyment. Not even now, after the foreign troops had withdrawn from France and all the sovereigns of the world had gone to Vienna.

The Marquis listened with profound attention. "Are those your impressions, *mon cher enfant?* Somehow they don't seem very favourable. But you English are very apt to judge us with severity. I hear very little of what is going on in France."

The train of his own thoughts had mastered Cosmo, who added, "What struck me most was the sense of security . . ." he paused for an instant and the ambassador, bending forward in the chair with the air of a man attempting an experiment, insinuated gently:

"Not such a bad thing, that sentiment."

In the ardour of his honesty Cosmo did not notice either the attitude or the tone, though he caught the sense of the words.

"Was it of the right kind," he went on, as if communing with himself, "or was it the absence of sound thought, and almost of all feeling? M. le Marquis, I am too young to judge, but one would have thought, listening to the talk one heard on all sides, that such a man as Bonaparte had never existed."

"You have been in the society of returned exiles," said the Marquis after a moment of meditation. "You must judge them charitably. A class that has been under the ban for years lives on its passions and on prejudices whose growth stifles not only its sagacity but its visions of the reality." He changed his tone. "Our present Minister of Foreign Affairs never communicates with me personally. The only personal letter I had from him in the last four months was on the subject of procuring some truffles that grow in this country for the King, and there were four pages of most minute directions as to where they were to be found and how they were to be packed and transmitted to Paris. As to my dispatches, I get merely formal acknowledgments. I really don't know what is going on except through travellers who naturally colour their information with their own desires. M. de Talleyrand writes me short notes now and then, but as he has been himself for months in Vienna he can't possibly know what is going on in France. His acute mind, his extraordinary talents are fit to cope with the international situation, but I suppose he too is uneasy. In fact, my dear young friend, as far as I can judge, uneasy suspense is the prevailing sentiment all round the basin of the Mediterranean. The fate of nations still hangs in the balance."

Cosmo waited a moment before he whispered, "And the fate of some individual souls perhaps."

The ambassador made no sound till after a whole minute had elapsed, and then it was only to say:

"I suppose that like many of your young and even old countrymen, you have formed a project of visiting Elba."

Cosmo at once adopted a conversational tone. "Half-formed at most," he said. "I was never one of those who like to visit prisons and gaze at their fellow beings in captivity. A strange taste indeed! I will own to you, M. le Marquis," he went on boyishly, "that the notion of captivity is very odious to me, for men, and for animals too. I would sooner look at a dead lion than a lion in a cage. Yet I remember a young French friend of mine telling me that we English were the most curious nation in the world. But as you said, everybody seems to be doing Elba. I suppose there are no difficulties."

"Not enough difficulties," said the ambassador blandly. "I mean for the good of all concerned."

"Ah," said Cosmo, and repeated thoughtfully, "All concerned! The other day in Paris I met Mr. Wycherley on his way home. He seemed to have had no difficulty at all, not even in Elba. We had quite a long audience. Mr. Wycherley struck me as a man of blunt feelings. Apparently the Emperor— after all, the imperial title is not taken away from him yet——"

The Marquis lowered his head slowly. "No, not yet."

"Well, the Emperor said to him: 'You have come here to look at a wild beast,' and Mr. Wycherley, who doesn't seem to be at a loss for words, answered at once: 'I have come here to look at a great man.' What a crude answer! He is telling this story to everybody. He told me he is going to publish a pamphlet about his visit."

"Mr. Wycherley is a man of good company. His answer was polite. What would have been yours, my young friend?"

"I don't think I will ever be called to make any sort of answer to the great man," said Cosmo.

The Marquis got up with the words: "I think that on the whole you will be wise not to waste your time. I have here a letter from the French Consul in Leghorn quoting the latest report he had from Elba. It states that Bonaparte remains shut up for days together in his private apartments. The reason given is that he fears attempts on his life being made by emissaries sent from France and Italy. He is not visible. Another report states that lately he has expressed great uneasiness at the movements of the French and English frigates."

The Marquis laid a friendly hand on Cosmo's shoulder. "You cannot complain of me; I have given you the very latest intelligence. And now let us join whatever company my daughter is receiving. I think very few people." He crossed the room, followed by Cosmo, and Cosmo noticed a distinct lameness in his gait. At the moment of opening the door the Marquis d'Armand said:

"Your arm, *mon jeune ami*. I am suffering from rheumatism considerably this evening."

Cosmo hastened to offer his arm, and the Marquis with his hand on the door said:

"I can hardly walk. I hope I shall be able to go to the audience I have to-morrow with the King of Sardinia. He is an excellent man but all his ideas and feelings came to a standstill in '98. It makes all conversation with him extremely difficult even for me. His ministers are more reasonable, but that is only because they are afraid."

A low groan escaped the ambassador. He remained leaning with one hand on Cosmo's shoulder and with the other clinging to the door-handle.

"Afraid of the people?" asked Cosmo.

"The people are being corrupted by secret societies," the Marquis said in his bland tone. "All Italy is seething with conspiracies. What, however, they are afraid most of is the Man of Elba."

Cosmo for an instant wondered at those confidences, but a swift reflection that probably those things were known to everybody who was anybody in Europe made him think that this familiar talk was merely the effect of the Marquis's kindness to the son of his old friend. "I think I can proceed now," said the Marquis, pushing the door open. Cosmo recognized one of the rooms which he had passed in the morning. It was the only one of the suite which was fully lighted by a great central glass chandelier, but even in that only two rows of candles were lighted. It was a small reception. The rest of the suite presented but a dim perspective. A semi-circle of heavy armchairs was sparsely occupied by less than a dozen ladies. There was only one card table in use. All the faces were turned to the opening door, and Cosmo was struck by the expression of profound surprise on them all. In one or two it resembled thunderstruck imbecility. It didn't occur to him that the entrance of the French King's personal representative leaning on the shoulder of a completely unknown young man was enough to cause a sensation. A group of elderly personages, conversing in a remote part of the room, became silent. The Marquis gave a general greeting by an inclination of his head, and Cosmo felt himself impelled towards a console between two windows against which the Marquis leaned, whispering to him, "If I were to sit down it would be such an affair to get up." The Countess de Montevesso advanced quickly across the room. Cosmo noticed that her dress had a long train. She smiled at Cosmo and said to the Marquis anxiously:

"You are in pain, Papa?"

"A little. . . . Take him away, my dear, now. He was good enough to lend me his shoulder as far as this."

"*Venez*, M. Latham," said Adèle, "I must introduce you at once to Lady William Bentick in order to check wild speculation about the appearance of a mysterious stranger. As it is, all the town will be full of rumours. People will be talking about you this very night."

Cosmo followed Adèle across the room. She moved slowly and talked easily with a flattering air of intimacy. She even stopped for a moment under the great chandelier. "Lady William is talking now with Count Bubna," she explained to Cosmo, who took a rapid survey of a tall, stout man in an Austrian general's uniform, with his hair tied up in a queue, with black moustaches and something cynical though not ill-natured in his expression. That personage interrupted suddenly his conversation with a lady, no longer very young, who was dressed very simply, and made his way to the ambassador, giving in passing a faintly caustic smile and a keen glance to Cosmo.

"Let me introduce to you Mr. Cosmo Latham," said Adèle. "He is the son of my father's very old friend. He and I haven't met since we were children together in Yorkshire. He has just arrived here."

Cosmo bowed, and in response to a slight gesture took a seat close to the lady, whose preoccupied air struck him with a sort of wonder. She seemed to have something on her mind. Cosmo could know nothing of the prevalent gossip that it was only the black eyes of Louise Durazzo that were detaining Lord William in Italy. He explained in answer to a careless inquiry as to the latest news from Paris that he had been travelling very leisurely and that he could not possibly have brought any fresh news. Lady William looked at him as if she had not seen him before.

"Oh, I am not very much interested in the news, except in so far that they may make a longer stay here unnecessary for us."

"I suppose everybody wants to see the shape of the civilized world settled at last," said Cosmo politely.

"All I want is to go home," declared Lady William. She was no longer looking at him and had the appearance of a person not anxious to listen to anybody's conversation. Cosmo glanced about the room. The card game had been resumed. The Austrian general was talking to the Marquis with Madame de Montevesso standing close to them, while other persons kept at a respectful distance. Lady William seemed to be following her own thoughts with a sort of impassive abstraction. Cosmo felt himself at liberty to go on with his observations, and sweeping his glance round noticed, sitting half hidden by the back of the armchair Adèle had vacated, the dark girl with round black eyes, whom he had seen that morning. To his extreme surprise she smiled at him and, not content with that, gave other plain signs of recognition. He thought he could do no less than get up and make her a bow. By the time he sat down again he became aware that he had attracted the notice of all the ladies seated before the fire. One of them put up her eyeglasses to look at him, two others started talking low together with side glances in his direction, and there was not one that did not look interested. This disturbed him much less than the fixed stare of the young creature, which became fastened on him unwinkingly. Even Lady William gave him a short look of curiosity.

"I understand that you have just arrived in Genoa."

"Yes. Yesterday afternoon late. This is my first appearance."

He meant that it was his first appearance in society and he continued:

"And I don't know a single person in this room even by name. Of course I know that it is Count Bubna who is talking to the Marquis, but that is all."

"Ah," said Lady William with a particular intonation which made Cosmo wonder what he could have said to provoke scepticism. But Lady William was asking herself how it was that this young Englishman seemed to be familiar with the freakish girl who was an object of many surmises in Genoa, and whose company, it was understood, Count Helion of Montevesso had imposed upon his wife. Meantime Cosmo, with the eyes

of all the women concentrated upon him with complete frankness, feel uncomfortable. Lady William noticed it and out of pure kindnes to him again.

"If I understood rightly you have known Madame de Montevess childhood."

"I can't call myself really a childhood's friend. I was so much from home," explained Cosmo. "But she lived for some years in my par house and everybody loved her there; my mother, my father, my sist and it seems to me, looking back now, that I too must have loved he that time; though we very seldom exchanged more than a few words in course of the day."

He spoke with feeling and glanced in the direction of the group ne the console where the head of Adèle appeared radiant under the sparklir crystals of the lustre. Lady William, bending sideways a little, leaned he cheek against her hand in a listening attitude. Cosmo felt that he wa: expected to go on speaking, but it seemed to him that he had nothing more to say. He fell back upon a general remark.

"I think boys are very stupid creatures. However, I wasn't so stupid as not to feel that Adèle d'Armand was very intelligent and quite different from us all. Her very gentleness set her apart. Moreover, Henrietta and I were younger. To my sister and myself she seemed almost grown up. A couple of years makes a very great difference at that age. Soon after she went away we children heard that she was married. She seemed lost to us then. Presently she went back to France, and once there she was lost indeed. When one looked towards France in those days it seems to me there was nothing to be seen but Napoleon. And then her marriage, too. A Countess de Montevesso didn't mean anything to us. I came here expecting to see a stranger."

Cosmo checked himself. It was impossible to say whether Lady William had heard him, or even whether she had been listening at all, but she asked:

"You never met Count Helion?"

"I haven't the slightest idea of the man. He is not in this room, is he? What is he like?"

Lady William looked amused for a moment at the artless curiosity of the Countess de Montevesso's young friend; but it was in an indifferent tone that she said:

"Count Helion is a man of immense wealth which he amassed in India somewhere. He is much older than his wife. More than twice her age."

Cosmo showed his surprise, and Lady William continued smoothly: "Of course all the world knows that Adèle has been a model wife."

Cosmo noted the faintest possible shade of emphasis on those last words and thought to himself: "That means she is not happy and that the world knows it." But, several men having approached the circle, the conversation became general. He vacated his seat by the side of Lady William and got introduced by Adèle to several people, amongst whom was a delicate young woman splendidly dressed and of a slightly Jewish type who, though she was the wife of General Count Bubna, commander-in-chief of the Austrian troops and the representative of Austria at the Court of Turin, behaved with a strange timidity and appeared almost too shy to speak. A simple Madame Ferrati, or so at least Cosmo heard her name, a lady with white tousled hair, had an aggressive manner. Cosmo remarked in the course of the evening that she seemed rather to be persecuting Lady William, who, however, remained amiably abstracted and did not seem to mind anything. The Marquis, getting away from the console, had seated himself near the little Madame Bubna. This, Cosmo thought, was an unavoidable sort of thing for him to do. A young man with a grave manner and something malicious in his eye, apparently a First Secretary of the Embassy, informed Cosmo shortly after they had been made known to each other that "the wife of the general would not naturally be received in Vienna society," and that this was the secret of Bubna sticking to his Italian command so long, even now when really all the excitement was over. Of course he was very much in love with his wife. He used to give her balls twice a week at the expense of the Turin Municipality. Old Bubna understood the art of pillaging to perfection, but apart from that he was a *parfait galant homme* and an able soldier. Bonaparte had a very great liking for him. Bubna was the only friend Bonaparte had in this room. He meant sympathy as man for man. Years ago when Bubna was in Paris he got on very well with the Emperor. Bonaparte knew how to flatter a man. It was worth while to sit up half the night to hear Bubna talking about Bonaparte. "I am posting you up like this," concluded the secretary, "because I see you are in the intimacy of the Marquis and of Madame de Montevesso here."

He went away then to talk to somebody else, and presently Madame de Montevesso, passing close to Cosmo, whispered to him, "Stay to the last," and went on without waiting for his answer. Cosmo amongst all the groups engaged in animated conversation felt rather lonely, totally estranged from the ideas those people were expressing to each other. He could not possibly be in sympathy with the fears and the hopes, strictly personal, and with the royalist-legitimist enthusiasms of these advocates of an order of things that had been buried for a quarter of a century and now was paraded like

a rouged and powdered corpse putting on a swagger of life and revenge. Then he reflected that in this room, at any rate, it was probably nothing but scandalous gossip and trivial talk of futile intrigues. There was no need for him to be indignant. He was even amused at himself, and looking about him in a kindlier frame of mind he perceived that the person nearest to him was that strange girl with the round eyes. She had kept perfectly still on her uncomfortable stool like a captured savage. Her green flounced skirt was spread on each side of the seat. The bodice of her dress, which was black, was cut low, her bare arms were youthfully red and immature. Her hair was done up smoothly and pulled up from her forehead in the manner of the portraits of the 15th Century.

"Why do they dress her in this bizarre manner?" thought Cosmo. It couldn't be Adèle's conception. Perhaps of the Count himself. Yet that didn't seem likely. Perhaps it was her own atrocious taste. But if so it ought to have been repressed. He reflected that there could be nothing improper in him talking to the niece of the house. He would try his conversational Italian. With the feeling of venturing on a doubtful experiment he approached her from the back, sat down at her elbow, and waited. She could not possibly remain unaware of him being there.

At last she turned her head for a point-blank stare, and once she had her eyes on him she never attempted to take them away. Cosmo uttered carefully a complimentary phrase about her dress, which was received in perfect silence. Her carmine lips remained as still as her round black eyes for quite a long time. Suddenly in a low tone, with an accent which surprised Cosmo but which he supposed to be Piedmontese, and with a sort of spiteful triumph, she said:

"I knew very well it would suit me. You think it does?"

Her whole personality had such an aggressive mien that Cosmo, startled and amused, hastened to say, "Undoubtedly," lest she should fly at his eyes.

She showed him her teeth in a grin of savage complacency, and the subject seemed exhausted. Cosmo set himself the task to daunt her by a steady gaze. In less than two seconds he regretted his venture. He felt certain that she would not be the one to look away first. There was not the slightest doubt about that. In order to cover his retreat he let his eyes wander vaguely about the room, smiled agreeably, and said: "Your uncle is not here. Shall I have the pleasure of seeing him this evening?"

"No," she said. "You won't see him this evening. But he knows you have been here this morning."

This was, strictly speaking, news to Cosmo, but he said at once and with great indifference:

"Why shouldn't he? Probably Madame de Montevesso has told him. I used to know your aunt when she was younger than you are, signorina."

"How do you know how old I am?"

Cosmo asked himself if she would ever wink those black eyes of hers.

"I know that you are not a hundred years old."

This struck her as humorous, because there was a sound as of a faint giggle which, generally speaking, is a silly kind of sound but in her case had a disturbing quality. It was followed by the hoarse declaration:

"Aunt didn't. I told Uncle. I looked a lot at you in the morning. Why didn't you look at me?"

"I was afraid of being indiscreet," said Cosmo readily, concealing his astonishment.

"What silliness," she commented scornfully. "And this evening too! I was looking at you all the time and you did nothing but look at all those witches here, one after another."

"I find all the ladies in the room perfectly charming," said Cosmo.

"You lie. I suppose you do nothing else from morning till night."

"I am sorry you have such a bad opinion of me, but it being what it is, hadn't I better go away?"

"Directly I set eyes on you I knew you were one of that sort."

"And did you impart your opinion of me to your uncle?" asked Cosmo. He could be no more offended with that girl than if she had been an unmannerly animal. Her peculiar stare remained unchanged but her general expression softened for a moment.

"No. But I took care to tell him that you were a very handsome gentleman. . . . You are a very handsome gentleman."

What surprised Cosmo was not the downright statement but the thought that flashed through his mind that it was as dreadful as being told that one was good to eat. For a time he stared without any thought of unwinking competition. He was not amused. Distinctly not. He asked:

"Where were you born?"

"How can I tell? In the mountains, I suppose. Somewhere where you will never go. How can it possibly concern you?"

Cosmo offered his apology for his indiscretion, and she received it with a sort of uncomprehending scorn. She said after a pause: "None of those witches, young or old, ever speak to me. And even you didn't want to speak to me. You only spoke to me . . . Oh, no! I know why you spoke to me."

"Why did I speak to you?" asked Cosmo thoughtfully. "Won't you tell me?"

Upon the firm roundness of that high-coloured face came a subtle change which suggested something in the nature of cunning, and the rough, somewhat veiled voice came from between the red lips which had no more charm or life than the painted lips carved in a piece of wood.

"If I were to tell you would be as wise as myself."

"Where would be the harm of me being as wise as yourself?" said Cosmo, trying to be playful but somehow missing the tone of playfulness so completely that he was struck by his failure himself.

"If you were as wise as myself you would never come to this house again and I don't want you to stay away," was the answer, delivered in a hostile tone.

Cosmo said, "You don't! Well, at any rate it can't be because of kindness, so I don't thank you for it." He said this with extreme amiability. Becoming aware that people were beginning to leave, he observed, out of the corner of his eye, that nobody went away without glancing in their direction. Then the departure of Lady William caused a general stir and gave Cosmo the occasion to get up and move away. Lady William gave him a gracious nod, and the Marquis, coming up to him, introduced him at the last moment to General Count Bubna just as that distinguished person was making ready to take his wife away. Everybody was standing up and for the first time Cosmo felt himself completely unobserved. Obeying a discreet sign of the Countess Montevesso, he moved unaffectedly in the direction of a closed door, the white and gold door he remembered well from his morning visit. When he had got near to it and within reach of the handle he turned about. He had the view of the guests' backs as they moved slowly out. Adèle looked over her shoulder for a moment with an affirmative nod. He understood it, hesitated no longer, opened the door, and slipped through without, so far as he could judge, being seen by anybody.

It was as he had thought. He found himself in Madame de Montevesso's boudoir in which he had been received that morning.

IV

He shut the door behind him gently and remained between it and the screen. He had expected to be followed at once by Adèle. What could be detaining her? But he remembered the remarkable proportions of that suite of reception rooms. He had seen some apartments in Paris, but nothing quite so long as that. The old Marquis would no doubt conduct the little Madame Bubna to the very door of the anteroom. The ambassador of The Most Christian King owed that attention to the representative of His Apostolic Majesty and Commander-in-Chief of the Austrian troops. This was the exact form which his thought took. The Christian King, the Apostolic Majesty — all those submerged heads were bobbing up out of the subsiding flood.

He pictured them to himself in their mental simplicity and with their grand air; the Marquis magnificent and ageing, and the dutiful daughter by his side with her radiant head and her divine form. It was impossible to believe that these two had also been submerged at one time.

All those people were mere playthings, reflected Cosmo without a pang. But who or what was playing with them? he thought further, boldly, and remained for a moment as if amused by the marvellousness of it, in the manner of people watching the changes on the stage. But what could have become of them?

She might next moment be opening the door. Could she have made him stay behind because she wanted to speak with him alone? Why, yes, obviously. Cosmo did not ask himself what she wanted to talk to him about. It was no wonder that he felt, it was a subtle emotion resembling impatience for the arrival of a promised felicity of an indefinite kind. All this was by no means poignant. It was merely delightfully disturbing.

"I shall have a tête-à-tête; that's clear," he thought, as he advanced into the room. The air all around him was delightfully warm. Whatever she would have to say would be wonderful because of her voice. He would look her in the face. She did not intimidate him and it was impossible to have too much of that. After all, he thought, immensely amused, it was only Adèle, Ad— —

His mental monologue was cut short by the shock of perceiving, seated on the painted sofa, a man who was looking at him in perfect silence and immobility. The fact was that Count Helion, having come into the boudoir sooner than his wife had expected him to do, had directed his eyes to the screen ever since he had heard the opening and the shutting of the door. One of his hands was resting on his thigh, the other hung down holding negligently a number of some gazette which was partly resting on the floor. Though not very big, that piece of paper attracted Cosmo's eyes; and it was in this way that he became aware of the brown fingers covered with rings, of the gaunt legs encased in silk stockings, and of the crossed feet in dress shoes with gold buckles, almost before he took in the impression of the broad but lean face which seemed to have been stained with walnut juice long enough for the stain to have worn down thin, letting the native pallor come through. The same tint extended to the bald top of the head. But what was really extraordinary was the hair: two patches of black behind each temple, obviously dyed. The man, as to whose identity Cosmo could have no doubt, got up, displaying the full length of his bony frame, in a tense and soldierly stiffness associated with cross-belts and a cowhide knapsack on the back. "A grenadier," thought Cosmo, startled by this unexpected meeting, which also caused him profound annoyance, as though he had been induced to walk into a trap. What he could not understand was why the man should make that grimace at him. It convulsed his whole physiognomy, involving his lips, his cheeks, and his very eyes in a sort of spasm. The most awful thing was that it stayed there. . . . "Why, it's a smile," thought Cosmo, with sudden relief. It was so sudden that it broke into a smile without any particular volition of his own. Thereupon the face of Count Helion recovered its normal aspect and Cosmo heard his voice for the first time. It proceeded from the depths of his chest. It was resonant and blurred and portentous with an effect of stiffness somehow in accord with the man's bearing. It informed Cosmo that Count Helion had been waiting in the Countess's boudoir on purpose to make his acquaintance, while in the man's eyes there was a watchfulness as though he had been uttering a momentous disclosure and was anxious as to its effect. A perfectly horizontal, jet-black moustache underlining the nose of Count Helion, which was broad at the base and thin at the end, suggested comic possibilities in that head, which had too much individuality to be looked upon by Cosmo simply as the head of Adèle's husband; and Cosmo hardly looked at it in that light. His hold on that fact was slippery. He preserved his equanimity perfectly and said that he himself had wondered whether he would have the pleasure of making the Count's acquaintance that evening. Both men sat down.

"My occupations kept me late to-night," said the Count. "The courier came in."

He pointed with his fingers to the gazette lying on the floor, and Cosmo asked if there were any news.

"In the gazette, no. At least nothing interesting. The world is full of vanities and scandals, rumours of conspiracies. Very poor stuff. I don't know any of those people the papers mention every day. That's more my wife's affair. For years now she has spent about ten months of every year in Paris or near Paris. I am a provincial. My interests are in the orphanage I have founded in my native country. I am also building an asylum for . . ."

He got up suddenly, approached the mantelpiece in three strides, and turned round exactly like a soldier in the ranks of a company changing front. He was wearing a blue coat cut away in front and having a long skirt, something recalling the cut of a uniform, though the material was fine and there was a good deal of gold lace about it, as also on his white satin waistcoat. Cosmo recalled the vague story he had heard about Count de Montevesso having served in more than one army before being given the rank of general by the King of Piedmont. The man had been drilled. Cosmo wondered whether he had ever been caned. He was a military adventurer of the commonest type. Some of them have been known to return with a fortune got by pillage and intrigue and possibly even by real talents of a sort in the service of oriental courts full of splendours and crimes, tyrannies and treacheries and dark drama of ambition, or love.

"He is the very thing," Cosmo exclaimed mentally, gating at the stiff figure leaning against the mantelpiece. Of course he got his fortune in India. What was remarkable about him was that he had managed to get away with his plunder, or at any rate a part of it, considerable enough to enable him to make a figure in the world and marry Adèle d'Armand in England. That was only because of the Revolution. In royal France he would not have had the ghost of a chance; and even as it was, only the odious laxity of London society in accepting rich strangers had given him his opportunity. Cosmo, forcing himself to envisage this dubious person as the husband of Adèle, felt very angry with the light-minded tolerance extended to foreigners characteristic of a certain part of London society. It was perfectly outrageous.

"Where the devil can my wife be?"

Those words made Cosmo start, though they had not been uttered very loudly. Almost mechanically he answered: "I don't know," and noticed that Count Helion was staring at him in a curiously unintelligent manner.

"I was really asking myself," muttered the latter and stirred uneasily, without however taking his elbow off the mantelpiece. "It's a natural thought since we are, God knows why, kept waiting for her here. I wasn't aware I had spoken. Living for many years amongst people who didn't understand any European language—I had hundreds of them in my palace in Sindh—I got into the habit of talking aloud, strange as it may appear to you."

"Yes," said Cosmo, with an air of innocence. "I suppose one acquires all sorts of strange habits in those distant countries. We in England have a class of men who return from India enriched. They are called nabobs. Some of them have most objectionable habits. Unluckily their mere wealth . . ."

"There is nothing to compare with wealth," interrupted the other in a soldierly voice and paused, then continued in the same tone of making a verbal report: "When I was in England I had the privilege to know many people of position. They were very kind to me. They didn't seem to think lightly of wealth."

Each phrase came curt, detached, but it was evident that the man did not mean to be offensive. Those statements originated obviously in sincere conviction; and after the Count had uttered them there appeared on his forehead the horizontal wrinkles of unintelligent worry. Cosmo asked himself whether the man before him was not really very stupid. Under the elevated eyebrows his eyes looked worn and empty of all thought.

"Lots of money, I mean," M. de Montevesso began again. "Not your savings and scrapings. Money that one acquires boldly and enough of it to be profuse with."

"Is he going to treat me to vulgar boasting?" thought Cosmo. He wished that Adèle would come in and interrupt this tête-à-tête which was so very different from the one he had been expecting.

"I daresay money is very useful," he assented, with airy scorn which he thought might put an end to the subject. But his interlocutor persisted.

"You can't know anything about it," he affirmed, then added unexpectedly: "Money will give you even ideas. Lots of ideas. The worst of it is that any one of them may turn out damnable. Well, yes. There is of course danger in money, but what of that?"

"It can scarcely be if it is used for good works, as you seem to use it," said Cosmo with polite indifference. He meant it to be final, but Count de Montevesso was not to be suppressed.

"It leads one into worries," he said. "For instance, that orphanage of mine, it is really a very large place. I am trying to be a benefactor to my native province, but I want it to be in my own way. Well, since the Restoration, the priests are trying to get hold of it. They want to turn it to the glory of God and to the service of religion. I have seen enough of all sorts of religions not to know what that means. No sooner had the King entered Paris than the Bishop wrote to me pointing out that there was no chapel and suggesting that I should build one and appoint a chaplain. That Bishop is . . ."

He threw up his head suddenly and Cosmo became aware of the presence of Adèle without having heard even the rustle of her dress. He stood up hastily. There was a short silence.

"I see the acquaintance is made," said Adèle, looking from one to the other. Her eyes lingered on Cosmo and then turned to her husband. "I didn't know you would be already here. I had to help my father to his room. I would have come at once here but he detained me." Again she turned to Cosmo. "You will pardon me."

"I found Count Helion here. I have not been alone for a minute," said Cosmo. "You owe me no apologies. I was delighted to make your husband's acquaintance, even if you were not here to introduce us to each other."

This was said in English and Count Helion by the mantelpiece waited till Cosmo had finished before he asked, "Where's Clelia?"

"I have sent her to bed," said Countess de Montevesso. "Helion, my father would like to see you this evening."

"I am at the orders of M. le Marquis."

The grenadier-like figure at the mantelpiece did not stir, and those words were followed only by a slight twitch in the muscles of the face which might have had a sardonic intention. "To-night, at once," he repeated. "But with Mr. Latham here?"

"Pray don't mind me, I am going away directly," said Cosmo. "It is getting late."

"In Italy it is never late. I hope to find you here when I return. As the husband of a daughter of the house of D'Armand I know what is due to the name of Latham. Am I really expected at once?"

Adèle moved forward a step or two, speaking rapidly. "There has been some news from Elba, or about Elba, which gives a certain concern to my father. As you have been to the public knowledge in direct touch with people from Elba my father would like to have your opinion."

Count Helion changed his attitude, and leaning his shoulders against the mantelpiece addressed himself to Cosmo.

"It was the most innocent thing in the world. It was something about the project for the exploitation of the Island of Pianosa. Napoleon sent his treasurer here to get in touch with a banker. I am a man of affairs. The banker consulted me—as a man who knew the spot. It's true I know the spot, but if you hear it said that it is because of my relations with the Dey of Algiers, pray don't believe it. I am in no way in touch with the Barbary States."

He made a step forward, and then another, and stood still. "You two had better sit down and talk. Yes, sit down and talk. Renew the acquaintance of your early youth . . . your early youth," he repeated in a faint voice. "Those youthful friendships . . ." he made a convulsive grimace which Cosmo had discovered to be the effect of a smile. "There is something so charming in those youthful friendships. As to myself I don't remember ever being youthful." He stepped out towards the door through which Cosmo had seen Clelia enter that morning. "Let me find you when I return, enjoying yourselves most sentimentally. Most delightful."

His long stiff back swayed in the doorway and the door came to with a crash.

Cosmo and Adèle looked at each other with a smile. Cosmo, hat in hand, asked just audibly, "I suppose I had better stay?" She made an affirmative sign and, moving away from him, put her foot on the marble fender of the fireplace where nothing was left but hot ashes hiding a reddish glow.

V

Cosmo, ill at ease, remained looking at her. He was in doubt what the sign she had made meant, a nervous and imperious gesture, which might have been a command for him to go or to stay. In his irresolution he gazed at her, thinking that she was lovely to an incredible degree and that the word "radiant" applied to her extraordinary aptness. Light entered into her composition. And it was not the cold light of marble. "She actually glows," he said to himself, amazed, "like ripe fruit in the foliage, like a big flower in the shade."

"Don't gaze at my blushes," said Madame de Montevesso in an even tone tinged with a little mockery and a little bitterness. "Would you believe that when I was a girl I was so shy that I used to blush crimson whenever anybody looked at me or spoke to me? It's a failing which does not meet with much sympathy. And yet my suffering was very real. It would reach such a pitch at times that I was ready to cry."

"Shall I go away?" asked Cosmo in a deadened voice. He waited for a moment while she seemed to debate in her mind the answer to the question. In his fear of being sent away he went on: "God knows I don't want to leave you. And after all the Count is coming back and . . ."

"Oh, yes, he is coming back. Sit down. Yes. It would be better. Sit down. . . ." Cosmo sat down where he could see her admirable shoulders, the roundness of her averted head, *coiffée en boucles* and girt with a gold circlet, the shadowy retreating view of her profile. The long drapery of her train flowed to the ground in a dark blue shimmer. . . . "He is inevitable. He has always been inevitable," came further from her lips which he couldn't see, for the mirror above the mantelpiece reflected nothing but her forehead with the gold mist of her hair above.

Cosmo remained silent. For nothing in the world would he have made a sound. He held his breath with expectation; and in the extreme tension of his whole being the lights grew dim around him, while her white shoulders, the thick clustering curls, the arm on which she leaned, and the other bare arm hanging inert by her side, seemed the only source of light in the room.

"You don't know me at all," began the Countess de Montevesso. "I don't charge you with forgetting; but the little you may remember of me cannot be of any use. It is only natural that I should be a stranger to you. But you cannot be a stranger to me. For one thing you were a boy and then you were not a child of outcasts without a country, of refugees with a ruined past and with no future. You were a young Latham, as rooted in your native soil as the old trees of your park. Even then there seemed to me something enviable about you."

She turned her head a little to glance at him. "You had no idea what it was like after we had gone to London. My ignorance of the world was so profound that I felt ill at ease in it. I hoped I had an attractive face, but I only discovered that I was pretty from the remarks of the people in the street I overheard. I spent my life by the side of my mother's couch. I never went out except attended by my father or by Aglae. My only amusement was to play a game of chess now and then with an old doctor, also a refugee, who looked after my mother, or listen to the conversation of the people who came to see us. Amongst them there were all the prominent men and women of the old régime. Refugees. They seldom spoke the truth to each other, and yet they were no more stupid than the rest of the world. Nobody could be more good-natured and better company, more frivolous or more inconsiderate. I have seen women of the highest rank work ten hours a day to get bread for their children, but they also slandered one another, told falsehoods about their conduct and their work, and quarrelled among themselves in the style of washerwomen. Morals were even looser than in the times before the Revolution. Manners were forgotten. Every transgression was excused in those who were regarded as good royalists. I don't mean this to apply to the great body of the refugees. Some of them led irreproachable lives. Round our Princes there were some most absurd intrigues. I didn't know much of all this, but I remember my poor father's helpless indignations and my own appalled disgust at the things I could not help hearing and seeing."

She turned her head to look at Cosmo. "I am telling you all this to give you some idea of the air I had to breathe," she said in a changed tone. "I don't think it contaminated me. I felt its odiousness; but all this seemed without remedy. I didn't even suffer much from it. What I suffered most from was our domestic anxieties; my mother's fears lest the small resources we had to live on should fail us altogether. Our daily crust of bread seemed to depend on political events in Europe, and they were going against us. Battles, negotiations, everything. A blight seemed to have fallen on the royalist cause. My mother didn't conceal her distress. What touched me more still was the careworn, silent anxiety of my poor father."

She paused, looking at Cosmo intently, meeting his eyes fixed on her face. "I was getting on for sixteen," she continued. "No one ever paid the slightest attention to me. The only genuine passion in my heart was filial love. . . . But is it any good in going on? And then I can't tell what you may have heard already."

"All I have heard," said Cosmo in a tone of profound respect, "is that Adèle de Montevesso's life has been irreproachable."

"I remember the time when all the world was doing its best to make it impossible. Would it shock you very much if I told you that I don't care at all about its good opinion now? There was a time when it would put the worst construction possible on my distress, on my bewilderment, on my very innocence."

"Why should the world do that to you?" asked Cosmo.

"Why? But I see you know nothing. I met my husband first at a select concert that was given by the music-master of the late Queen of France. My mother was feeling a little better and insisted on my going out a little. Those were small fashionable affairs. I had a good voice myself, and that evening I sang with Madame Seppio. An English gentleman—his name doesn't matter—presented M. de Montevesso to me as a friend of his just returned from India and anxious to be introduced to the best society. What with my usual shyness and the unattractive appearance of the man, I don't think I received his attentions very well. There was really no reason I should notice him particularly. It wasn't difficult to see that he had not the manners of a man of the world. Where could he have acquired them? He had left his village at seventeen, he enlisted in the Irish Regiment which served in France, then he deserted, perhaps. I only know that some years afterwards he was a captain in the service of Russia. From there he made his way to India. I believe the governor-general used him as a sort of unofficial agent amongst native princes, but he got into some scrape with the company. By what steps he managed to get on to the back of an elephant and command the army of a native prince I really don't know. And even if I had known then it would not have made him more interesting in my eyes. I was relieved when he made me a deep bow with his hand on his heart and went away. He left a most fugitive impression, but the very next morning he sent his English friend to ask my parents for my hand. That friend was a nobleman, a man of honour, and the offers he was empowered to make were so generous that my parents thought they must tell me of them. I was so astonished that at first I couldn't speak. I simply went away and shut myself up in my room. They were not people to press me for an answer. The poor worried dears thought that I wouldn't even consent to contemplate this marriage; while I, shut up in my room—I was afraid, remembering the way they had spoken to me of that offer, that they would reject it without consulting me any further. I sent word by Aglae that I would give my answer next day and that I begged to be left to myself. Then I escaped from the house, followed by Aglae, who was never so frightened in her life, and went to see the wife of that friend of my present husband. I begged her to send at once for General de Montevesso—at that time he called himself General. The King of Sardinia had given him this rank in acknowledgment of some service that his great wealth had enabled him to render to the Court of Turin. That lady of course had many scruples about doing something so highly unconventional, but at last, overcome by the exaltation of my feelings, she consented."

"She did that?" murmured Cosmo. "What an extraordinary thing!"

"Yes. She did that, instead of taking me home. People will do extraordinary things to please a man of fabulous wealth. She sent out two or three messengers to look for him all over the town. They were some time in finding him. I waited. I was perfectly calm. I was calmer than I am now, telling you my story. I was possessed by the spirit of self-sacrifice. I had no misgivings. I remember even how cold I was in that small drawing room with a big coal fire. He arrived out of breath. He was splendidly dressed and behaved very ceremoniously. I felt his emotion without sharing it. I, who used to blush violently at the smallest provocation, didn't feel the slightest embarrassment in addressing that big stiff man so much older than myself. I could not appreciate what a fatal mistake I was committing by telling him that I didn't care for him in the least and probably never should; but that if he would secure my parents' future comfort my gratitude would be so great that I could marry him, without reluctance and be his loyal friend and wife for life. He stood there stiff and ominous and told me that he didn't flatter himself with the possibility of inspiring any deeper feeling.

"We stood there facing each other for a bit. I felt nothing but an inward glow of satisfaction at having, as I thought, acted honourably. As to him I think he was simply made dumb with rage. At last he bowed with his hands on his heart and said that he would not even ask now for the favour of kissing my hand. I appreciated his delicacy at that moment. It would have been an immense trial to my shyness. I think now that he was simply afraid of putting my hand to his lips lest he should lose his self-control and bite it. He told me later, in one of those moments when people don't care what they say, that at that moment he positively hated me, not the sight of me, you understand, but my aristocratic insolence."

She paused, and in the youthful sincerity of his sympathy Cosmo uttered a subdued exclamation of distress. Madame de Montevesso looked at him again and then averted her face.

"I heard afterwards some gossip to the effect that he had been jilted by a girl to whom he was engaged, the daughter of some captain on half-pay, and that he proposed to me simply to show her that he could find a girl prettier, of higher rank, and in every way more distinguished that would consent to be his wife. I believe that it was this that prevented him from drawing back before my frankness. As to me, I went home, seeing nothing, hearing nothing, caring for nothing, as though I had done with the world, as though I had taken the veil. I can find no other comparison for the peace that was in me. I faced my mother's reproaches calmly. She was of course very much hurt at my not confiding in her at this crisis of my life. My father, too. But how could I have confided in them in this matter on which their security and welfare depended? How could I have confided in any of the men and women around me who seemed to me as if mad, whose conduct and opinions I despised with youthful severity as foolish and immoral? There was one human being in the world in whom I might perhaps have confided, that perhaps would have understood me. That was your father, Cosmo. But he was three hundred miles away. There was no time. Tell me, did he understand? Has he cast me out of his thoughts for ever?"

"My father," said Cosmo, "has lived like a hermit for years. There was nothing to make him forget you. Yes, he was a man in whom you could have confided. He would have understood you. That doesn't mean to say that he would have approved. I wish he had been by your side. He would have brought pressure on your parents with the authority of an old and tried friend."

"And benefactor," struck in the Countess de Montevesso. "My father, I believe, had an inkling of the truth. He begged me again and again to think well of what I was doing. I told him that I was perfectly satisfied with what I had done. It was perfectly true then. I had satisfied my conscience by telling my suitor that I could never love him. I felt strangely confident that I could fulfil the duties of my new position, and I was absorbed by the happiness of having saved my parents from all anxiety for the future. I was not aware of having made any sacrifice. Probably if I had been twenty or more I would have been less confident; perhaps I wouldn't have had the courage! But at that age I didn't know that my whole life was at stake. Three weeks afterwards I was married.

"As you see, there was no time lost. During that period our intercourse was of the most formal kind only I never even attempted to observe him with any attention. He was very stiff and ceremonious, but he was in a hurry, because I believe he was afraid from his previous experience that I would change my mind. His usual answer to the expression of all my wishes and to most of my speeches was a profound bow—and, sometimes, I was amused. In the lightness of my heart a thought would come to me that a lifetime on such terms would be a funny affair. I don't say he deceived me in anything. He had brought an immense fortune out of India and the world took him at its face value. With no more falsehood than holding his tongue and watching his behaviour he kept me in the dark about his character, his family, his antecedents, his very name. When we first were married he was ostentatious and rather mean at the same time. His long life in India added the force of oriental jealousy to that which would be in a sense natural to a man of his age. Moreover, his character was naturally disagreeable. The only way he could make the power of his great fortune felt was by hurting the feelings of other people, of his servants, of his dependents, of his friends. His wife came in for her share. An older and cleverer woman with a certain power of deception and caring for the material pleasures of life could have done better for herself and for him in the situation in which I was placed, but I, almost a child, with an honest and proud character and caring nothing for what wealth could give, I was perfectly helpless. I was being constantly surprised and shocked by the displays of evil passions and his fits of ridiculous jealousy which were expressed in such a coarse manner that they could only arouse my resentment and contempt.

"Meantime we lived in great style—dinner parties, concerts. I had a very good voice. I daresay he was anxious enough to show off his latest acquisition, but at the same time he could not bear me being looked at or even spoken to. A fit of oriental jealousy would come over him, especially when I had been much applauded. He would express his feelings to me in barrack-room language. At last, one evening he made a most scandalous scene before about two hundred guests, and then went out of the house, leaving me to make the best of it before all those people. It caused the greatest possible scandal. The party of course broke up. I spent the rest of the night sitting in my bedroom, too overcome to take off my splendid dress and those jewels with which he always insisted I should bedeck myself. With the first signs of dawn he returned, and coming up into my room found me sitting there. He told me then that living with me was too much of a torture for him and proposed I should go back to my parents for a time.

"We had been married for a little over a year then. For the first time since the wedding I felt really happy. They, poor dears, were delighted. We were all so innocent together that we thought this would be the end of all our troubles, that the man was chivalrous enough to have seen his mistake in the proper light, and to bear the consequences nobly. Hadn't I told him I could never love him, exactly in so many words?

"I ought to have known that he was incapable of any generosity. As a matter of fact I didn't think much about it. I, who had overcome my shyness enough to become, young as I was, a perfect hostess in a world which I knew so little—because after all that sort of thing was in my tradition—I was really too stupid, too unsophisticated for those ten months to have been a lesson to me. I had learned nothing, any more than one learns from a nightmare or from a period of painful illness. I simply breathed freely. I became again the old Adèle. I dismissed M. de Montevesso from my thoughts as though he had never lived. Can you believe this, Cosmo? It is astonishing how facts can fail to impress one; brutalities, abuse, scenes of passion, mad exhibitions of jealousy, as long as they do not attack your conception of your moral personality. All this fell off me like a poisoned robe, leaving hardly a smart behind. I raised my head like a flower after a thunderstorm. Don't think my character is shallow, Cosmo. There were depths in me that could be reached, but till then I had been only tormented, shocked, surprised, but hardly even frightened. It was he who had suffered. But my turn was to come."

"I don't think you were ever a person of shallow feelings."

"One's feelings must mature like everything else, and I assure you I had not yet stopped growing. The next six months were to finish my education. For by that time I had lost all my illusions. While I was breathing freely between my father and mother, forgetting the world around us, Montevesso was going about the town with his complaints and his suspicions; regretting he had let me go and enraged that I should have gone from him so easily. And you may be sure he found sympathizers. A rich man, you understand! Who could refuse sympathy to so much wealth? He was obviously a much ill-used man, all the faults of course were on my side; in less than a month I found myself the centre of underhand intrigues and the victim of a hateful persecution. Friends, relatives, mere acquaintances in the world of emigration entered M. de Montevesso's service. They spied on my conduct and tampered with the servants. There were assemblies in his house where my character was torn to shreds. Some of those good friends offered him their influence in Rome for the annulation of the marriage, for a consideration of course. Others discovered flaws in the marriage contract. They invented atrocious tales. There were even horrid verses made about that scandal; till at last he himself became disgusted with the wretches and closed his house and his purse to them. Years later he showed me a note of their names and the amounts paid for all those manifestations of sympathy. He must have been impressed and disgusted by the retrospect, because it was a big lot of money. As to the names, they were aristocratic enough to flatter his plebeian pride. He showed the list to me just to hurt my feelings.

"Some sinners have been stoned, but I, an innocent girl of seventeen, had been pelted with mud beyond endurance. It was impossible to induce him to come to any sort of arrangement that would leave me in peace. All the world, influenced by his paid friends, was against me. What could I do? Calumnies are hard to bear. Harder than truth. Even my parents weakened. He promised to make amends. Of course I went back to him, as one would crawl out of the mud amongst clean thorns that can but tear one's flesh. He received me back with apologies that were as nearly public as such things can be. It was a vindication of my character. But directly he had me with him again he gave way to his fits of hatred as before, such hatred as only black jealousy can inspire. It was terrible. For even jealousy has its gradations, coloured by doubts and hopes, and his was the worst, the hopeless kind, since he could never forget my honest declaration."

The Countess of Montevesso's voice died out and then Cosmo looked up. She was a little pale, which made her eyes appear darker than ever he had seen them before. Cosmo was too young yet to understand the full meaning of this confession, but his very youth invested the facts with a sort of romantic grandeur, while the woman before him felt crushed by the feelings of their squalid littleness. Without looking at him she said:

"We went travelling for a year and a half, stayed for a time in Paris, where he began to make me scenes again, and then we went oh to Italy. The pretext was to make me known to some of his relations. I don't believe he could remember his mother, and his father, an old dealer in rabbit skins, I believe, had died some time before. As to the rest, I think his heart failed him notwithstanding the brutal pride he used at times to display to me. He took me to see some decayed people living in old ruined houses whom I verily believe he bribed to pass for his more distant connections. It was a pilgrimage amongst the most squalid shams, something that you cannot conceive, yet I didn't rebel against the horrible humiliation of it. It was part of the bargain. Sometimes I thought that he would kill me in one of those wild places in some lost valley where the people, only a degree removed from peasants in their dress and speech, fawned upon him as the wealthy cousin and benefactor. I am certain that during those wanderings he was half distracted. It was I who went through all this unmoved. But I don't suppose my life was ever in any danger. At that time none of his moods lasted long enough to let him carry out any definite purpose. And then he is not a man of criminal instincts. After all, he is perhaps a great adventurer. He has commanded armies of a hundred thousand men. He has in a sense faced the power of England in India. The very fact that he had managed to get out of it with so much wealth and with quite a genuine reputation shows that there is something in him. I don't know whether it's that obtained for him a very gracious reception from Bonaparte when he dragged me back to Paris."

VI

Madame de Montevesso paused, looking at the white ashes in which the sparks had not died out yet. "Yes," she went on, "I lived near Paris through the whole time of the Empire. I had a charming house in the country. Monsieur de Montevesso had established me in a style which he considered worthy of himself if not of me. He could never forgive me for being what I am. He was tolerated by the returned emigration for my sake, but he grew weary of his own unhappiness and resolved to live by himself in his own province where he could be a great personage. Perhaps he is not altogether a bad man. He consented eagerly to my parents, who had obtained permission to return to France, joining me in the country. I tasted again some happiness in the peace of our semi-retired life and in their affection. Our world was that of old society, the world of returned nobles. They hated and despised the imperial power, but most of them were ready to cringe before it. Yes, even the best were overawed by the real might under the tinsel of that greatness. Our circle was very small and composed of convinced royalists, but I could not share their hatreds and their contempts. I felt myself a Frenchwoman. I had liberal ideas. . . ."

She noticed Cosmo's eyes fixed on her with eager and friendly curiosity, and paused with a faint smile.

"You understand me, Cosmo?" she asked. The latter gave a little nod without detaching his eyes from the face which seemed to him to glow with the light of generous feelings, but already Madame de Montevesso was going on.

"I did not want to be patronized by all those returned duchesses who wanted to teach me how to feel and how to behave. Their own behaviour was a mixture of insolence and self-seeking before that government which they feared and despised. I didn't fear it but neither could I despise it. My heart was heavy during all those years but it was not downcast. All Europe was aflame and the blaze scorched and dazzled and filled one with awe and with forebodings; but then one always heard that fire purifies all which it cannot destroy. The world would perhaps come out better from it."

"Well, it's all over," said Cosmo, "and what has it done? The smoke hangs about yet and I cannot see, but how do you feel?"

Madame de Montevesso, leaning on her elbow on the mantelpiece, with one foot on the fender, looked down at the ashes in which a spark gleamed here and there.

"I feel a little cold," she said, "and dazed perhaps. One doesn't know where to look."

Cosmo got up and made a step forward. His voice, however, was subdued. "Formerly there was a man."

"A man, yes. One couldn't help looking towards him. There was something unnatural in that uniqueness, but do you know, Cosmo, the man was nothing. You smile, you think you hear a royalist speaking, a woman full of silly aristocratic prejudice; a woman who sees only a small Corsican squire who hadn't even the sense to catch the opportunity by the hair as it flew by and be the restorer of the Bourbon dynasty. You imagine all that of me! . . . Of me!"

She kept her pose, desolate, as if looking down at the ashes of a burnt-up world.

"I don't think you could be stupid if you tried," he said. "But if the man was nothing, then what has done it?"

Madame de Montevesso remained silent for a while before murmuring the word "Destiny," and only then turned her head slightly towards Cosmo. "What are you staring at in that corner?" she asked, after another period of silence.

"Was I staring?" he said with a little start. "I didn't know. Your words evoked a draped figure with an averted head."

"Then it wasn't that," she said, looking at him with friendly eyes. "Whatever your fancy might have seen it was not Destiny. One must live a very long time to see even the hem of her robe. Live a very, very long time," she repeated in a tone of such weariness, tinged by fear, that Cosmo felt impelled to step forward, take up the hand that hung by her side, and press it to his lips. When released, it fell slowly to its previous position. But Madame de Montevesso did not move.

"That's very nice," she said. "It was a movement of sympathy. I have had very little of that in my life. There is something in me that does not appeal to the people with whom I live. My father, of course, loves me; but that is not quite the same thing. Your father, I believe, sympathized with the child and I am touched to see that the son seems to understand something of the woman; of an almost old woman."

Cosmo would have been amused at the tone of unaffected conviction in which she called herself an old woman had it not been for the profound trouble on that young face bent downwards, and at the melancholy grace of the whole attitude of that woman who had once been the child Adèle; a foreign, homeless child, sheltered for a moment by the old walls of his ancestral home, and the sharer of its life's stately intimacies.

"No," he said, marvelling that so much bitter experience should have been the lot of such a resplendent figure. "No. Destiny works quickly enough. We are both still young, and yet think of what we have already seen."

He fancied she had shuddered a little. He felt ashamed at the thought of what she had lived through, how she had been affected in her daily life by what to him had been only a spectacle after all, though his country had played its part, the impressive part of a rock upraising its head above the flood. But he continued: "Why, the Man of Destiny himself is young yet. You must have seen him many times."

"No. Once or twice a year I went to the Tuileries in the company of some reconciled royalist ladies and very much against my wish. It was expected from Madame de Montevesso and I always came away thankful to think that it was over for a time. You could hardly imagine how dull that Empire time was. All hopes were crushed. It was like a dreadful overdressed masquerade with the everlasting sound of the guns in the distance. Every year I spent a month with my husband to save appearances. That was in the bond. He used then to invite all the provincial grandees for a series of dinners. But even in the provinces one felt the sinister moral constraint of that imperial glory. No doubt all my movements were noticed and recorded by the proper people. Naturally I saw the Emperor several times. I saw him also in theatres, in his carriage driving about, but he spoke to me only once."

"Only once!" exclaimed Cosmo under his breath.

"You may imagine I tried to make myself as inconspicuous as possible, and I did not belong to the Court. It was on the occasion of a ball given to the Princess of Baden. There was an enormous crowd. Early in the evening I found myself standing in the front row in the Galerie de Diane between two women who were perfect strangers to me. By and by the Court came in, the Empress, the Princess, the Chamberlains in full dress, and took their place on a platform at the end. In the intervals of dancing the Emperor came down alone, speaking only to the women. He wore his imperial dress of red velvet, laced in all the seams, with white satin breeches, with diamonds on the hilt of his sword and the buckles of his shoes and on his cap with white plumes. It was a well-designed costume but with his short thick figure and the clumsiness of his movements he looked to me frightful and like a mock king. When he came opposite me he stopped. I am certain he knew who I was, but he asked me my name. I told him.

"'Your husband lives in his province?'

"'Yes, sire.'

"'Your husband employs much labour, I hear. I am grateful to him for giving work to the people. This is the proper use of wealth. Hasn't he served in the English army in India?'

"His tone was friendly. I said I didn't know that, but I did know that he had fought against them there.

"He smiled in a fascinating manner and said, 'That's very possible. A soldier of fortune. He is a native of Piedmont, is he not?'

"'Yes, sire.'

"'But you are French, entirely French. We have a claim on you. How old are you?'

"I told him. He said, 'You look younger.' Then he came nearer to me and, speaking in a confidential tone, said, 'You have no children. I know. I know. It isn't your fault, but you should try to make some other arrangement. Believe me, I am giving you good advice.'

"I was dumb with astonishment. He gave me again a very gracious smile and went on. That is the only conversation I ever had with the Emperor."

She fell silent with downcast eyes, then she added: "It was very characteristic of him." Cosmo was mainly struck by the fact that he knew so little of her, that this was the first intimation he had of the Montevessos being childless. He had never asked himself the question before, but this positive if indirect statement was agreeable to him.

"I did not make any other arrangements," began Madame de Montevesso with a slightly ironic intonation. "I was only too thankful to be left alone. At the time the Russian campaign began I paid my annual visit to Monsieur de Montevesso. Except for the usual entertainments to local people I was alone with Count Helion, and as usual when we were quite alone he behaved in a tolerable way. There was nobody and nothing that could arouse his jealousy and the dormant hatred he nurses for me deep down in his heart. We had only the slight discussion, at the end of which he admitted, gnashing his teeth, that he had nothing to reproach me with except that I was what I was. I told him I could not help it and that as things were he ought rather to congratulate himself on that fact. He gave me only a black look. He can restrain himself wonderfully when he likes. Upon the whole I had a quiet time. I played and sang to myself, I read a little, I took long walks, I rode almost every day, attended by Bernard. That wasn't so agreeable. You remember Bernard?"

Cosmo nodded.

"For years he had been a very devoted and faithful servant to us but I suppose he, too, like so many of his betters, fell under the spell of Monsieur de Montevesso's wealth. When my parents rejoined me in France he had his wish at last and married Aglae, my mulatto maid. He was quite infatuated with her and now he makes her terribly wretched. She is really devoted to me, and there cannot be any doubt that Bernard has been bribed by my husband to play the part of a spy. It seems incredible but I have had it from the Count in so many words. Bernard let himself be corrupted years ago, when M. de Montevesso first sent me back to my parents in a rage and next day was nearly out of his mind with agony at having done so. Yes, it dates as far back as that. That man so faithful to us in our misfortunes allowed himself to be bought with the greatest ease. Everybody, from the highest to the lowest, was in a conspiracy against a poor girl whose only sin was her perfect frankness. When Bernard came over to France with my parents I was already aware of this, but Aglae wanted to marry him and so I said nothing. She probably would not have believed me then."

"And could you bear that wretch near you all those years?" exclaimed Cosmo, full of indignation. She smiled sadly. She had borne the disclosure and had kept the secret of greater infamies. She had all her illusions about rectitude destroyed so early that it did not matter to her now what she knew of the people about her.

"Oh, Cosmo," she exclaimed suddenly, "I am a hardened woman now, but I assure you that sometimes when I remember the girl of sixteen I was, without an evil thought in her head and in her ignorance surrounded by the basest slanderers and intrigues, tears come into my eyes. And since the baseness of selfish passions I have seen seething round the detestable glory of that man in Elba, it seems to me that there is nowhere any honesty on earth—nowhere!" The energy of that outburst, contrasted with the immobility of the pose, gave to Cosmo the sensation of a chill.

"I will not mention us two," said Cosmo, "herein this room. But I know of at least two honest men on earth. They are your father and mine. Why didn't you write to Father, Adèle?"

"I tell you I was a child. What could I write to him? Hasn't he retired out of the world for so many years only not to see and not to hear? That's one of your honest men. And as to my poor father, who is the soul of honour, such is the effect of long misfortune on the best characters and of temptations associated with his restored rank, that there have been moments when I watched his conduct with dread. Caste prejudices are an awful thing, but thank God he had never a thought of vengeance in his mind. He is not a courtier."

"I have heard about it," interrupted Cosmo, "from the Marquis himself. He is a dear old man."

The two by the mantelpiece exchanged dim smiles.

"I had to come here with him," said Adèle. "He cannot do without me. I too was glad to get away from the evil passions and the hopeless stupidities of all the people that had come back without a single patriotic feeling, without a single new idea in their heads, like merciless spectres out of a grave, hating the world to which they had returned. They had forgotten nothing and learned nothing."

"I have seen something of that myself," murmured Cosmo. "But the world can't be put back where it was before you and I were born."

"No! But to see them trying to do it was intolerable. Then my husband appeared on the scene, hired this Palazzo, and insisted on us all living here. It was impossible to raise a rational objection to that. Father was never aware of half I went through in my life. I learned early to suppress every expression of feeling. But in the main we understand each other without talking. When he received Count Helion's letter offering us this house he just looked at me and said, 'I suppose we must.' For my part, I go through life without raising any objections to anything. One has to preserve one's dignity in some way; and is there another way open to me? Yes, I have made up my mind; but I must tell you, Cosmo, that notwithstanding that amazing tour we made ten years ago amongst M. de Montevesso's problematic relations, those two sisters and that niece have been a perfect novelty to me. I only hope I never betrayed my surprise or any feeling at all about it." The Countess raised her eyes to Cosmo's face. "I have spoken of it to you as I have never spoken to anybody in my life, because of old memories which are so much to me and because I could not mistrust anybody of your name. Have you been wearied by this long tale?"

"No," said Cosmo. "But have you thought how it is going to end?"

"To end?" she said in a startled tone which affected Cosmo profoundly. "To end? What do you mean? Everything is ended already."

"I was thinking of your endurance," said Cosmo.

"Do I look worn out?" she asked.

Cosmo raised his head and looked at her steadily. The impression of her grace and her strength filled his breast with an admiring and almost oppressive emotion. He could find nothing to say, not knowing what was uppermost in his mind, pity or admiration, mingled with a vague anger.

"Well, what do you see in my face?"

"I never have seen such serenity on any face," said Cosmo. "How sure of itself your soul must be!"

Her colour became heightened for a moment, her eyes darkened as she said in a grateful tone, "You are right, Cosmo. My face is not a mask."

But he hardly heard her. He was lost in wonder at the sudden disorder of his thoughts. When he regained his mental composure he noticed that Madame de Montevesso seemed to be listening.

"I wonder whether the Count is still with my father," she said. "Ring that bell on the table at your hand, Cosmo."

Cosmo did so and they waited, looking at each other. Presently the door swung open, and at the same time the cartel above it began to strike the hour. Cosmo counted eleven and then Madame de Montevesso spoke to Bernard, who waited in silence.

"Is M. le Comte still with my father?"

"I haven't seen him come out yet, Madame la Comtesse."

"Tell your wife not to wait for me, Bernard."

"Yes, Madame la Comtesse." Bernard backed out respectfully through the door.

"How fat he is, and what sleek hair," marvelled Cosmo. "And what a solemn manner. No wonder I did not recognize him at once. He showed me into your father's room, you know. He looks a Special Envoy's confidential man all over. And to think that he is your household spy! I wonder at your patience."

"Perhaps if I had anything to conceal I would have had less patience with the spy," she said, equably. "I believe that when we lived in Paris he wrote every week to M. de Montevesso, because, you know, he can write quite well. I wonder what he found to write about. Lists of names, I suppose. Or perhaps his own views of the people who called with bits of overheard conversations."

"It's incredible," murmured Cosmo. "It's fantastic. What contempt he must have for your husband."

"The most remarkable thing," said Madame de Montevesso, "is that I am convinced that he doesn't write any lies."

"Yes," said Cosmo, "I assume that. And do you mean that the Count is paying him every week for that sort of thing. It's an ugly farce."

"Don't you think," said the Countess, "that something serious may come of it some day?" Cosmo made a hopeless gesture.

"The man you married is mad," he said with intense conviction.

"There have been times when I felt as if I were mad myself," murmured Madame de Montevesso. "Take up your hat," she added quickly.

She had heard footsteps outside the door. A moment after, Count Helion came in and fixed his black glance on his wife and Cosmo. He did not open his lips and remained ominously by the door for a time. The strain of the silence was made sinister by the stiff bearing of the man, the immobility of the carven brown face, crossed by the inky-black moustache in harsh contrast with the powdered head. He might have been a sergeant come at the stroke of the hour to tell those two people that the firing squad was waiting for them outside the door. Madame de Montevesso broke the dumb spell.

"I did my best to entertain Mr. Latham, but we had given you up. He was just going."

She glanced serenely at Cosmo, whom the sweetness of her tone, her easy self-possession before that barrack-room figure, stung to the heart. At that moment no words could have expressed the intensity of his hatred for the Count of Montevesso, at whom he was looking with a smile of the utmost banality. The latter moved forward stiffly.

"Your father hopes you will see him for a moment presently," he said to his wife. "He has not gone to bed yet."

"Then I will go to him at once."

Madame de Montevesso extended her hand to Cosmo, who raised the tips of her fingers to his lips ceremoniously.

"I will see Mr. Latham out," said the Count, bowing to his wife, who went out of the room without looking at him. Cosmo, following her with his eyes, forgot Count Helion's existence. He forgot it so thoroughly that it was with a perceptible start that he perceived the Count's eyes fixed on him in an odd way. "He will never look at ease anywhere," thought Cosmo scornfully. A great part of his hatred had evaporated. "I suppose he means to be pilot. I wonder how he looked on the back of an elephant."

"It was very good of you to wait so long for my return," said Count Helion. "I have been detained by an absurd discussion arising out of probably false reports."

"The time passed quickly," said truthful Cosmo; but, before the black weary glance of the other, hastened to add with assumed care, "We talked of old times."

"Old times," repeated Count Helion without any particular accent. "My wife is very young yet, though she must be older than you are. Isn't she older?"

Cosmo said curtly that he really did not know. When they were running about as children together she was the tallest of the three.

"And now," took up the inexpressive voice of Count de Montevesso, "without her high heels she would be a little shorter than you. As you stood together you looked to me exactly the same height. And so you renewed the memories of your youth. They must have been delightful."

"They were no doubt more delightful for me than they could have been for Mme. la Comtesse," said Cosmo, making a motion towards taking leave.

"A moment. Let me have the honour to see you out." Count Helion walked round the room blowing out the candles in three candelabras in succession and taking up the fourth in his hand.

"Why take this trouble?" protested Cosmo. "I know my way."

"Every light has been extinguished in the reception rooms; or at least ought to have been. I detest waste of all kinds. It is perhaps because I have made my own fortune, and by God's favour it is so considerable in its power for good that it requires the most careful management. It is perhaps a peculiar point of view, but I have explained it to Mme. de Montevesso."

"She must have been interested," muttered Cosmo between his teeth, following across the room and round the screen the possessor of these immensely important riches, who, candelabra in hand, preceded him by a pace or two and threw open the door behind the screen. Cosmo, crossing in the wake of Count Helion the room of the evening reception, saw dimly the disarranged furniture about the mantelpiece, the armchair in which Lady William had sat, the great sofa in which little Countess Bubna had been shyly ensconced, the card table with the chairs pushed back and all the cards in a heap in the middle. The swaying flames of the candles, leaping from one long strip of mirror to another, preceded him into the next salon where all the furniture stood ranged expectantly against the walls. The next two salons were exactly alike except for the colour of the hangings and the size of the pictures on the walls. As to their subjects, Cosmo could not make them out.

Not a single lackey was to be seen in the anteroom of white walls and red benches; but Cosmo was surprised at the presence of a peasant-like woman, who must have been sitting there in the dark for some time. The light of the candelabra fell on the gnarled hands lying in her lap. The edge of a dark shawl shaded her features with the exception of her ancient chin. She never stirred. Count Helion, disregarding her as though she had been invisible, put down the candelabra on a little table and wished Cosmo good-night with a formal bow. At the same time he expressed harshly the hope of seeing Cosmo often during his stay in Genoa. Then with an unexpected attempt to soften his tone he muttered something about his wife—"the friend of your childhood."

The allusions exasperated Cosmo. The more he saw of the grown woman, the less connection she seemed to have with the early Adèle. The contrast was too strong. He felt tempted to tell M. de Montevesso that he by no means cherished that old memory. The nearest he came to it was the statement that he had the privilege to hear much of Madame de Montevesso in Paris. M. de Montevesso, contemplating now the dark peasant-like figure huddled up on the crimson seat against a white wall, hastened to turn towards Cosmo the black weariness of his eyes.

"Mme. de Montevesso has led a very retired life during the Empire. Her conduct was marked by the greatest circumspection. But she is a person of rank. God knows what gossip you may have heard. The world is censorious."

Brusquely Cosmo stepped out into the outer gallery. Listening to M. de Montevesso was no pleasure. The Count accompanied him as far as the head of the great staircase and stayed to watch his descent with a face that expressed no more than the face of a soldier on parade, till, all at once, his eyes started to roll about wildly as if looking for some object he could snatch up and throw down the stairs at Cosmo's head. But this lasted only for a moment. He reëntered the anteroom quietly and busied himself in closing and locking the door with care. After doing this he approached the figure on the bench and stood over it silently.

VII

The old woman pushed back her shawl and raised her wrinkled soft face without much expression to say:

"The child has been calling for you for the last hour or more."

Helion de Montevesso walked all the length of the anteroom and back again; then stood over the old woman as before.

"You know what she is," she began directly the Count had stopped. "She won't give us any rest. When she was little one could always give her a beating but now there is no doing anything with her. You had better come and see for yourself."

"Very unruly?" asked the Count de Montevesso.

"She is sixteen," said the old woman crisply, getting up and moving towards the stairs leading to the upper floor. A stick that had been lying concealed in the folds of her dress was now in her hand. She ascended the stairs more nimbly than her appearance would have led one to expect, and the Count of Montevesso followed her down a long corridor, where at last the shuffle of her slippers and the tapping of her stick ceased in front of a closed door. A profound silence reigned in this remote part of the old palace which the enormous vanity of the upstart had hired for the entertainment of his wife and his father-in-law in the face of the restored monarchies of Europe. The old peasant woman turned to the stiff figure which, holding the candelabra and in its laced coat, recalled a gorgeous lackey.

"We have put her to bed," she said, "but as to holding her down in it, that was another matter. Maria is strong but she got weary of it at last. We had to send for Father Paul. Shameless as she is she would not attempt to get out of her bed in her nightdress before a priest. The Father promised to stay till we could fetch you to her, so I came down, but I dared not go further than the anteroom. A valet told me you had still a guest with you, so I sent him away and sat down to wait. The wretch to revenge himself on me put out the lights before he went."

"He shall be flung out to-morrow," said M. de Montevesso in a low tone.

"I hope I have done nothing wrong, Helion."

"No," said M. de Montevesso in the same subdued tone. He lent his ear to catch some slight sound on the other side of the door. But the stillness behind it was like the stillness of a sick room to which people listen with apprehension. The old woman laid her hand lightly on the sleeve of the gorgeous coat. "You are a great man . . ."

"I am," said Count Helion without exultation.

The old woman, dragged out at the age of seventy from the depths of her native valley by the irresistible will of the great man, tried to find utterance for a few simple thoughts. Old age with its blunted feelings had alone preserved her from utter bewilderment at the sudden change; but she was overpowered by its greatness. She lived inside that palace as if enchanted into a state of resignation. Ever since she had arrived in Genoa, which was just five weeks ago, she had kept to the upper floor. Only the extreme necessity of the case had induced her to come so far downstairs as the white anteroom. She was conscious of not having neglected her duty.

"I did beat her faithfully," she declared with the calmness of old age and conscious rectitude. The lips of M. de Montevesso twitched slightly. "I did really, though often feeling too weary to raise my arm. Then I would throw a shawl over my head and go in the rain to speak to Father Paul. He had taught her to read and write. He is full of charity. He would shrug his shoulders and tell me to put my trust in God. It was all very well for him to talk like that. True that on your account I was the greatest person for miles around. I had the first place everywhere. But now that you made us come out here just because of your fancy to turn the child into a Contessa, all my poor senses leave my old body. For, you know, if I did beat her, being entrusted with your authority, everybody else in the village waited on a turn of her finger. She was full of pride and wilfulness then. Now since you have introduced her amongst all these *grandissimi signori* of whom she had only heard as one hears of angels in heaven, she seems to have lost her head with the excess of pride and obstinacy. What is one to do? The other day on account of something I said she fastened her ten fingers into my gray hair. . . ." She threw her shawl off and raised her creased eyelids. . . . "This gray hair, on the oldest head of your family, Helion. If it hadn't been for Maria she would have left me a corpse on the floor." The mild bearing of the old woman had a dignity of its own, but at this point it broke down and she became agitated.

"Many a time I sat up in my bed thinking half the night. I am an old woman. I can read the signs. This is a matter for priests. When I was a big girl in our village they had to exorcise a comely youth, a herdsman. I am not fit to talk of such matters. But you, Helion, could say a word or two to Father Paul. He would know what to do . . . or get the Bishop . . ."

"Amazing superstition," Count Helion exclaimed in a rasping growl. "The days of priests and devils are gone," he went on angrily, but paused as if struck with a sudden doubt or a new idea. The old woman shook her head slightly. In the depths of her native valley all the days were alike in their hopes and fears as far back as she could remember. She did not know how she had offended her brother and emitted a sigh of resignation.

"What's the trouble now?" Count Helion asked brusquely.

The old woman shrugged her shoulders expressively. Count Helion insisted. "There must be some cause."

"The cause, as I am a sinner, can be no other but that young signore that came out with you and to whom you bowed so low. I didn't know you had to bow to anybody unless perhaps to the King who has come back lately. But then a king is anointed with holy oils! I couldn't believe my eyes. What kind of prince was that?" She waited, screwing her eyes up at Count Helion, who looked down at her inscrutably and at last condescended to say:

"That was an Englishman."

She moaned with astonishment and alarm. A heretic! She thought no heretic could be good-looking. Didn't they have their wickedness written on their faces?

"No," said Count Helion. "No man has that, and no woman, either."

Again he paused to think. "Let us go in now," he added.

The big room (all the rooms in that Palazzo were big unless they happened to be mere dark and airless cupboards), which they entered as quietly as if a sick person had been lying in there at the point of death, contained amongst its gilt furniture also a few wooden stools and a dark walnut table brought down from the farmhouse for the convenience of its rustic occupants. A priest sitting in a gorgeous armchair held to the light of a common brass oil lamp an open book, the shadow of which darkened a whole corner of the vast space between the high walls decorated with rare marbles, long mirrors, and heavy hangings. A few small pieces of washing were hung out to dry on a string stretched from a window latch to the back of a chair. A common brazier stood in the fireplace and, near it, a gaunt, bony woman dressed in black with a white handkerchief on her head was stirring something in a little earthen pot. Ranged at the foot of a dais bearing a magnificent but dismantled couch of state were two small wooden bedsteads, on one of which lay the girl whom Cosmo knew only as "Clelia, my husband's niece," with a hand under her cheek. The other cheek was much flushed; a tangle of loose black hair covered the pillow. Whether from respect for the priest or from mere exhaustion she was keeping perfectly still under her bedclothes pulled up to her very neck so that only her head remained uncovered.

At the entrance of the Count the priest closed his book and stood up, but the woman by the mantelpiece went on stirring her pot. Count Helion returned a "*Bonsoir, Abbé*" to the priest's silent bow, put down the candelabra on a console, and walked straight to the bedstead. The other three people, the gaunt woman still with her pot in her hand, approached it too but kept their distance.

The girl Clelia remained perfectly still under the downward thoughtful gaze of Count Helion. In that face half buried in the pillow one eye glittered full of tears. She refused to make the slightest sound in reply to Count Helion's questions, orders, and remonstrances. Even his coaxings, addressed to her in the same low, harsh tone, were received in obstinate silence. Whenever he paused he could hear at his back the old woman whispering to the priest. At last even that stopped. Count Helion resisted the temptation to grab all that hair on the pillow and pull the child out of bed by it. He waited a little longer and then said in his harsh tone:

"I thought you loved me."

For the first time there was a movement under the blanket. But that was all. Count Helion turned his back on the bed and met three pairs of eyes fixed on him with different expressions. He avoided meeting any of them. "Perhaps if you were to leave us alone," he said.

They obeyed in silence, but at the last moment he called the priest back and took him aside to a distant part of the room where the brass oil lamp stood on the walnut-wood table. The full physiognomy of Father Paul Carpi with its thin eyebrows and pouting mouth was overspread by a self-conscious professional placidity that seemed ready to see or hear anything without surprise. Count de Montevesso was always impressed by it. "Abbé," he said brusquely, "you know that my sister thinks that the child is possessed. I suppose she means by a devil."

He looked with impatience at the priest, who remained silent, and burst out in a subdued voice:

"I believe you people are hoping now to bring him back into the world again, that old friend of yours." He waited for a moment. "Sit down, Abbé."

Father Carpi sank into the armchair with some dignity while Count Helion snatched a three-legged stool and planted himself on it on the other side of the table. "Now, wouldn't you?"

Something not bitter, not mocking, but as if disillusioned seemed to touch the lips of Father Carpi at the very moment he opened them to say quietly:

"Only as a witness to the reign of God."

"Which of course would be your reign. Never mind, a man like me can be master under any reign." He jerked his head slightly towards the bed. "Now what sort of devil would it be in that child?"

The deprecatory gesture of Father Carpi did not detract from his dignity. "I should call it dumb myself," continued Count Helion. "We will leave it alone for a time. What hurts me often is the difficulty of getting at your thoughts, Abbé. Haven't I been a good enough friend to you?" To this, too, Father Carpi answered by a deferential gesture and deprecatory murmur. Count Helion had restored the church, rebuilt the presbytery, and had behaved generally with great munificence. Father Carpi, sprung from shopkeeping stock in the town of Novi, had lived through times difficult for the clergy. He had been contented to exist. Now, at the age of forty or more, the downfall of the Empire, which seemed to carry with it the ruin of the impious forces of the Revolution, had awakened in him the first stirrings of ambition. Its immediate object was the chaplaincy to the Count of Montevesso's various charitable foundations.

There was a man, one of the great of this world, whom, without understanding him in any deeper sense or ever trying to judge his nature, he could see plainly enough to be unhappy. And that was a great point.

For the unhappy are more amenable to obscure influences, religious and others. But Father Carpi was too intelligent to intrude upon the griefs of that man with the mysterious past either religious consolation or secular advice. For a long time now he had watched and waited, keeping his thoughts so secret that they seemed even hidden from himself. To the outbreaks of that rough, arrogant, contemptuous, and oppressive temper he could oppose only the gravity of his sacerdotal character as Adèle did her lofty serenity, that detachment, both scornful and inaccessible, which seemed to place her on another plane.

Father Carpi had never been before confronted so directly by the difficulties of his position as at that very moment and on the occasion of that intolerable and hopeless girl. To gain time he smiled, a slight, non-committal smile.

"We priests, M. le Comte, are recommended not to enter into discussion of theological matters with people who, whatever their accomplishments and wisdom, are not properly instructed in them. As to anything else I am always at Monseigneur's service."

He gave this qualification to Count Helion because it was not beyond the bounds of respect due from a poor, parish priest to a titled great man of his province.

"Have you been much about amongst the town people?" asked Count Helion.

"I go out every morning about seven to say mass in that church you may have noticed near by. I have visited also once or twice an old friend from my seminary days, a priest of a poor parish here. We rejoice together at the return of the Holy Father to Rome. For the rest I had an idea. Monseigneur, that you did not wish me to make myself prominent in any way in this town."

"Perhaps I didn't. It may be convenient, though, to know what are the rumours current amongst the populace. That class has its own thoughts. I suppose your friend would know something of that."

"No doubt. But I can tell you, Monseigneur, what the people think. They think that if they can't be Genoese as before, they would rather be French than Piedmontese. That, Monseigneur, is a general feeling even amongst the better class of citizens."

"Much would they gain by it," mumbled Count de Montevesso. "Unless the Other were to come back. Abbé," he added sharply, "is there any talk of him coming back?"

"That indeed would be a misfortune." Father Carpi's tone betrayed a certain emotion which Count Helion noticed, faint as it was.

"Whatever happens you will have always a friend in me," he said, and Father Carpi acknowledged the assurance by a slight inclination of his body.

"Surely God would not allow it," he murmured uneasily. But the stare of his interlocutor augmented his alarm. He was still more startled when he heard Count de Montevesso make the remark that the only thing which seemed to put a limit to the power of God was the folly of men. He had too poor an opinion of Count de Montevesso to be shocked by the blasphemy. To him it was only the proof that the Count had been very much upset by something, some fact or some news.

"And people are very foolish just now both in Paris and in Vienna," added Count de Montevesso after a long pause.

It was news then. Father Carpi betrayed nothing of his anxious curiosity. The inward unrest which pervaded the whole basin of the Western Mediterranean was strongest in Italy perhaps and was very strong in the heart of Father Carpi, who was both an Italian and a priest. Perhaps he would be told something! He almost held his breath, but Count de Montevesso took his head between his hands and said only:

"One is pestered by folly of all sorts. Abbé, see whether you can bring that child to reason."

However low in the scale of humanity Father Carpi placed the Count de Montevesso, he never questioned his social position. Father Carpi was made furious by the request, but he obeyed. He approached the rustic bedstead and looked at the occupant with sombre disgust. Nothing was obscure to him in the situation. If he couldn't tell exactly what devil possessed that creature he remembered perfectly her mother, a rash sort of girl who was found drowned years ago in a remarkably shallow pond amongst some rocks not quite a mile away from the presbytery. It might have been an accident. He had consented to bury her in consecrated ground not from any compassion, but because of the revolutionary spirit which had penetrated even the thick skulls of his parishioners and probably would have caused a riot and shaken the precarious power of the Church in his obscure valley. He stood erect by the head of the couch, looking down at the girl's uncovered eye whose sombre iris swam on the glistening white. He could have laughed with contempt and fury. He regulated his deep voice so that it reached Count de Montevesso at the other side of the room only as a solemn admonishing murmur.

"You miserable little wretch," he said, "can't you behave yourself? You have been a torment to me for years."

The sense of his own powerlessness overcame him so completely that he felt tempted for a moment to throw everything up, walk out of the room, seek refuge amongst sinners that would believe either in God or in the devil.

"You are a scourge to us all," he continued in the same equable murmur. "If you don't speak out, you little beast, and put an end to this scene soon I will exorcise you."

The only effect of that threat was the sudden immobility of the rolling eye. Father Carpi turned towards the Count.

"It is probably some sort of malady," he said coldly. "Perhaps a doctor could prescribe some remedy."

Count Helion came out of his listless attitude. A moment ago a doctor was in the house in conference with M. le Marquis. Perhaps he was still there. Count Helion got up impetuously and asked the Abbé to go along to the other side and find out.

"Take a light with you. All the lights are out down there. Knock at the Marquis's door and inquire from Bernard, and if the doctor is still there bring him along."

Father Carpi went out hastily and Count de Montevesso, keeping the women outside, paced the whole length of the room. The fellow called himself a doctor whatever else he might have been. Whether he did any good to the child or not—Count de Montevesso stopped and looked fixedly at the bed—this was an extremely favourable opportunity to get in touch with him personally. Who could tell what use could be made of him in his other capacities, apart from the fact that he probably could really prescribe some remedy? Count de Montevesso's heart was softened paternally. His progress from European barrack-rooms to an Eastern palace left on his mind a sort of bewilderment. He even thought the girl attractive. There she was, a prey of some sort of illness. He bent over her face and instantly a pair of thin bare arms darted from under the blankets and clasped him round the neck with a force that really surprised him. "That one loves me," he thought. He did not know that she would have hung round anybody's neck in the passion of obtaining what she wanted. He thought with a sort of dull insight that everybody was a little bit against her. He abandoned his neck to the passionate clasp for a little time, then disengaged himself gently.

"What makes you behave like this?" he asked. "Do you feel a pain anywhere?"

No emotion could change the harshness of his voice, but it was very low and there was an accent in it which the girl could not mistake. She sat up suddenly with her long wild hair covering her shoulders. With her round eyes, the predatory character of her face, the ruffled fury of her aspect, she looked like an angry bird; and there was something bird-like in the screech of her voice.

"Pain? No. But if I didn't hate them so I would like to die. I would . . ."

Count de Montevesso put one hand at the back of her head and clapped the other broad palm over her mouth. This action surprised her so much that she didn't even struggle. When the Count took his hands away she remained silent without looking at him.

"Don't scream like this," he murmured harshly but with obvious indulgence. "Your aunts are outside and they will tell the priest all about it."

Clelia drew up her knees, clasped her hands round them outside the blanket, and stared.

"It is just your temper!" suggested Count Helion reproachfully.

"All those dressed-up witches despise me. I am not frightened. And the worst of them is that yellow-haired witch, your wife. If I had gone in there in my bare feet they could not have stared more down on me. . . . I shall fly at their faces. I can read their thoughts as they put their glasses to their eyes. 'What animal is this?' they seem to ask themselves. I am a brute beast to them."

A shadow seemed to fall on Count de Montevesso's face for the moment. Clelia unclasped her fingers, shook her fists at the empty space, then clasped her legs again. These movements, full of sombre energy, were observed silently by the Count of Montevesso. He uttered the word *"Patienza,"* which in its humility is the word of the ambitious, of the unforgiving who keep a strict account with the world; a word of indomitable hope. "You wait till you are a little older. You will have plenty of people at your feet; and then you will be able to spurn anybody you like."

"You mean when I am married," said Clelia in a faraway voice and staring straight over her knees.

"Yes," said the Count de Montevesso, "but you will first have to learn to be gentle."

This recommendation apparently missed the ear for which it was destined. For a whole minute Clelia seemed to contemplate some sort of vision with her predatory and pathetic stare. One side of her nightgown had slipped off her shoulder. Suddenly she pushed her scattered hair back, and extending her arm towards Count Helion patted him caressingly on the cheek.

When she had done patting him he asked, unmoved: "Now, what is it you want?"

She was careful not to turn her face his way while she whispered: "I want that young signor that came to-day to make eyes at my aunt."

"Impossible."

"Why impossible? I was with them in the morning. They did nothing but look at each other. But I went for him myself."

"That Englishman! You can't have an Englishman like this. I am thinking of something better for you, a marquis or a count."

This was the exact truth, not a sudden idea to meet a hopeless case.

"You have hardly had time to have a good look at him," added Count Helion.

"I looked at him this evening with all my eyes, with all my soul. I would have sat up all night to look at him. But he got up and turned his back on me. He has no eyes for anybody but my aunt."

"Did you speak together, you two?"

"Yes," she said, "he sat down by me and all those witches stared as if he had been making up to a monster. Am I a monster? He too looked at me as if I had been one."

"Was he rude to you?" asked the Count de Montevesso.

"He was as insolent as all the people I have seen since we came to this town. His heart was black as of all the rest of them. He was gentle to me as one is gentle to an old beggar for the sake of charity. Oh, how I hated him."

"Well, then," said Count de Montevesso in a harsh unsympathetic tone, "you may safely despise him."

Clelia threw herself half out of bed on the neck of Count Helion, who preserved an unsympathetic rigidity though he did not actually repulse her wild and vehement caress.

"Oh, dearest uncle of mine," she whispered ardently! into his ear, "he is handsome! I must have him for myself."

There was a knocking at the door. Count Helion tore the bare arms from his neck and pushed the girl back into bed.

"Cover yourself up," he commanded hurriedly. He arranged the blanket at her back. "Lie still and say nothing of all this, and then you need have no fear. But if you breathe a word of this to anybody, then . . . Come in," he shouted to the renewed knocking and had just time to shake his finger at Clelia menacingly before the Abbé and the doctor entered the room.

PART III

I

Cosmo walked away with no more than one look back, just before turning the corner, at the tensely alert griffins guarding the portals of the Palazzo. At the entrance of his inn a small knot of men on the pavement paused in their low conversation to look at him. After he had passed he heard a voice say, "This is the English milord." He found the dimly lit hall empty and he went up the empty staircase into the upper regions of silence. His face, which to the men on the pavement had appeared passionless and pale as marble, looked at him suddenly out of the mirror over the fireplace, and he was startled as though he had seen a ghost.

Spire had been told not to wait for his return. His empty room had welcomed him with a bright flame on the hearth and with lighted candles. He turned away from his own image and stood with his back to the fire looking downwards and vaguely oppressed by the profound as if expectant silence around him. The strength and novelty of the impressions received during that day, the intimacy of their appeal, had affected his fortitude. He felt mortally weary and began to undress; but after he got into bed he remained for a time in a sitting posture. For the first time in his life he tasted of loneliness. His father was at least thirty-five years his senior. An age! His sister was just a young girl. Clever, of course. He was very fond of her, but the mere fact of her being a girl raised a wall between them. He had never made any real friends. He had nothing to do; and he did not seem to know what to think of anything in the world. Now, for instance there was that vanquished fat figure in a little cocked hat. . . . Still an emperor.

Cosmo came with a start out of a deep sleep that seemed to have lasted only a moment. But he knew at once where he was, though at first he had to argue himself out of the conviction of having parted from Count Helion at the top of a staircase less than five minutes ago. Meantime he watched Spire flooding the room with brilliant sunshine, for the three windows of the room faced east.

"Very fine morning, sir," said Spire over his shoulder. "Quite a spring day."

A delicious freshness flowed over Cosmo. It did not bring joy to him, but dismay. Daylight already! It had come too soon. He had had no time yet to decide what to do. He had gone to sleep. A most extraordinary thing! His distress was appeased by the simple thought that there was no need for him to do anything. After drinking his chocolate, which Spire received on a tray from some woman on the other side of the door, he informed him that he intended to devote the whole day to his correspondence. A table having been arranged to that end close to an open window, he started writing at once. On retiring without a sound Spire left the goose-quill flying over the paper. It was past noon before Cosmo, hearing him come in again on some pretence or other, raised his head for the first time and dropped the pen to say: "Give me my coat, I will go down to the dining room."

By that time the murmur of voices in the piazza had died out. The good Genoese had gone indoors to eat. Coming out of his light-filled room Cosmo found the corridors cold and dark like subterranean passages cut in rock, and the hall downstairs gloomy like a burial vault. In contrast with it the long dining room had a festive air, a brilliancy that was almost crude. In a corner where the man who called himself Doctor Martel had his table this glare was toned down by half-closed shutters and Cosmo made his way there. Cantelucci's benefactor, seated sideways with one arm thrown over the chair's back, took Cosmo's arrival as a matter of course, greeted him with an amiable growl, and declared himself very sharp set. Presently laying down his knife and fork he enquired what Cosmo had been doing that morning. Writing? Really? Thought that perhaps Cosmo had been doing the churches. One could see very pretty girls in the morning, waiting for their turn at the confessional.

Cosmo, raising suddenly his eyes from his plate, caught his companion examining him keenly. The doctor burst into a loud laugh till Cosmo's grave face recalled him to himself.

"I beg your pardon. I remembered suddenly a very funny thing that happened to me last night. I am afraid you think me very impolite. It was extremely funny."

"Won't you tell me of it?" asked Cosmo coldly.

"No, my dear sir. You are not in the mood. I prefer to apologize. There is a secret in it which is not mine. But as to the girls I was perfectly serious. If you seek female beauty you must look to the people for it and in Genoa you will not look in vain. The women of the upper classes are alike everywhere. You must have remarked that."

"I have hardly had time to look about me as yet," said Cosmo. He was no longer annoyed with the doctor, not even after he heard him say:

"Surely yesterday evening you must have had an opportunity. You came home late."

"I wonder who takes the trouble to watch my movements?" remarked Cosmo carelessly.

"Town-police spies, of course," said the doctor grimly; "and perhaps one or two of the most enterprising thieves. You must make up your mind to that. After all, why should you care?"

"Yes, why should I?" repeated Cosmo nonchalantly. "Do they report to you?"

The doctor laughed again. "I see you haven't forgiven me my untimely merriment; but I will answer your question. No doubt I could hear a lot if I wanted to, both from the police and the thieves. But as a matter of fact it was my courier who told me. He was talking with some friends outside this inn when you came home. You know, you are a noticeable figure."

"Oh, your courier. I suppose he hasn't got much else to do!"

"I see you are bent on quarrelling, Mr. Latham," said the other, while two unexpected dimples appeared on his round cheeks. "All right. Only hadn't we better wait for some other opportunity? Don't you allow your man to talk while he is assisting you to dress? I must confess I let my fellow run on while he is shaving me in the morning. But then I am an easy-going sort of tramp. For I am just a tramp. I have no Latham Hall to go back to."

He pushed his chair away from the table, stretched his legs, plunged his hands in his pockets complacently. How long was it he had been a tramp? he mused aloud. Twenty years? Or a little more. From one end of Europe to the other. From Madrid to Moscow, as one might say. Exactly like that Corsican fellow. Only he hadn't dragged a tail of two hundred thousand men behind him, and had done no more blood-letting than his lancet was equal to.

He looked up at Cosmo suddenly.

"The lancet's my weapon, you know. Not bayonet or sabre. Cold steel anyhow. Of course I found occasion to fire off my pistols more than once, in the course of my travels, and I must say for myself that whenever I fired them it settled the business. One evening, I remember, in Transylvania, stepping out of a wretched inn to take a look round, I ran against a coalition of three powerful Haiduks in tarry breeches, with moustaches a foot long. The moonlight was bright as day. I took in the situation at a glance and I assure you two of them never made a sound as they fell, while the third just grunted once. I fancy they had designs on my poor horse. He was inside the inn, you know. A custom of the country. Men and animals under the same roof. I used to be sorry for the animals. When I came in again the Jew had just finished frying the eggs. He had been very surly before but when he served me I noticed that he was shaking like a leaf. He tried to propitiate me by the offer of a sausage. I was simply ravenous. It made me ill for two days. That's why I haven't forgotten the occurrence. He nearly managed to avenge those bandits. Luckily I had the right kind of drugs in my valise, and my iron constitution helped me to pull through. But I should like to have seen Bonaparte in that predicament. He wouldn't have known what to do. And, anyhow, the sausage would have finished him. His constitution is not like mine. He's unhealthy, sir, unhealthy."

"You had occasion to observe him often?" asked Cosmo, simply because he was reluctant to go back to his writing.

"Our paths seldom crossed," stated the other simply. "But some time after the abdication I was passing through Valence—it's a tramp's business, you know, to keep moving—and I just had a good look at him outside the post-house. You may take it from me, he won't reach the term of the Psalmist. Well, Mr. Latham, when I take a survey of the past, here we are, the Corsican and I, within, say, a hundred miles of each other, at the end of twenty years of tramping, and, frankly, which of us is the better off when all's said and done?"

"That's a point of view," murmured Cosmo wearily. He added, however, that there were various ways of appreciating the careers of the world's great men.

"There are," assented the other. "For instance, you would say that nothing short of the whole of Europe was needed to crush that fellow. But Pozzo di Borgo thinks that he has done it all by himself."

At the name of the Emperor's Corsican enemy Cosmo raised his head. He had caught sight in Paris of that personage at one or other of those great receptions from which he used to come away disgusted with the world and dissatisfied with himself. The doctor seemed inwardly amused by his recollection of Pozzo di Borgo.

"He said to me," he continued, "'Ah! If Bonaparte had had the sense not to quarrel with me he wouldn't be in Elba now.' What do you think of that, Mr. Latham? Is that a point of view?"

"I should call it mad egotism."

"Yes. But the most amusing thing is that there is some truth in it. The private enmity of one man may be more dangerous and more effective than the hatred of millions on public grounds. Pozzo has the ear of the Russian Emperor. The fate of the Bourbons hung on a hair. Alexander's word was law—and who knows!"

Cosmo, plunged in abstraction, was repeating to himself mechanically, "The fate of the Bourbons hung on a hair—the fate of the Bourbons." . . . Those words seemed meaningless. He tried to rouse himself. "Yes, Alexander," he murmured vaguely. The doctor raised his voice suddenly in a peevish tone.

"I am not talking of Alexander of Macedon, Mr. Latham." His vanity had been hurt by Cosmo's attitude. The young man's faint smile placated him, and the incongruous dimples reappeared on the doctor's cheeks while he continued: "Here you are. For Pozzo, Napoleon has always been a starveling squireen. For the Prince, he has been principally the born enemy of good taste. . . ."

"The Prince?" repeated Cosmo, struggling to keep his head above the black waters of melancholia which seemed to lap about his very lips. "You have said the Prince, haven't you? What Prince?"

"Why, Talleyrand, of course. He did once tell him so, too. Pretty audacious! What? . . . Well, I don't know. Suppose you were master of the world, and somebody were to tell you something of the sort to your face—what could you do? Nothing. You would have to gulp it, feeling pretty small. A private gentleman of good position could resent such a remark from an equal, but a master of the world couldn't. A master of the world, Mr. Latham, is very small potatoes; and I will tell you why: it's because he is alone of his kind, stuck up like a thief in the pillory, for dead cats and cabbage stalks to be thrown at him. A devil of a position to be in unless for a moment. But no man born of woman is a monster. There never was such a thing. A man who would really be a monster would arouse nothing but loathing and hatred. But this man has been loved by an army, by a people. For years his soldiers died for him with joy. Now, didn't they?"

Cosmo perceived that he had managed to forget himself. "Yes," he said, "that cannot be denied."

"No," continued the doctor. "And now, within twenty yards of us, on the other side of the wall there are millions of people who still love him. Hey! Cantelucci!" he called across the now empty length of the room. "Come here."

The innkeeper, who had been noiselessly busy about a distant sideboard, approached with deference, in his shirt-sleeves, girt with a long apron of which one corner was turned up, and with a white cap on his head. Being asked whether it was true that Italians loved Napoleon, he answered by a bow and "Excellency."

"You think yourself that he is a great man, don't you?" pursued the doctor, and obtained another bow and another murmured "Excellency."

The doctor turned to Cosmo triumphantly. "You see! And Bonaparte has been stealing from them all he could lay his hands on for years. All their works of art. I am surprised he didn't take away the wall on which *The Last Supper* is painted. It makes my blood boil. I love Italy, you know." He addressed again the motionless Cantelucci.

"But what is it that makes you people love this man?"

This time Cantelucci did not bow. He seemed to make an effort: "Signore, it is the idea."

The doctor directed his eyes again to Cosmo in silence. At last the innkeeper stepped back three paces before turning away from his English clients. The dimples had vanished from the doctor's full cheeks. There was something contemptuous in the peevishness of his thin lips and the extreme hardness of his eyes. They softened somewhat before he addressed Cosmo.

"Here is another point of view for you. Devil only knows what that idea is, but I suspect it's vague enough to include every illusion that ever fooled mankind. There must be some charm in that gray coat and that old three-cornered hat of his, for the man himself has betrayed every hatred and every hope that have helped him on his way."

"What I am wondering at," Cosmo said at last, "is whether you have ever talked like this to anybody before."

The doctor seemed taken aback a little.

"Oh. You mean about Bonaparte," he said. "If you had gone to that other inn, Pollegrini's, more suitable to your nationality and social position, you would have heard nothing of that kind. I am not very communicative really, but to sit at meals like two mutes would have been impossible. What could we have conversed about? One must have some subject other than the weather and, frankly, what other subject would we have had here in Genoa, or for that matter in any other spot of the civilized world? I know there are amongst us in England a good many young men who call themselves revolutionists and even republicans. Charming young men, generous and all that. Friends of Boney. You might be one of them."

As he paused markedly Cosmo murmured that he was hardly prepared to state what he was. That other inn, the Pollegrini, was full when he arrived.

"Well, there had been three departures this morning," the doctor informed him. "You can have your things packed up this afternoon and carried across the Place. You know, by staying here you make yourself conspicuous to the spies, not to speak of the thieves; they ask themselves: 'What sort of inferior Englishman is that?' With me it is different. I am known for a man who has his own work to do. People are curious. And as my work is confidential I prefer to keep out of the way rather than have to be rude. But for you it would be more amusing to live over there. New faces all the time; endless gossip about all sorts of people."

"I do not think it is worth while to change now," said Cosmo coldly.

"Of course not, if you are not going to prolong your stay. If you project a visit to Elba, Livorno is the port for that. And if you are anxious to hear about Napoleon you will hear plenty of gossip about him there. Here you have nothing but my talk."

"I have found it very interesting," said Cosmo, rising to go away. The doctor smiled without amiability. He was determined never to let Cosmo guess that he knew of his acquaintance with the people occupying the palace guarded by the symbolic griffins. Of that fact he had been made aware by the Count de Montevesso who, once, he had got the doctor into Clelia's room, decided to take him into his confidence—on the ground that one must be frank with a medical man. The real reason was, however, that knowing Doctor Martel to be employed on secret political work by the statesmen of the Alliance, and having a very great idea of his occult influences in all sorts of spheres, he hoped to get from him another sort of assistance. His last words were, "You see yourself the state the child is in. I want that popinjay moved out of Genoa."

The only answer of the doctor to this, and the last sound during that professional visit that Count de Montevesso heard from him, was a short wooden laugh. That man of political intrigues, confidential missions (often he had more than one at a time on his hands), inordinately vain of his backstairs importance, was not mercenary. He had always preserved a most independent attitude towards his employers. To him the Count de Montevesso was but a common stupid soldier of fortune of no importance and of no position except as the son-in-law of the Marquis d'Armand. He had never seen him before, but his marital life was known to him as it was known to the rest of the world. To be waylaid by a strange priest just as he was leaving the Marquis's room was annoying enough, but he could not very well refuse the request since it seemed to be a case of sudden illness. He was soon enlightened as to its nature by Clelia, who had treated him and the Count to another of her indescribable performances. Characteristically enough the doctor had never been for a moment irritated with the girl. He behaved by her tempestuous bedside like a man of science, calm, attentive, impenetrable. But it was afterwards, when he had been drawn aside by the Count for a confidential talk, that he had asked himself whether he were dreaming or awake. His scorn for the man helped him to preserve his self-command, and to the end the Count was not intelligent enough to perceive its character.

The doctor left the Palazzo about an hour after Cosmo (but not by the same staircase) and on his way to his inn gave rein to his indignation. Did the stupid brute imagine that he had any sort of claim on his services? Ah, he wanted that popinjay removed from Genoa! Indeed! And what the devil did he care for it? Was he expected to arrange a neat little assassination to please that solemn wooden imbecile? The doctor's sense of self-importance was grievously hurt. Even in the morning after a good-night's rest he had not shaken off the impression. However, he was reasonable enough not to make Cosmo in any way responsible for what he defined to himself as the most incredibly offensive experience of his life. He only looked at him when he came to lunch with a sort of acid amusement as the being who had had the power to arouse a passion of love in the primitive soul of that curious little savage. As the meal proceeded, the doctor seemed to notice that his young countryman was somehow changed. He watched him covertly. What had happened to him since last evening? Surely he hadn't been smitten himself by the little savage that under no circumstances could have been made fit to be a housemaid in an English family.

After he had been left by Cosmo alone in the dining room, the doctor's body continued to loll in the chair while his thoughts continued to circle around that funny affair, of which you couldn't say whether it was love at first sight or a manifestation of some inherited lunacy. Quite a good-looking young man. Out of the common too, in a distinguished way. Altogether a specimen of one's countrymen one could well be proud of, mused further the doctor, whose tastes had been formed by much intercourse with all kinds of people. Characteristically enough, too, he felt for a moment sorry in his grumpy contemptuous way for the little dishevelled savage with a hooked nose and burning cheeks and her thin sticks of bare arms. The doctor was humane. The origin of his reputation sprang from his humanity. But his thought, as soon as it left Clelia, stopped short as it were before another image that replaced it in his mind. He had remembered the Countess of Montevesso. He knew her of old, by sight and reputation. He had seen her no further back than last night by the side of the old Marquis's chair. Now he had seen the Count de Montevesso himself, he could well believe all the stories of a lifelong jealousy. The doctor's hard, active eyes stared fixedly at the truth. It was not because of that little savage that gloomy self-tormenting ass of a drill sergeant to an Indian prince wanted young Latham removed from Genoa. Oh, dear no. That wasn't it at all. It was much more serious.

Before he walked out of the empty dining room Doctor Martel concluded that it would be perhaps just as well for young Latham not to linger too long in Genoa.

II

Cosmo, having returned to his room, sat down again at the writing table: for was not this day to be devoted to correspondence? Long after the shade had invaded the greater part of the square below he went on, while the faint shuffle of footsteps and the faint murmur of voices reached him from the pavement like the composite sound of agitated insect life that can be heard in the depths of a forest. It required all his courage to keep on, piling up words which dealt exclusively with towns, roads, rivers, mountains, the colours of the sky. It was like labouring the description of the scenery of a stage after a great play had come to an end. A vain thing. And still he travelled on. Having at last descended into the Italian plain (for the benefit of Henrietta), he dropped his pen and thought: "At this rate I will never arrive in Genoa." He fell back in his chair like a weary traveller. He was suddenly overcome by that weary distaste a frank nature feels after an effort at concealing an overpowering sentiment.

But had he really anything to conceal? he asked himself.

Suddenly the door flew open and Spire marched in with four lighted candles on a tray. It was only then that Cosmo became aware how late it was. "Had I not better tear all this up?" he thought, looking down at the sheets before him.

Spire put two candlesticks on the table, disposed the two others, one each side of the mantelpiece, and was going out.

"Wait!" cried Cosmo.

It was like a cry of distress. Spire shut the door quietly and turned about, betraying no emotion. Cosmo seized the pen again and concluded hastily:

I have been in Genoa for the last two days. I have seen Adèle and the Marquis. They send their love. You shall have lots about them in my next. I have no time now to tell you what a wonderful person she has become. But perhaps you would not think so.

After he had signed it the thought struck him that there was nothing about Napoleon in his letter. He must put in something about Napoleon. He added a P.S.:

You can form no idea of the state of suspense in which all classes live here from the highest to the lowest, as to what may happen next. All their thoughts are concentrated on Bonaparte. Rumours are flying about of some sort of violence that may be offered to him, assassination, kidnapping. It's difficult to credit it all, though I do believe that the Congress in Vienna is capable of any atrocity. A person I met here suggested that I should go to Livorno. Perhaps I will. But I have lost, I don't know why, all desire to travel. Should I find a ship ready to sail for England in Livorno, I may take passage in her and come home at once by sea.

Cosmo collected the pages, and while closing the packet asked himself whether he ought to tell her that. Was it the fact that he had lost all wish to travel? However, he let Spire take the packet to the post and during the man's absence took a turn or two in the room. He had got through the day. Now there was the evening to get through somehow. But when it occurred to him that the evening would be followed by the hours of an endless night, filled by the conflict of shadowy thoughts that haunt the birth of a passion, the desolation of the prospect was so overpowering that he could only meet it with a bitter laugh. Spire, returning, stood thunderstruck at the door.

"What's the matter with you? Have you seen a ghost?" asked Cosmo, who ceased laughing suddenly and fixed the valet with distracted eyes.

"No, sir, certainly not. I was wondering whether you hadn't better dine in your room."

"What do you mean? Am I not fit to be seen?" asked Cosmo captiously, glancing at himself in the mirror as though the crisis through which he had passed in the last three or four minutes could have distorted his face. Spire made no answer. The sound of that laugh had made him lose his conventional bearing; while Cosmo wondered what had happened to that imbecile and glared at him suspiciously.

"Give me my coat," he said at last. "I am going downstairs."

This broke the spell and Spire, getting into motion, regained his composure.

"Noisy company down there, sir. I thought you might not like it."

Cosmo felt a sudden longing to hear noise, lots of it, senseless, loud, common, absurd noise; noise loud enough to prevent one from thinking, the sort of noise that would cause one to become, as it were, insensible.

"What do you want?" he asked savagely of Spire, who was hovering at his back.

"I am ready to help you with your coat, sir," said Spire, in an apathetic voice. He had been profoundly shocked. After his master had gone out, slamming the door behind him, he busied himself with a stony face in putting the room to rights, before he blew out the candles and left it to get his supper.

"Didn't you advise me this morning to go to Livorno?" asked Cosmo, falling heavily into the chair. Doctor Martel was already at table, and, except that he had changed his boots for silk stockings and shoes, he might not have moved from there all the afternoon.

"Livorno," repeated that strange man. "Did I? Yes. The road along the Riviera di Levante is delightful for any person sensible to the beauties of Italian landscapes." He paused with a sour expression in the noise of voices filling the room, and muttered that no doubt Cantelucci found that sort of thing pay but that the place was becoming impossible.

Cosmo was just thinking that there was not half enough uproar there. The naval officers seemed strangely subdued that evening. The same old lieutenant with sunken cheeks and a sharp nose, in the same shabby uniform, was at the head of the table. Cantelucci, wearing a long-skirted maroon coat, now glided about the room, unobtrusive and vigilant. His benefactor beckoned to him.

"You would know where to find a man with four good horses for the signore's carriage?" he asked; and accepting Cantelucci's low bow as an affirmative, addressed himself to Cosmo. "The road's perfectly safe. The country's full of Austrian troops."

"I think I would prefer to go by sea," said Cosmo, who had not thought of making any arrangements for the journey. Instantly Cantelucci glided away, while the doctor emitted a grunt and applied himself to his dinner. Cosmo thought desperately, "Oh, yes, the sea, why not by sea, away from everybody?" He had been rolling and bumping on the roads, good, bad, and indifferent, in dust or mud, meeting in inns ladies and gentlemen for days and days between Paris and Genoa, and for a moment he was fascinated by the notion of a steady gliding progress in company of three or four bronzed sailors over a blue sea in sight of a picturesque coast of rocks and hills crowded with pines, with opening valleys, with white villages, and purple promontories of lovely shape. It was like a dream which lasted till the doctor was heard suddenly saying, "I think I could find somebody that would take your travelling carriage off your hands"—and the awakening came with an inward recoil of all Cosmo's being, as if before a vision of irrevocable consequences.

The doctor lowered his eyelids. "He is changed," he said to himself. "Oh yes, he is changed." This, however, did not prevent him from feeling irritated by Cosmo's lack of response to the offer to dispose of his travelling carriage.

"There are many people that would consider themselves lucky to have such an offer made to them," he remarked, after a period of silence. "It is not so easy at this time to get rid of a travelling carriage. Nor yet to have an opportunity to hire a dependable man with four good horses if you want to go by land. I mean at a time like this when anything may happen any day."

"I am sure I am very much obliged to you," said Cosmo, "but I am really in no hurry."

The doctor took notice of Cosmo's languid attitude and the untouched plate before him.

"The trouble is that you don't seem to have any aim at all. Isn't that it?"

"Yes. I confess," said Cosmo carelessly. "I think I want a rest."

"Well, Mr. Latham, you had better see that you get it, then. This place isn't restful, it is merely dull. And then suppose you were suddenly to perceive an aim, such for instance as a visit to Elba—you may be too late if you linger unduly. You know, you are not likely to see a specimen like that one over there again in your lifetime. And even he may not be with us very long."

"You seem very positive about that," said Cosmo, looking at his interlocutor searchingly. "This is the third or fourth time that I hear that sort of allusion from you. Have you any special information?"

"Yes, of a sort. It has been my lot to hear much of what is said in high places, and the nature of my occupation has given me much practice in appreciating what is said."

"In high places!" interjected Cosmo.

"And in low, too," retorted the doctor a little impatiently, "if that is the distinction you have in your mind, Mr. Latham. However, I told you I have been in Vienna quite recently, and I have heard something there."

"From Prince Talleyrand?" was Cosmo's stolid suggestion.

The doctor smiled acidly. "Not a bad guess. I did hear something at Prince Talleyrand's. I heard it from Montrond. You know whom I mean?"

"Never heard of him. Who is he?"

"Never heard of Montrond? Oh, I forgot, you have been shut up in that tight island of ours. Monsieur Montrond has the advantage to live near the rose. You understand me? He is the intimate companion to the Prince. Has been for many years. The Prince told somebody once that he liked Montrond because he was not 'excessively' scrupulous. That just paints the man for you. I was talking with Monsieur Montrond about Bonaparte's future—and I was not trying to be unkind, either. I pointed out that one could hardly expect him to settle down if the French Government were not made to pay him the money guaranteed under the Treaty. He could see the moment when he would find himself without a penny. That's enough to make any human being restive. He was bound to try and do something. A man must live, I said. And Montrond looks at me, sideways, and says deliberately: 'Oh, here we don't see the necessity.' You understand that after a hint like this I dropped the subject. It's a point of view like another, eh, Mr. Latham?"

Cosmo was impressed. "I heard last night," he said, "that he is taking precautions for his personal safety."

"He remembered perhaps what happened to a certain Duc d'Enghien, a young man who obviously didn't take precautions. So you heard that story? Well, in Livorno you will hear many sorts of stories. Livorno is an exciting place, and an excellent point to start from for a visit to Elba, which would be a great memory for your old age. And if you happen to observe anything remarkable there I would thank you to drop me a line, care of Cantelucci. You see, I have put some money into a deal of oil, and I don't know how it is, everything in the world, even a little twopenny affair like that, is affected by this feeling of suspense that man's presence gives rise to: hopes, plans, affections, love affairs. If I were you, Mr. Latham, I would certainly go to Livorno." He waited a little before he got up, muttering something about having a lot of pen work to do, and went out, Cantelucci hastening to open the door for him.

Cosmo remained passive in his chair. The room emptied itself gradually, and there was not even a servant left in it when Cosmo rose in his turn. He went back to his room, threw a few pieces of wood on the fire, and sat down. He felt as if lost in a strange world.

He doubted whether he ought not to have called that day at the Palace, if only to say good-bye. And suddenly all the occurrences and even words of the day before assailed his memory. The morning call, the mulatto girl, the sunshine in Madame de Montevesso's boudoir, the seduction of her voice, the emotional appeal of her story, had stirred him to the depths of his soul. Where was the man who could have imagined the existence of a being of such splendid humanity, with such a voice, with such amazing harmony of aspect, expression, gesture—with such a face in this gross world of mortals in which Lady Jane and Mrs. R.'s daughters counted for the most exquisite products offered to the love of men? And yet Cosmo remembered now that even while all his senses had been thrown into confusion by the first sight of Madame de Montevesso he had felt dimly that she was no stranger, that he had seen her glory before: the presence, the glance, the lips. He did not connect that dim recognition with the child Adèle. No child could have promised a woman like this. It was rather like the awed recollection of a prophetic vision. And it had been in Latham Hallbut not in a dream; he was certain no man ever found the premonition of such a marvel in the obscure promptings of slumbering flesh. And it was not in a vision of his own; such visions were for artists, for inspired seers. She must have been foretold to him in some picture he had seen in Latham Hall, where one came on pictures (mostly of the Italian school) in unexpected places, on landings, at the end of dark corridors, in spare bedrooms. A luminous oval face on the dark background—the noble full-length woman, stepping out of the narrow frame with long draperies held by jewelled clasps and girdle, with pearls on head and bosom, carrying a book and a pen (or was it a palm?) and—yes! he saw it plainly with terror—with her left breast pierced by a dagger. He saw it there plainly as if the blow had been struck before his eyes. The released hilt seemed to vibrate yet, while the eyes looked straight at him, profound, unconscious in miraculous tranquillity.

Terror-struck as if at the discovery of a crime, he jumped up, trembling in every limb. He had a horror of the room, of being alone within its four bare walls on which there were no pictures except that awful one which seemed to hang in the air before his eyes. Cosmo felt that he must get away from it. He snatched up his cloak and hat and fled into the corridor. The hour was late and everything was very still. He did not see as much as a flitting shadow on the bare rough walls of the unfinished palace awaiting the decoration of marbles and bronzes that would never cover its nakedness now. The dwelling of the Grazianis stood as dumb and cold in all its lofty depths as at that desolate hour of the dreadful siege, when its owner lay dead of hunger at the foot of the great flight of stairs. It was only in the hall below that Cosmo caught from behind one of the closed doors faint, almost ghostly, murmurs of disputing voices. The two hanging lanterns could not light up that grandly planned cavern in all its extent, but Cosmo made out a dim shape of the elderly lieutenant sitting all alone and perfectly still against the wall, with a bottle of wine before him. By the time he had reached the pavement Cosmo had mastered his trembling and had steadied his thoughts. He wanted to keep away from that house for hours, for hours. He glanced right and left, hesitating. In the whole town he knew only the way to the Palazzo and the way to the port. He took the latter direction. He walked by the faint starlight falling into the narrow streets resembling lofty unroofed corridors as if the whole town had been one palace, recognizing on his way the massive shape of one or two jutting balconies he remembered seeing before, and also a remarkable doorway, the arch of which was held up by bowed giants with flowing beards, like two captive sons of the god of the sea.

III

At the moment when Cosmo was leaving his room to escape the haunting vision of an old picture representing a beautiful martyr with a dagger in her breast. Doctor Martel was at work finishing what he called a confidential memorandum which he proposed to hand over to the Marquis d'Armand. The doctor applied very high standards of honour and fidelity to his appreciation of men's character. He had a very great respect for the old Marquis. He was anxious to make him the recipient of that crop of valuable out-of-the-way information interesting to the French Bourbons which he had gathered lately.

Having sat up half the night, he slept late and was just finishing shaving when, a little before eleven o'clock, there was a knock at his door and Cantelucci entered. The innkeeper offered no apology for this intrusion, but announced without preliminaries that the young English gentleman had vanished during the night from the inn. The woman who took the chocolate in the morning upstairs found no servant ready to receive it as usual. The bedroom door was ajar. After much hesitation she had ventured to put her head through. The shutters being open, she had seen that the bed had not been slept in. . . . The doctor left off dabbing his cheeks with eau de cologne and turned to stare at the innkeeper. At last he shrugged his shoulders slightly.

Cantelucci took the point immediately. Yes. But in this case it was impossible to dismiss the affair lightly. The young English signore had not been much more than forty-eight hours in Genoa. He had no time to make many acquaintances. And in any case, Cantelucci thought, he ought to have been back by this time.

The doctor picked up his wig and adjusted it on his head thoughtfully, like a considering cap. That simple action altered his physiognomy so completely that Cantelucci was secretly affected. He made one of his austerely deferential bows, which seemed to put the whole matter into the doctor's hands at once.

"You seem very much upset," said the doctor. "Have you seen his servant? He must know something."

"I doubt it. Excellency. He has been upstairs to open the shutters, of course. He is now at the front door, looking out. I did speak to him. He had too much wine last evening and fell asleep with his head on the table. I saw him myself before I retired."

The doctor preserving a sort of watchful silence, Cantelucci added that he, himself, had retired early on account of one of those periodical headaches he had suffered from since the days of his youth when he had been chained up in the dungeons of St. Elmo for months.

The doctor thought the fellow did look as though he had had a bad night. "Why didn't you come to see me? You know I can cure worse ailments."

The innkeeper raised his hands in horror at the mere idea. He would never have dared to disturb His Excellency for such a trifle as a headache. But the cause of his trouble was quite other. A partisan of the revolutionary French from his early youth, Cantelucci had been an active conspirator against the old order of things. Now that kings and priests were raising their heads out of the dust he had again become very busy. The latest matter in hand had been the sending of some important documents to the conspirators in the South. He had found the messenger, had taken steps for getting him away secretly, had given him full instructions the last thing before going to bed. The young fellow was brave, intelligent, and resourceful, beyond the common. But somehow the very perfection of his arrangements kept the old conspirator awake. He reviewed them again and again. He could not have done better. At last he fell asleep, but almost immediately, it seemed to him, he was roused by the old crone whose task it was to light the fires in the morning. Sordid and witchlike, she conveyed to him in a toothless mumble the intelligence that Checca was in the kitchen, all in tears and demanding to see him at once.

This Checca was primarily and principally a pretty girl, an orphan left to his care by his late sister. She was not consulted when her uncle, of whom she stood in awe, married her to the middle-aged owner of a wine-shop in the low quarter of the town extending along the shore near the harbour. He was good-natured, slow-witted, and heavy-handed at times. But Checca was much less afraid of him than of her austere uncle. It amused her to be the padrona of an osteria which in the days of Empire was a notable resort for the officers of French privateers. But on the peace that clientèle had disappeared and Checca's husband, leaving the wine-casks to her management, employed his leisure in petty smuggling operations which kept him away from home.

Cantelucci connected his niece's irruption with some trouble that men might have got into. He was vexed. He had other matters to think of. He was astonished by the violence of her grief. When she could speak at last her tale turned out to be more in the nature of a confession. The old conspirator could hardly believe his ears when he heard that the man whom he had trusted had committed the crime of betraying the secrecy of his mission by going to the osteria late at night to say good-bye to Checca. She assured him that he had been there only a very few moments.

"What, in a wine-shop! Before all the people! With spies swarming everywhere!"

"No," she said. It was much later. Everybody was gone. He had scratched at the barred door.

"And you were on the other side waiting to let him in—miserable girl," Cantelucci hissed ferociously.

She stared at her terrible uncle with streaming eyes. "Yes, I was." She had not the heart to refuse him. He stayed only a little moment. . . . (Cantelucci ground his teeth with rage. It was the first he had heard of this affair. Here was a most promising plot endangered by this *bestialita*.) . . . Only one little hug, and then she pushed him out herself. Before she had finished putting up the bar she heard a tumult in the street. Shots, too. Perhaps she would have rushed out but her husband was home for a few days. He came down to the wine-shop very cross and boxed her ears, she did not know why. Perhaps for being in the shop at that late hour. That did not matter; but he drove her before him up the stairs and she had to sham sleep for hours till he began to snore regularly. She had grown so desperate that she took the risk of running out and telling her uncle all about it. She thought he ought to know. What brought her to the inn really was a faint hope that Attilio, having eluded the assassins (she was sure they were assassins), had taken refuge there unscathed—or wounded perhaps. She said nothing of this, however. Before Cantelucci's stony bearing she broke down. "He is dead— *poverino*. My own hands pushed him to his death," she moaned to herself crazily, standing in front of her silent uncle before the blazing kitchen fire in the yet slumbering house.

Rage kept Cantelucci dumb. He was as shocked by what he had heard as the most rigid moralist could desire. But he was a conspirator, and all he could see in this was the criminal conduct of those young people who ought to have thought of nothing but the liberation of Italy. For Attilio had taken the oath of the Carbonari; and Checca belonged to the women's organization of that secret society. She was an *ortolana*, as they called themselves. He had initiated her and was responsible for her conduct. The baseness—the stupidity—the frivolity—the selfishness!

By severe exercise of self-restraint he refrained from throwing her out into the street all in tears as she was. He only muttered awfully at her, "Get out of my sight, you little fool," with a menacing gesture; but she stood her ground; she never flinched before his raised hand. And as it fell harmless by his side she seized it in both her own, pressing it to her lips and breast in turn, whispering the while all sorts of endearing names at the infuriated Cantelucci. He heard the sounds of his staff beginning the work of the day, their voices, their footsteps. They would wonder—but his niece did not care. She clung to his hand, and he did not get rid of her till he had actually promised to send her news directly he had heard something himself. And she even thought of the means. There was that fine sailor with black whiskers in attendance on the English officers frequenting the hotel. He was a good-natured man. He knew the way to the wine-shop.

This reminded her of her husband. What if he should wake in her absence? And still distracted, she ran off at last, leaving Cantelucci to face the situation.

He was dismayed. He did not really know what had happened—not to his messenger but to the documents. The old conspirator, battling with his thoughts, moved so silent and stern amongst his people that nobody dared approach him for a couple of hours. And when they did at last come to him with the news of the young "milord's" disappearance he simply swore at them. But as the morning advanced he came to the conclusion that for various reasons it would be best for him to seek his old benefactor. He did so with a harassed face which caused the doctor to believe in the story of a sleepless night. Of course he spoke only of Cosmo's absence.

The doctor, leaning back against the edge of his dressing table, gazed silently at the innkeeper. He was profoundly disturbed by the intelligence. "Got your snuffbox on you?" he asked.

The alacrity of Cantelucci in producing his snuffbox was equalled by the deferential flourish with which he held it out to his benefactor.

"The young English signore," he remarked, "visited the Palazzo of the Griffins the evening before."

The doctor helped himself to a pinch. "He didn't spend the night there, though," he observed. "You know who lives in the Palazzo, don't you, Cantelucci?"

"Some Piedmontese general, I understand, Your Excellency," said Cantelucci, who had been in touch with Count Helion ever since the Austrian occupation, and had even forwarded secretly one or two letters for the Count to Elba. But these were addressed to a grain merchant in Porto

Ferraio. "I will open all my mind to Your Excellency," continued Cantelucci. "An English milord is a person of consequence. If I were to report his disappearance the police would be coming here to make investigation. I don't want any police in my house."

The doctor lost his meditative air. "I daresay you don't," he said grimly.

"I recommend myself to Your Excellency's protective influence," murmured Cantelucci insinuatingly.

The doctor let drop the pinch of snuff between his thumb and finger. "And he may have come back while we are talking here," he said hopefully. "Go down, Cantelucci, and send me my courier."

But the doctor's man was already at the door, bringing the brushed clothes over his arm. While dressing, the doctor speculated on the mystery. It baffled all his conjectures. A man may go out in the evening for a breath of fresh air and get knocked on the head. But how unlikely! He spoke casually to his man who was ministering to him in gloomy silence.

"You will have to step over to the police presently and find out whether anything has happened last night. Do it quietly."

"I understand," said the courier surlily. The thought that the fellow had been drunk recently crossed the doctor's mind.

"Whom were you drinking with last night?" he asked sharply.

"The English servant," confessed the courier-valet grumpily. "His master let him off his services last night."

"Yes. And you made him pay the shot." With these words the doctor left the room. While crossing the great hall downstairs he had the view of Spire's back framed in the entrance doorway. The valet had not apparently budged from there since seven. So Mr. Latham had not returned. In the dining room there were only two naval officers at the table reserved for them: the elderly gentleman in his usual place at the head, and a round-faced florid person in a bobbed wig, who might have been the ship's surgeon. During their meal the doctor did not hear them exchange a single remark. They went away together, and after the last of the town customers had left the room, too, the doctor sat alone before his table, toying with a half-empty glass thoughtfully. His grave face was startlingly at variance with the short abrupt laugh which he emitted as he rose, pushing his chair back. It was provoked by the thought that only last evening he had been urging half jestingly his young countryman to leave Genoa in one of the conventional ways, by road or sea, and now he was gone with a vengeance—spirited away, by Jove! The doctor was startled at the profound change of his own feelings. Count Helion's venomous, "I don't want that popinjay here" did not sound so funny in his recollection now. Very extraordinary things could and did happen under the run of everyday life. Was it possible that the word of the riddle could be found there? he asked himself.

This investigator of the secret discontents and aspirations of his time had never shut his ears to the mere social gossip that came in his way. He had lived long, he remembered much. For instance, he could remember things that were said about Sir Charles Latham long before Cosmo was born. As to the story of the Montevesso marriage, that had made noise enough in its time in society and also amongst the French émigrés. Its celebration, the subsequent differences, reconciliations, recriminations, and final arrangement had kept idle tongues wagging for years. Of course it was that match which had given that dubious Montevesso his social standing; and what followed had invested that absurd individual with the celebrity of a character out of a Molière comedy: "Le Jaloux." The elderly jealous husband. Comic enough. But that was the sort of comedy that soon takes a tragic turn. A special provocation, a sudden opportunity are enough. What puzzled the doctor was the suddenness of the problem. Yet one could not tell what an orientalized brute, no stranger probably to palace murders, had not the means of doing. He might have been harbouring in that barn of a palace some retainers of a deadly kind. A Corsican desperado, or a couple of rascals from his own native mountains. Had he not two unattractive old peasant women concealed there?

The doctor believed that unlikely things happened every day. This view was not the result of inborn credulity but of much acquired knowledge of a secret sort. A serious, fastidious, and obviously earnest-minded young man, like Latham, was particularly liable to get into trouble of a grave kind. A manifestation of perfectly innocent sympathy could do it, and even less. An unguarded glance. An unconscious warmth of tone. Confound it! Yet he could not let a young countryman of his, a nice, likable young gentleman, vanish from under his nose without taking some steps.

The doctor stepped out into the hall, attractively dim and cool in the middle of the day. Spire had disappeared, but the doctor had given up the hope of Cosmo's return. In a dark corner he perceived the shadowy shape of a cocked hat, and made out the old lieutenant leaning back against the wall with his arms crossed and his chin on his breast. He had a bottle of wine and a glass standing in front of him.

"I suppose," thought the doctor, "this is what he comes ashore for."

The product of twenty years of war. The reeking loom that converted such as he into food for guns had stopped suddenly. There would be no demand for heroes for a long, long time, and somehow the fact that the fellow had all his limbs about him made him even more pathetic. The doctor had almost forgotten Cosmo. He did not notice Spire coming down the stairs, and he started at the sound of the words, "I beg your pardon, sir," uttered almost in his ears. The elderly valet was very much shaken. He said in a low murmur, "I am nearly out of my mind, sir. My master . . ."

"I know," interrupted the doctor. He pounced upon Spire like a bird of prey. "Come, what do you know about it?"

This reception roused Spire's dislike of that sour and off-hand person like no medical man he had ever seen and certainly no gentleman. On the principle, "like master like man," Spire was more sensitive to manner than to any trait of personality. He pulled himself together and steadied his voice. "I know nothing, sir, except that you were the last person seen speaking to Mr. Latham."

"You don't think I have got him in my pocket, do you?" asked Doctor Martel, noting the hostile stare. "Don't you attend your master when he retires for the night?"

"I got dismissed early last night. I am sorry to say I sat downstairs after supper very late, listening to tales about one thing and another. I . . . I went to sleep there," added Spire with a sort of desperation.

"Listening to tales," repeated the doctor jeeringly. "Pretty tales they must have been, too. Zillers is no company for a respectable English servant. You ought to be ashamed of yourself. Well, and then?"

"I went up, sir, and . . ."

"In the middle of the night," suggested the doctor.

"It was pretty late. I . . ."

He faltered at the remembrance. The waking up in the cold dark kitchen, the cold dark staircase, the light shining through the keyhole of Mr. Cosmo's bedroom, the first vague feeling that there was something wrong, the empty room. And most awful of all, the bed not slept in, and the candles in the candelabras burning low. He remembered his horror, incredulity, his collapse into an armchair where he sat till broad daylight in a pitiable state of mental agitation.

A slight tremor passed through his portly frame before he forced himself to speak.

"Mr. Latham had emptied his pockets, sir, as if he were making ready to go to bed. All the change and the keys were lying on the mantelpiece. One would think he had been kidnapped. Of course it can't be," he added in a low, intense tone.

"Do you mean to say he disappeared without his hat?" asked the doctor.

"No, sir, hat and cloak aren't there." And to the doctor's further questions Spire confessed that he had spoken to no one in the house that morning. He would only have been told lies. He did not think much of the people in the inn.

"So I took the liberty of speaking to you, sir. Mr. Latham may turn up any moment and I don't know that he would like to find that I have been to the police already."

"No, perhaps he wouldn't," assented the doctor reflectively.

"That's just it, sir," murmured Spire. "Mr. Cosmo is a very peculiar young gentleman. He doesn't like notice to be taken."

"Doesn't he? Well then, you had better wait before you go to the police. We had better give him till four o'clock."

"Very well, sir," said Spire, fighting down his feeling that nothing in the world would be worse than this waiting. The doctor nodded dismissal, then at the last moment:

"By the by, hadn't you better look up all the papers that may be lying about?"

Spire was favourably impressed by the suggestion.

"Yes, sir, we have a small strong box with us. I will go and do it at once."

During that colloquy, conducted in low tones at the foot of the grand staircase, nobody had appeared in the hall. Not even the vigilant Cantelucci. But the elderly lieutenant had raised his head, and his dull uninterested eyes followed the doctor across the hall and out through the door into the sunshine of the square. In all its vast and paved extent only very few figures were moving. The doctor's tastes and even his destiny had made of him a nocturnal visitor to the abodes of the great. At this time of the day, however, there was almost as little risk of being seen entering the Palace of the Griffins as in the middle of the night. The populace, the shopkeepers, the Austrian garrison, the gendarmes, the *sbirri*, the spies, and even the conspirators were indulging in midday repose. The very team of dapple-gray horses, harnessed to an enormous two-wheeled cart drawn up in the shade, dozed over their empty nosebags. Dogs slumbered in the doorways in utter abandonment; and only the bronze griffins seated on their narrow pedestals of granite before the doorway of the Palace preserved their alert wide-awake pose of everlasting watchfulness. They were really very fine.

And the doctor gave them an appreciative glance before crossing the empty quadrangle. He felt the only wide-awake person in a slumbering world. He wondered if he would succeed in getting admitted to the Palace. If not, he confessed to himself, he would be at a loss what to do next. Very disagreeable. He had, however, the memorandum for the Marquis in his pocket as a pretext for his visit.

All was still without and within; but in the noble anteroom at the foot of the marble staircase he was met by a sight characteristic of the easy Italian ways. Extended face downward on one of the red and gold benches, one of the footmen in shirt-sleeves and with his breeches untied at the knees was sleeping profoundly. His dishevelled head rested on his forearm. At an unceremonious poke in the ribs he jumped up to his feet, looking scared and wild. But Doctor Martel was ready for him.

"What's the matter, my friend?" he asked softly. "Is there a price set on your head?"

The man remained open-mouthed as if paralysed by the caustic enquiry.

"Fetch the major-domo here," commanded the doctor, thinking that he had seldom seen a more bandit-like figure. While waiting, the doctor reflected that a livery coat was a good disguise. It occurred to him also that in the house of a man having such retainers all sorts of things might happen. This was Italy. The silence as of a tomb, which pervaded the whole house, though nothing extraordinary in the hour of siesta, produced the effect of sinister mystery. The arrival of the sleek Bernard did not destroy that bad impression. The doctor, who had never seen him before by daylight, said to himself that this was no doubt only another kind of villain. On learning that the Marquis had been very ill during the night and that Bernard could not think of taking in his name, the doctor inquired whether Madame de Montevesso would see him on most important business. To his great relief (because he had been asking himself all along how he could contrive to get private speech with the Countess) Bernard raised no objections. He simply went away. And again the dumbness around him grew oppressive to Doctor Martel. He fell into a brown study. This palace, famed for the treasures of art, for the splendours of its marbles and paintings and gildings, was no better than a gorgeous tomb. Men's vanity erected these magnificent abodes only to receive in them the unavoidable guest. Death, with all the ceremonies of superstitious fear. The sense of human mortality evoked by this dumb palazzo was very disagreeable. He was relieved by the return of the noiseless Bernard, all in black and grave like a sleek caretaker of that particular tomb, who stood before him saying in a low voice: "Follow me, please."

Bernard introduced the doctor into a comparatively small, well-lighted boudoir. At the same moment Madame de Montevesso entered it from her bedroom by another door. The doctor had an impression of a gown with a train, trimmed with ribbons and lace, surmounted by a radiant fair head. The face was pale. Madame de Montevesso had been up most of the night with her father. The Marquis was too ill to see anybody.

The doctor expressed his regret in a formal tone. Meantime he took out of his pocket the memoir and begged Madame la Comtesse to keep it under lock and key till she could hand it over to her father. He was also in possession of information which, he said, would be of the greatest interest to the French court; but he could disclose it only to the French King or to Monsieur de Jaucourt. He was ready to proceed to Paris should the Marquis be impressed sufficiently by the memoir to procure for him a private audience from the King or the minister.

This curt, businesslike declaration called out a smile on that charming face—just a flicker—a suspicion of it. He could not be offended with that glorious being. He felt only that he must assert himself.

"I cannot deal with lesser people," he said simply. "This must be understood in Paris. I make my own conditions. I am not a hireling. Your father has known me for years. Monsieur le Marquis and I met in other, dangerous times, in various parts of Europe. Each of us was risking his life."

The Marquis had often talked with his daughter of his past. She had heard from him of a certain agent Martel, a singular personage. Her curiosity was aroused. She said:

"I know. I believe he was indebted to you for his safety on one occasion. I can understand my father's motives. But you will forgive me for saying that as to yours . . ."

"Oh! It was not the love of absolutism. The fact is, I discovered early in life that I was not made for a country practice. I started on my travels with no definite purpose, except to do a little good—here and there. I arrived in Italy while it was being revolutionized by Jacobins. I was not in love with them either. Humane impulses, circumstances, and so on, did the rest."

He looked straight at her. This tête-à-tête was a unique experience. She was a marvellous being somehow and a very great lady. And yet she was as simple as a village maid—a glorified village maid. The trials of a life of exile and poverty had stripped her of the faintest trace of affectation or artificiality of any kind. The doctor was lost in wonder. What humanizing force there was in the beauty of that face to make him talk like that the first time he saw her! And suddenly the thought, "her face has been her fortune," came to him with great force, evoking by the side of her noble unconscious grace the stiff wooden figure of Count de Montevesso. The effect was horrible, but the doctor's hard gray eyes betrayed neither his horror nor his indignation. He only asked Madame de Montevesso, who was locking up his memoir in the drawer of a little writing table, if it would be safe there, and was told that nobody ever came into the room but a confidential mulatto maid who had been with the Countess for years.

"Yes, as far as you know," the doctor ventured significantly. With this beginning he found no difficulty in discovering that Madame de Montevesso knew nothing of the composition of the household. She did not know how many servants there were. She had not been interested enough to look over the Palazzo. Apart from the private apartments and the suite of rooms for small receptions she had seen nothing of it, she confessed, looking a little surprised. It was clear that she knew nothing, suspected nothing, had lived in that enormous and magnificent building like a lost child in a forest. The doctor felt himself at the end of his resources, till it occurred to him to say that he hoped that she was not specially anxious about her father. No, Madame de Montevesso was not specially anxious. He seemed better this morning. Doctor Martel was very much gratified; and then, by a sudden inspiration, added that it would be a pleasure to give the good news to Mr. Latham whom he hoped to see this evening.

Madame de Montevesso turned rigid with surprise for a moment at the sound of that name. "You have met Mr. Latham . . ." she faltered out.

"Oh! By the merest chance. We are staying at the same inn. He shares my table. He is very attractive."

Madame de Montevesso looked no longer as though she expected her visitor to go away. The doctor had just time to note the change before he was asked point-blank:

"Did Mr. Latham tell you that he was a friend of ours?"

He answered evasively that he knew very little about Mr. Latham, except what he could see for himself—that Mr. Latham was very superior to the young men of fashion coming over in such numbers from England since the end of the war. That generation struck him as very crude and utterly uninteresting. It was different, as far as Mr. Latham was concerned. A situation had arisen which would make a little information as to his affairs very desirable.

"Desirable?" repeated Madame de Montevesso in a whisper.

"Yes, helpful. . . ."

The deliberate stress which he put on that word augmented Madame de Montevesso's bewilderment.

"I don't quite understand. In what way? Helpful for you—or helpful for Mr. Latham?"

"You see," said the doctor slowly, "though our acquaintance was short my interest was aroused. I am a useful person to know for those who travel in Italy."

Madame de Montevesso sank into a *bergère*, pointing at the same time to a chair which faced it. But the doctor, after a slight bow, only rested his hand on its high back. At the end of five minutes Adèle was in possession of all the doctor knew about Cosmo's disappearance. She sat silent, her head drooped, her eyes cast down. The doctor was beginning to feel restive when she spoke, without looking up.

"And this is the real motive for your visit here."

The doctor was moved by the hopeless tone. It might have been an attempt to appear indifferent, but, only in a moment, she seemed to have become lifeless.

"Well," he said, "on the spur of the moment it seemed the only thing to do. . . . There is somebody in the next room. May I shut the door?"

"It's only my maid," said Madame de Montevesso. "She couldn't hear us from there."

"Well, then perhaps we had better leave the door as it is. It's best to avoid all appearance of secrecy." The doctor was thinking of Count Helion, but Madame de Montevesso made no sign. The doctor lowered his voice still more.

"I wanted to ask you if you had seen him yesterday—last night. No? But he may have called without your knowledge."

She admitted that it was possible. People had been sent away from the door on account of her father's illness. There had been no reception in the evening. But Mr. Latham would have asked for her. She thought she would have been told. The doctor suggested that Mr. Latham might have asked for the Count. Madame de Montevesso had only seen her husband for a moment in her father's bedroom the day before, and not at all yet this day. For all she knew he may have been away for the day on a visit in the country. "But I know nothing of his interests, really," she said in a little less deadened voice.

She could not explain to the doctor that she was a stranger in that house; an unwilling visitor with an unsympathetic host whose motives one cannot help suspecting. Beyond the time she spent by arrangement every year at Count de Montevesso's country house she knew nothing of his life. What could have been the motives which brought him to Genoa, she had and could have not the slightest idea. She only felt that she ought not to have accepted his pressing invitation to this hired palazzo. But then she could not have come with her father to Genoa. And yet he could not have done without her. And indeed it seemed but a small thing. The alarming thought crossed her mind that, all unwittingly, she had taken a fatal step.

The doctor, who had quite an accurate notion of the state of affairs, hastened to say:

"After all, I don't know that this is of any importance. I have heard that Mr. Latham was busy writing all yesterday. If he had come to Italy with some sort of purpose," he continued as if arguing with himself, "one could . . ." Then sharply: "You couldn't tell me anything, could you?" he asked Adèle.

"This is the first time I have seen him for ten years." Madame de Montevesso raised her eyes, full of trouble, to the doctor's face. "Since we were children together in Yorkshire. We talked of old times. Only of old times," she repeated.

"Of course—very natural," mumbled the doctor. He made the mental remark that one did not disappear like this after talking of old times. And aloud he said, "I suppose Mr. Latham made the acquaintance of Count de Montevesso."

"Certainly."

"I presume that they had an opportunity to have a conversation together."

"I don't think that Cosmo—that Mr. Latham made any confidences to Count de Montevesso." While saying those words Adèle looked the doctor straight in the face.

He was asking himself whether she could read his thoughts, when she got up suddenly and walked away to the window, without haste and with a grace of movement which aroused the doctor's admiration. He could not tell her what he had in his mind. He looked irresolutely at the figure in the window. It was growing enigmatic in its immobility. He began to feel some little awe, when he heard unexpectedly the words:

"You suspect a crime?"

The doctor could not guess the effort which went to the uttering of those few words. It was the stunning force of the shock which enabled Adèle de Montevesso to appear so calm. It was the general humanity of Doctor Martel's disposition which dictated his answer.

"I suspect some imprudence," he admitted in an easy tone. At that moment he drew the gloomiest view of Cosmo's disappearance, from the sinister conviction that twenty-four hours was enough to arrange an assassination. "The difficulty is to imagine a cause for it. To find the motive. . . ."

Madame de Montevesso continued to face the window as if lost in the contemplation of a vast landscape. "And you came to look for it here," she said.

"I don't think I need to apologize," he said, with a movement of annoyance like a man who has received a home thrust. "Of course I might have simply gone about my own affairs, which are of some importance to a good many people. My advice to Mr. Latham was to leave Genoa, since he did not seem to have any object in remaining and seemed to have a half-formed wish to visit Elba. I suggested Leghorn as the best port for crossing over."

It was impossible to say whether the woman at the window was listening to him at all. She did not stir, she seemed to have forgotten his existence. But that immobility might have been also the effect of concentrated attention. He made up his mind to go on speaking.

"His mind, his imagination seemed very busy wit! Napoleon. It seemed to me the only reason for his travels." He paused.

"I believe the only reason for Mr. Latham coming to Genoa was to see us." Madame de Montevesso turned round and moved back towards the *bergère*. She was extremely pale. "I mean Father and myself," she explained. "He came to see me the day before yesterday in the morning. I invited him to our usual evening reception. He stayed after everybody else was gone. I asked him to. But my father needed me and I had to leave Mr. Latham with Monsieur de Montevesso."

The doctor interrupted her gently. "I know, Madame. I was in the Palazzo with the Marquis, in the very room, when he sent for your husband."

"I forgot," confessed Madame de Montevesso simply. "But Mr. Latham got back to his inn safely."

"Yes. He was writing letters next day till late in the evening, and seems to have been spirited away in the middle of that occupation. But people like Mr. Latham are not spirited out of their bedrooms by main force. I advised the servant to wait till four o'clock, then I came straight here."

"Till four o'clock," repeated Madame de Montevesso under her breath.

The doctor, a man of special capacity in confronting enigmatical situations, showed himself as perplexed before this one as the most innocent of mortals.

"I don't know. It seems to me that a man who puts on his hat and cloak before vanishing like this must turn up again. He ought to be given a chance to do so at any rate. He left all his money behind, too. I mean even to the small change."

The glimpse of helpless concern in that man affected Adèle with a feeling of actual bodily anguish. She got brusquely out of the *bergère* and moved into the middle of the room. The doctor, letting go the back of the chair, turned to face her.

"I am appalled," she murmured.

This came out as if extracted from her by torture. It moved the doctor more than anything he had heard for years. His voice sank into a soothing murmur.

"I do believe, Madame, that if there had been a murder committed last night anywhere in this town I would have heard something about it this morning. My inn is just the place for such news. I will go back there now. I shall question his servant again. He may give us a gleam of light."

Her intent, distressed gaze was unbearable, yet held him bound to the spot. It was difficult to abandon a woman in that state! He became aware of the sound of voices outside the door. Some sort of dispute. He hastened to make his bow, and Madame de Montevesso, moving after him, whispered eagerly: "Yes! A gleam of light! Do let me know. I won't draw a free breath till I hear something."

Her extended arms dropped by her side a moment before the door flew open and Bernard was heard announcing with calm formality:

"Signorina Clelia."

The doctor, turning away from Madame de Montevesso, saw "that little wretch" standing just within the room, evidently very much taken aback by the unexpected meeting. He guessed that she had snatched at some opportunity to escape from the old women. It had given her no time to pull on her stockings, a fact made evident by the shortness of the dark petticoat which, with a white jacket, comprised all her costume. She had managed to thrust her bare feet into a pair of old slippers, and her loose hair, tied with a blue ribbon at the back of her head, produced a most incongruous effect of neatness. Her invasion was alarming and inexplicable. The doctor, as he passed out, compressed his lips and stared fiercely with some idea of scaring her into good behaviour. She met this demonstration with a round stupid stare of astonishment. The next moment he found himself outside in the corridor alone with Bernard, who had shut the door quietly and remained with his back to it. The exasperated doctor looked him up and down coolly.

"How long have you been in the habit of hanging about your lady's door, my friend?" he asked with ominous familiarity.

The simple-minded factotum of the London days, the love-lorn naïve swain of the mulatto maid, was a figure of the past now. The doctor was confronted by a calm unmoved servant of much experience, somewhat inclining to stoutness, made respectable by the black well-fitting clothes. He did not flinch at the question, but he took his time. At last he said with the utmost placidity:

"Many years now. Pretty near all my life."

The tone was well calculated to surprise the doctor. Taking advantage of the latter's silence, Bernard paused before he continued reasonably: "Was I to let her rush in unannounced on Madame la Comtesse while you were there? I tried to send her away but she would think nothing of filling the air with her screams. I kept her back as long as it was prudent. . ." He raised his open hand, palm outwards, warning the doctor to remain silent, while with conscientious gravity he applied his big ear to the door. When he came away he did not apparently intend to take any further notice of the doctor, but stood there with an air of perfect rectitude.

"Is that your constant practice?" asked the astonished doctor, with curiosity rather than indignation. "Suppose I told on you," he added with a glance at the door. "Suppose somebody else gave you away. . . ."

"You would not be thanked," was the unexpected answer.

"I wouldn't be believed—is that it? Well, I confess that I can hardly believe my own eyes."

"Oh, you would be believed," was the ready but dispassionate admission. Bernard's trust in his interlocutor's acuteness was not deceived.

"Do you mean that you have been found out already?" said the doctor in a changed tone. "Whew! You don't say! Well, stranger things have happened. Whose old retainer are you?"

"I have always belonged to Madame la Comtesse," said the old retainer without looking at the doctor, who, after some meditation, accepted the statement at its face value.

"I am staying at Cantelucci's inn," he said in an ordinary conversational tone. "And I would be glad to see you there any time you like to call. Especially if you had anything to tell me of Mr. Latham." Bernard not responding in any way to that invitation, the doctor added, "You know what I mean?"

"Oh, yes, I know what you mean." That answer came coldly from the lips of the respectable servant, who said nothing more while conscientiously escorting the doctor to the anteroom at the foot of the grand staircase. A little bowed old woman in black clothes clung to the balustrade half way down the marble steps, in the act of descending, while another, taller and upright, hovered anxiously on the landing above. Bernard's scandalized, "Go away! Go back!" sounded irresistibly authoritative. The doctor had no doubt that it would send the two crones back to their lair, but he did not stop to see.

Bernard went up the staircase slowly to the first landing, where he watched the retreat of the two weird apparitions down a long and dim corridor. They were very much intimidated by this man in black and with a priestly aspect. One of them, however, made a stand, and screamed in an angry cracked voice, "Where's the child? The child! We are looking for her."

"Why don't you take her back to your village and keep her there?" he cried out sternly. "I have seen her. She won't get lost."

A distant door slammed. They had vanished as if blown away by his voice; and Bernard with a muttered afterthought, "More's the pity," continued up one flight of stairs after another till he reached the wilderness of the garrets that once upon a time had been inhabited by a multitude of servants and retainers. The room he entered was low and sombre, with rough walls and a vast bare floor. His wife Aglae sat on the edge of the bed, with her hands in her lap and downcast eyes which she did not raise at his entrance. He looked at her with a serious and friendly expression before he sat down by her side. And even then she did not move. He took her tragic immobility in silence as a matter of course. His face, which had never been very mobile, had acquired with years a sort of blank dignity. It had been the work of years, of those married years which had crushed the last vestiges of pertness out of the more emotional Aglae. When she whispered to him, "Bernard, this thing kill me a little every day," he felt moved to put his arm round his wife's waist and made a mental remark which always occurred to him poignantly on such occasions, that she had grown very thin. In the trials of a life which had not kept its promise of contented bliss, he had been most impressed by the loss of that plumpness which years ago was so much appreciated by him. It seemed to give to that plaint which he had heard before more than once an awful sort of reality, a dreadful precision. . . . A little. . . . Every day.

He took his arm away brusquely and got up.

"I thought I would find you here," he remarked in an indifferent marital tone. "That man has gone now," he added.

With a deep sigh the maid of Madame de Montevesso struggled out of the depths of despondency, only to fall a prey to anxiety.

"Oh, Bernard, what did that man want with Miss Adèle?"

Bernard knew enough to have formed a conjecture that English fellow must have either left some papers or a message for the Marquis with Madame de Montevesso.

PART IV

I

In what seemed to him a very short time Cosmo found himself under the colonnade separating the town piled upon the hills from the flat ground of the waterside. A profound quietness reigned on the darkly polished surface of the harbour and the long, incurved range of the quays. This quietness that surrounded him on all sides through which, beyond the spars of clustered coasters, he could look at the night-horizon of the open sea, relieved that fantastic feeling of confinement within his own body with its intolerable tremors and shrinkings and imperious suggestions. Mere weaknesses all. His desire, however, to climb to the top of the tower, as if only there complete relief could be found for his captive spirit, was as strong as ever.

The only light on shore he could see issued in a dim streak from the door of the guardhouse which he had passed on his return from the tower on his first evening in Genoa. As he did not wish to pass near the Austrian sentry at the head of the landing-steps, Cosmo, instead of following the quay, kept under the portico at the back of the guardhouse. When he came to its end he had a view of the squat bulk of the tower across a considerable space of flat waste ground extending to the low rocks of the seashore. He made for it with the directness of a man possessed by a fixed idea. When he reached the iron-studded low door within the deep dark archway at the foot of the tower he found it immovable. Locked! How stupid! As if those heavy ship guns up there could be stolen! Disappointed, he leaned his shoulders against the side of the deep arch, lingering as people will before the finality of a closed door or of a situation without issue.

His superstitious mood had left him. An old picture was an old picture; and probably the face of that noble saint copied from an old triptych and of Madame de Montevesso were not at all alike. At most, a suggestion which may have been the doing of the copyist and so without meaning. A copyist is not an inspired person; not a seer of visions. He felt critical, almost ironic, towards the Cosmo of the morning, the Cosmo of the day, the Cosmo rushing away like a scared child from a fanciful resemblance, that probably did not even exist. What was he doing there? He might have asked the way to the public gardens. Lurking within the dark archway, muffled up in his blue cloak, he was a suspect figure like an ambushed spadassin waiting for his victim, or a conspirator hiding from the minions of a tyrant. "I am perfectly ridiculous," he thought. "I had better go back as soon as I can." This was his sudden conclusion, but he did not move. It struck him that he was not anxious to face his empty room. Was he ready to get into another panic? he asked himself scornfully. . . . At that moment he heard distinctly the sound of whispering as if through the wall, or from above or from the ground. He held his breath. The whispering went on, loquacious. When it stopped, another voice, as low but deeper and more distinct, muttered the words: "The hour is past."

Ha! Whispers in the air, sounds wandering without bodies, as mysterious as though they had come across a hundred miles, for he had heard no footsteps, no rustle, no sound of any sort. Nothing but the two voices. They were so weirdly disembodied and unbelievable that he had to clothe them in attributes: the excitable—the morose. They were quite near. But he did not know on which side of the arch within which he was hiding. For he was frankly hiding now—no doubt about it. He had remembered that he had left his pistols by his bedside. And he was certain he would hear the voices again. The wait seemed long before the fluent-loquacious came back through space and was punctually followed by the deep voice which this time emitted only an unintelligible grunt.

The disagreeable sense of having no means of defence in case of necessity prevented Cosmo from leaving the shelter of the deep arch. Two men, the excitable and the morose, were within a foot of him. Remembering that the tower was accessible on its seaward face, Cosmo surmised that they had just landed from a boat and had crept round barefooted, secret and, no doubt, ready to use their knives. Smugglers probably. That they should ply their trade within three hundred yards of the guardroom with a sentry outside did not surprise him very much. These were Austrian soldiers, ignorant of local conditions and certainly not concerned with the prevention of smuggling. Why didn't these men go about their business, then? The road was clear. But perhaps they had gone? It seemed to him he had been there glued to that door for an hour. As a matter of fact it was not ten minutes. Cosmo, who had no mind to be stabbed through a mere mistake as to his character, was just thinking of making a dash in the direction of the guardhouse when the morose but cautiously lowered voice began, close to the arch, abruptly: "Where did the beast get to? I thought a moment ago he was coming. Didn't you think too that there were footsteps—just as we landed?"

Cosmo's uplifted foot came down to the ground. Of the excitable whisperer's long rigmarole not a word could be made out. Cosmo imagined him short and thick. The other, whom Cosmo pictured to himself as lean and tall, uttered the word, "Why?" The excitable man hissed fiercely: "To say good-bye."—"Devil take all these women," commented the morose voice dispassionately. The whisper, now raised to the pitch of a strangled wheeze, remarked with some feeling: "He may never see her again."

It was clear they had never even dreamt of any human being besides themselves having anything to do on this part of the shore at this hour of the night. "Won't they be frightened when I rush out," thought Cosmo taking off his cloak and throwing it over his left forearm. If it came to an encounter he could always drop it. But he did not seriously think that he would be reduced to using his fists.

He judged it prudent to leave the archway with a bound which would get him well clear of the tower, and on alighting faced about quickly. He heard an exclamation but he saw no one. They had bolted! He would have laughed had he not been startled himself by a shot fired somewhere in the distance behind his back—the most brutally impressive sound that can break the silence of the night. Instantly, as if it had been a signal, a lot of shouting broke on his ear, yells of warning and encouragement, a savage clamour which made him think of a lot of people pursuing a mad dog. He advanced, however, in the direction of the portico, wishing himself out of the way of this odious commotion, when the flash of a musket shot showed him for a moment the tilted head in a shako and the white cross-belts of an Austrian soldier standing erect in the middle of the open ground. Cosmo stopped short, then inclined to the left, moving cautiously and staring into the darkness. The yelling had died out gradually away from the seashore, where he remembered a cluster of the poorer sort of houses nestled under the cliffs. He could not believe that the shot could have been fired at him, till another flash and report of a musket followed by the whizz of the bullet very near his hand persuaded him to the contrary. Thinking of nothing but getting out of the line of fire, he stooped low and ran on blindly till his shoulder came in contact with some obstacle extremely hard and perfectly immovable.

He put his hand on it, felt it rough and cold, and discovered it was a stone, an enormous square block such as are used in building breakwaters. Several others were lying about in a cluster like a miniature village on a miniature plain. He crept amongst them, spread his cloak on the ground, and sat down with his back against one of the blocks. He wondered at the marvellous eyesight of that confounded soldier. He was not aware that his dark figure had the starry sky for a background. "He nearly had me," he thought. His whole being recoiled with disgust from the risk of getting a musket ball through his body. He resolved to remain where he was till all that incomprehensible excitement had quieted down and that brute with wonderful powers of vision had gone away. Then his road would be clear. He would give him plenty of time.

The stillness all around continued, becoming more convincing, as the time passed, inits suggestion of everything being over, convincing enough to shame timidity itself. Why this reluctance to go back to his room? What was a room in an inn, in any house? A small portion of space forced off with bricks or stones in which innumerable individuals had been alone with their good and evil thoughts, temptations, fears, troubles of all sorts, and had gone out without leaving a trace. This train of thought led him to the reflection that no man could leave his troubles behind . . . never . . . never. . . . "It's no use trying," he thought with despair. Why should he go to Livorno? What would be the good of going home? Lengthening the distance would be like lengthening a chain. What use would it be to get out of sight? . . . "If I were to be struck blind to-morrow it wouldn't help me." He forgot where he was till the convincing silence round him crumbled to pieces before a faint and distant shout which recalled him to the sense of his position. Presently he heard more shouting, still distant but much nearer. This took his mind from himself and started his imagination on another track. The man hunt was not over, then! The fellow had broken cover again and had been headed towards the tower. He depicted the hunted man to himself as long-legged, spare, agile, for no other reason than because he wished him to escape. He wondered whether the soldier with the sharp eyes would give him a shot. But no shot broke the silence which had succeeded the distant shouts. Got away perhaps? At least for a time. Very possibly he had stabbed somebody and . . . by heaven! here he was!

Cosmo had caught the faint sound of running feet on the hard ground. And even before he had decided that it was no illusion it stopped short and a bulky object fell hurtling from the sky so near to him that Cosmo instinctively drew in his legs with a general start of his body which caused him to knock his hat off against the stone. He became aware of a man's back almost within reach of his arm. There could be no doubt he had taken a leap over the stone and had landed squatting on his heels. Cosmo expected him to rebound and vanish, but he only extended his arm to seize the hat as it rolled past him and at the same moment pivoted on his toes, preserving his squatting posture.

"If he happens to have a knife in his hand he will plunge it into me," thought Cosmo. So without moving a limb he hastened to say in a loud whisper: "Run to the tower. Your friends are waiting for you." It was a sudden inspiration. The man without rising flung himself forward full length and, propped on his arms, brought his face close to Cosmo. His white eyeballs seemed to be starting out of his head. In this position the silence between them lasted for several seconds.

"My friends, but who are you?" muttered the man.

And then the recognition came, instantaneous and mutual. Cosmo simply said, "Hallo!" while the man, letting himself fall to the ground, uttered in a voice faint with emotion, "My Englishman!"

"There were two of them," said Cosmo.

"Two? Did they see you?"

Cosmo assured him that they had not. The other, still agitated by the unexpectedness of that meeting, asked, incredulous and even a little suspicious: "What am I to think, then? How could you know that they were my friends?"

Cosmo disregarded the question. "You will be caught if you linger here," he whispered.

The other, as though he had not heard the warning, insisted: "How could they have mentioned my name to you?"

"They mentioned no names. . . . Run."

"I don't think they are there now," said the fugitive.

"Yes. There was noise enough to scare anybody away," commented Cosmo. "What have you done?"

The other made no answer, and in the pause both men listened intently. The night remained dark. Cosmo thought: "Some smuggling affair," and the other muttered to himself, "I have misled them." He sat up by the side of Cosmo and put Cosmo's hat, which he had been apparently holding all the time, on the ground between them.

"You are a cool hand," said Cosmo. "The soldiers . . ."

"Who cares for the soldiers? They can't run."

"They have muskets, though."

"Oh, yes. I heard the shots and wondered at whom they were fired."

"At me. That's why I have got in here. There is one of them who can see in the dark," explained Cosmo, who had been very much impressed. His friend of the tower emitted a little chuckle.

"And so you have hidden yourself in here. Soldiers, water, and fire soon make room for themselves. But they did not know who they were after. They got the alarm from that beast."

He paused suddenly, and Cosmo asked: "Who was after you?"

"One traitor and God knows how many *sbirri*. If they had been only ten minutes later they would have never set eyes on me."

"I wonder they didn't manage to cut you off, if they were so many," said Cosmo.

"They didn't know. Look! Even now I have deceived them by doubling back. You see I was in a house." He seemed to hesitate.

"Oh, yes," said Cosmo. "Saying good-bye."

The man by his side made a slight movement and preserved a profound silence for a time.

"As I have no demon," he began slowly, "to keep me informed about other people's affairs, I must ask you what you were doing here?"

"Why, taking the air like that other evening. But why don't you try to get away while there is time?"

"Yes, but where?"

"You were going to leave Genoa," said Cosmo. "Either on a very long or a very deadly journey."

Again the man by his side made a movement, of surprise and remained silent for a while. This was very extraordinary, as though some devil having his own means to obtain knowledge had taken on himself for a disguise the body of an Englishman of the kind that travels and stays in inns. The acquaintance of Cosmo's almost first horn in Genoa was very much puzzled and a little suspicious, not as before something dangerous but as before something inexplicable, obscure to his mind like the instruments that fate makes use of sometimes in the affairs of men.

"So you did see two men a little while ago waiting for me?"

"I did not see them. They seemed to think you were late," was the surprising answer.

"And how do you know they were waiting for me?"

"I didn't," said Cosmo naturally. And the other muttered a remark that he was glad to hear of something that Cosmo did not know. But Cosmo continued: "Of course I didn't, not till you jumped in here."

The other made a gesture requesting silence and lent his ear to the unbroken stillness of the surroundings.

"Signore," he said suddenly in a very quiet and distinct whisper, "it may be true that I was about to leave this town, but I never thought of leaving it by swimming. No doubt the noise was enough to frighten anybody away, but it has been quiet enough now for a long time and I think that I will crawl on as far as the tower to see whether perchance they didn't think it worth while to bring their boat back to the foot of the tower. I have put my enemies off the track and I fancy they are looking for me in very distant places from here. The treachery, signore, was not in the telling them where I was. Anybody with eyes could have seen me walking about Genoa. No, it was in the telling them who I was."

He paused again to listen and suddenly changed his position, drawing in his legs.

"Well," said Cosmo, "I myself wonder who you are." He noticed the other's eyes rolling, and the whisper came out of his lips much faster and, as it were, more confidential.

"Attilio, at your service," the mocking whisper fell into Cosmo's ear. "I see the signore is not so much of a wizard as I thought." Then with great rapidity: "Should the signore find something, one never knows, Cantelucci would be the man to give it to."

And suddenly with a half turn he ran off on all fours, looking for an instant monstrous and vanishing so suddenly that Cosmo remained confounded. He was trying to think what all this might mean, when his ears were invaded by the sound of many footsteps and before he could make a move to get up he found himself surrounded by quite a number of men. As a matter of fact there were only four; but they stood close over him as he sat on the ground, their dark figures blotting all view, with an overpowering effect. Very prudently Cosmo did not attempt to rise; he only picked up his hat, and as he did so it seemed to him that there was something strange about the feel of it. When he put it on his head some object neither very hard nor very heavy fell on the top of his head. He repressed the impulse to have a look at once. "What on earth can it be?" he thought. It felt like a parcel of papers. It was certainly flat. An awestruck voice said, "That's a foreigner." Another muttered, "What's this deviltry?" As Cosmo made an attempt to rise with what dignity he might, the nearest of the band stooped with alacrity and caught hold of his arm above the elbow as if to help him up, with a muttered, "*Permesso, signore.*" And as soon as he regained his feet his other arm was seized from behind by someone else without any ceremony. A slight attempt to shake himself free convinced Cosmo that they meant to stick on.

"Would it be an accomplice?" wondered a voice.

"No. Look at his hat. That's an Englishman."

"So much the worse. They are very troublesome. Authority is nothing to them."

All this time one or another would take a turn to peer closely into Cosmo's face, in a way which struck him as offensive. Cosmo had not the slightest doubt that he was in the hands of the municipal *sbirri.* That strange Attilio had detected their approach from afar. "He might have given me a warning," he thought. His annoyance with the fugitive did not last long; but he began to be angry with his captors, of which every one, he noticed, carried a cudgel.

"What authority have you to interfere with me?" he asked haughtily. The wretch who was holding his right arm murmured judicially: "An Inglese, without a doubt." A stout man in a wide-brimmed hat, who was standing in front of him, grunted: "The authority of four against one," then addressed his companions to the general effect that he didn't know what the world was coming to if foreigners were allowed to mix themselves up with conspirators. It looked as if they had been at a loss what to do with their captive. One of them insinuated: "I don't know. Those foreigners have plenty of money and are impatient of restraint. A poor man may get a chance."

Cosmo thought that probably each of them was provided with a stiletto. Nothing prevented them from stabbing him in several places, weighting his body with some stones from the seashore, and throwing it into the water. What an unlucky reputation to have! He remembered that he had no money with him. The few coins he used to carry in his pocket were lying on his mantelpiece in the bedroom at the inn. This would have made no difference if those men had been bandits, since they would not be aware of the emptiness of his pockets. "I could have probably bribed them to let me go," he thought, after he had heard the same man add with a little laugh, "I mean obliging poor men. Those English *signori* are rich and harmless."

Cosmo regretted more than ever not being able to make them an offer. It would have been probably successful, as they seemed to be in doubt what to do next. He mentioned he was living at the Casa Graziani. "If one of you will go with me there you shall be recompensed for your trouble." No answer was made to that proposal except that one of the men coughed slightly. Their chief in a hat with an enormous brim seemed lost in deep thought, and his immobility in front of Cosmo appeared to the latter amusingly mysterious and sinister. A sort of nervous impatience came over Cosmo, an absurd longing to tear himself away and make a dash for liberty, and then an absurd discouragement as though he were a criminal with no hiding-place to make for. The man in the big hat jerked up his head suddenly and disclosed the irritable state of his feelings at the failure of getting hold of that *furfante*. "As to that Englishman," he continued in his rasping voice not corresponding to his physical bulk, "let him be taken to the guardroom. He will have to show his papers."

Cosmo was provoked to say: "Do you expect a gentleman to carry his papers with him when he goes out for a walk?"

He was disconcerted by an outburst of laughter on three sides of him. The leader in the hat did not laugh; he only said bitterly; "We expect papers from a man we find hiding."

"Well, I have no papers on me," said Cosmo, and immediately in a sort of mental illumination thought, "Except in my hat." Of course that object reposing on the top of his head was a bundle of papers, dangerous documents. Attilio was a conspirator. Obviously! The mysterious allusion to something he was to find and hand over to Cantelucci became clear to Cosmo. He felt very indignant with his mysterious acquaintance. "Of course he couldn't foresee I was going to get into this predicament," he thought, as if trying to find an excuse for him already.

"*Avanti*," commanded the man in front of him.

The grip on his arm of the two others tightened, resistance was no use though he felt sorely tempted again to engage in a struggle. If only he could free himself for a moment, dash off into the darkness, and throw that absurd packet away somewhere before they caught him again. It was a sort of solution; but he discovered in himself an unsuspected and unreasoning loyalty. "No! Somebody would find it and take it to the police," he thought. "If we come near the quay I may manage to fling it on the water."

He said with lofty negligence: "You needn't hold my arms."

This suggestion was met by a profound silence. Neither of the men holding him relaxed his grasp. Another was treading close on his heels, while the police-hound in the big hat marched a couple of paces in front of him, importantly.

Before long they approached the guardhouse close enough for Cosmo to see the sentry at the foot of the steps, who challenged them militarily. The shim in the hat advanced alone and made himself known in the light streaming through the door. It was too late to attempt anything. As he was impelled by his two captors inside the guardroom, which was lighted by a smoky lamp and also full of tobacco smoke, Cosmo thought, "I am in for it. What a horrible nuisance! I wonder whether they will search me?"

At Cosmo's entrance with his escort several soldiers reclining on the floor raised their heads. It was a small place which may have been used as a store for sails or cordage. The furniture consisted of one long bench, a rack of muskets, a table, and one chair. A sergeant sitting on that chair rose and talked with the head *sbirro* for a time in a familiar and interested manner about the incidents of the chase, before he even looked at Cosmo. Cosmo could not hear the words. The sergeant was a fine man with long black moustaches and a great scar on his cheek. He nodded from time to time in an understanding manner to the man in the hat, whom the light of the guardroom disclosed as the possessor of very small eyes, a short thick beard, and a pear-shaped yellow physiognomy which had a pained expression. At the suggestion of the *sbirri* (they had let him go) Cosmo sat down on a bench running along the wall. Part of it was occupied by a soldier stretched at full length with his head on his knapsack and with his shako hung above him on the wall. He was profoundly asleep. "Perhaps that's the fellow who took those shots at me," thought Cosmo. Another of the *sbirri* approached Cosmo and with a propitiatory smile handed him his cloak. Cosmo had forgotten all about it.

"I carried it behind the signore all the way," he murmured with an air of secrecy; and Cosmo was moved to say: "You ought to have brought it to me at Cantelucci's inn," in a significant tone. The man made a deprecatory gesture and said in a low voice: "The signore may want it to-night."

He was young. His eyes met Cosmo's without flinching.

"I see," whispered Cosmo. "What is going to be done with me?" The man looked away indifferently and said: "I am new at this work; but there is a post of royal gendarmerie on the other side of the harbour."

He threw himself on the bench by Cosmo's side, stretched his legs out, folded his arms across his breast, and yawned unconcernedly.

"Can I trust him?" Cosmo asked himself. Nobody seemed to pay any attention to him. The *sbirro* in the hat bustled out of the guardroom in great haste; the other two remained on guard; the sergeant sitting astride the chair folded his arms on the back of it and stared at the night through the open door. The *sbirro* by Cosmo's side muttered, looking up at the ceiling: "I think Barbone is gone to find a boatman." From this Cosmo understood that he was going to be taken across the harbour and given up to the gendarmes. He thought, "If they insist upon searching me I would have to submit and in any case a hat is not a hiding-place. I may just as well hand the packet over without a struggle." A bright idea struck him. "If those fellows take me over there in a boat to save themselves the trouble of walking round the harbour I will simply contrive to drop my hat overboard—even if they do hold my arms during the passage." He was now convinced that Attilio belonged to some secret society. He certainly was no common fellow. He wondered what had happened to him. Was he slinking and dodging about the low parts of the town on his way to some refuge; or had he really found the excitable man and the grumpy man still waiting under the tower with a boat? Most unlikely after such an alarming commotion of yells and shots. He feared that Attilio, unable to get away, could hardly avoid being caught to-morrow, or at the furthest next day. He himself obviously did not expect anything better; or else he would not have been so anxious to get rid of those papers. Cosmo concluded that conspirators were perfectly absurd with their passion for documents, which were invariably found at a critical time and sent them all to the gallows.

He noticed the eyes of the sergeant, a Croat, with pendent black moustaches, fixed on his hat, and at once felt uneasy as if he had belonged to a secret society himself. His hat was the latest thing in men's round hats which he had bought in Paris. But, almost directly, the sergeant's eyes wandered off to the doorway and resumed their stare. Cosmo was relieved. He decided, however, to attempt no communication with the young police fellow whose lounging attitude, abandoned and drowsy, and almost touching elbows with him, seemed to Cosmo too suggestive to be trustworthy. And indeed, he reflected, what could he do for him?

His excitement about this adventure was combined in a strange way with a state of inward peace which he had not known for hours. He wondered at his loyalty to the astute Attilio. He would have been justified in regarding the transaction as a scurvy trick; whereas he found that he could not help contemplating it as a matter of trust. He went on exercising his wits upon the problem of those documents (he was sure those were papers of some kind) which he had been asked to give to Cantelucci (how surprised he would be), since apparently the innkeeper was a conspirator too. Yet, he thought, it would be better to destroy them than to let them fall into the hands of the Piedmontese justice, or the Austrian military command. "I must contrive," he thought, "to get rid of them in the boat. I can always shake my hat overboard accidentally." But the packet would float and some boatman would be sure to find it during the day. On the other hand, by the time daylight came the handwriting would probably have become illegible. Or perhaps not? Fire, not water, was what he needed. If there had been a fire in that inexpressibly dirty guardroom he would have made use of it at once under the very noses of those wild-looking Croats. But would that have been the proper thing to do in such a hurry?

He had not come to any conclusion before Barbone returned, accompanied by a silver-haired, meek old fellow, with a nut-brown face, bare-footed and bare-armed, and carrying a pair of sculls over his shoulder, whom Barbone pushed in front of the sergeant. The latter took his short pipe out of his mouth, spat on one side, looked at the old man with a fixed savage stare, and finally nodded. At Cosmo he did not look at all, but to Barbone he handed a key with the words, "Bring it back." The *sbirri* closed round Cosmo and Barbone uttered a growl with a gesture towards the door. Why Barbone should require a key to take him out of doors Cosmo could not understand. Unless it were the key of liberty. But it was not likely that the fierce Croat and the gloomy Barbone should have indulged in symbolic actions. The mariner with the sculls on his shoulder followed the group patiently to where, on the very edge of the quay, the Austrian soldier with his musket shouldered paced to and fro across the streak of reddish light from the garrison door. He swung round and stood, very martial, in front of the group, but at the sight of the key exhibited to him by Barbone moved out of the way. The air was calm but chilly. Below the level of the quay there was the clinking of metal and the rattling of small chains, and Cosmo then discovered that the key belonged to a padlock securing the chain to which quite a lot of small rowing boats were moored. The young policeman said from behind into Cosmo's ear, "The signore is always forgetting his cloak," and threw it lightly on Cosmo's shoulders. He explained also that every night all the small boats in the port were collected and secured like this on both sides of the port and the Austrians furnished the sentry to look after them on this side. The object was that there should be no boats moving after ten o'clock, except the galley of the *dogana* and of course the boat of the English man-of-war.

"Come and see me at noon at Cantelucci's inn," whispered Cosmo, to which the other breathed out a "Certainly, Excellency," feelingly before going up the steps.

Cosmo found himself presently sitting in a boat between two *sbirri*. The ancient fellow shoved off and shipped his oars. From the quay, high above, Barbone's voice shouted to him, "The gendarmes will take charge of your boat for the rest of the night." The old boatman's only answer was a deep sigh, and in a very few strokes the quay with the sentry receded into the darkness. One of the *sbirri* remarked in a tone of satisfaction, "Our service will be over after we have given up the signore there." The other said, "I hope the signore will consider we have been kept late on his account." Cosmo, who was contemplating with immense distaste the prospect of being delivered up to the gendarmes, emitted a mirthless laugh, and after a while said in a cold tone: "Why waste your time in pulling to the other side of the harbour? Put me on board the nearest vessel. I'll soon find my way to the quay from one *tartane* to another, and your service would be over at once."

The fellow on his left assumed an astonishing seriousness: "Most of those *tartanes* have a dog on board. We could not expose an illustrious stranger to get bitten by one of these ugly brutes."

But the other had no mind for grave mockery. In a harsh and overbearing tone he ordered the boatman to pull well into the middle of the harbour away from the moored craft.

It was like crossing a lake overshadowed by the hills with the breakwaters prolonging the shore to seaward. The old man raised and dipped his oars slowly, without a sound, and the long trails of starlight trembled on the ripples on each side of the boat. When they had progressed far enough to open the harbour entrance Cosmo detected between the end of the jetties far away—he was glancing casually about—a dark speck about the size of a man's head, which ought not to have been there. The air was perfectly still and the stars thick on the horizon. It struck him at once that it could be nothing than either the English man-of-war's boat or the boat of the *dogana*, since no others were allowed to move at night. His thoughts were, however, so busy with speculating as to what he had better do that he paid no more attention to that remarkable speck. He looked absently at the silver-haired boatman pulling an easy stroke and asked himself: Was it or was it not time to lose his hat overboard? How could he contrive to make it look plausible in this absurd calm? Then he reproached himself for reasoning as if those two low fellows (whose proximity had grown extremely irksome to him) had wits of preternatural sharpness. If he were to snatch it and fling it away they would probably conclude that he was trying to make himself troublesome, or simply mad, or anything in the world rather than guess that he had in his hat something which he wanted to destroy. He undid quietly the clasp of his cloak and rested his hands on his knees. His guardians did not think it necessary now to hold his arms. In fact they did not seem to pay much attention to him. Cosmo asked himself for a moment whether he would island up suddenly and jump into the water. Of course he knew that fully clothed and in his boots they would very soon get hold of him, but the object would have been attained. However, the prospect of being towed behind a boat to the custom-house quay by the collar of his coat and being led into the presence of the gendarmes looking like a drowned rat was so disagreeable that he rejected that plan.

By that time the boat had reached little more than half way across the harbour. The great body of the shipping was merged with the shore. The nearest vessels were a polacca brig and xebec lying at anchor. Both were shadowy, and the last, with her low spars, a mere low smudge on the dim sheen of the water. From time to time the aged boatman emitted a moan. The boat seemed hardly to move. Everything afloat was silent and dark. The crews of the coasters were ashore or asleep; and if there were any dogs on board any of them they too seemed plunged in the same slumber that lay over all things of the earth, and by contrast with which the stars of heaven looked intensely wakeful. In the midst of his perplexities Cosmo enjoyed the feeling of peace that had come to him directly his trouble had begun.

"We will be all night getting across," growled suddenly the man on his left. ". . . I don't know what Barbone was thinking of to get this antiquity out of his bed."

"I told him there was hardly any breath in my old body," declared the boatman's tranquil voice.

Apparently in order to speak he had to cease rowing, for he rested on his oars while he went on in the grave-like silence. "But he raged like a devil; and rather than let him wake up all the neighbours I came out. I may just as well die in the boat as in bed."

Both *sbirri* exclaimed indignantly against Barbone, but neither offered to take the sculls. With a painful groan the old man began to pull again. Cosmo asked: "What's that dark thing between the heads of the jetties?" One of his captors, turning his head to look, said, "That must be the galley. I wish she would come this way. We would ask her for a tow." The other man remarked sarcastically, "No fear, they are all snoozing in her except one perhaps to keep a lookout. It's an easy life. . . . *Voga, vecchio, yoga.*"

Cosmo thought suddenly that if by any chance the man-of-war boat happened to be pulling that way he would hail her without hesitation, and, surely, the officer in charge would not leave him in the hands of those villains without at least listening to his tale. Unluckily their way across the harbour did not take them near the man-of-war. The light at her mizzen peak seemed to Cosmo very far away; so that if it had not burned against the dark background of the land it would have seemed more distant than any star, and not half as brightly vigilant. He took his eyes from it and let them rest idly on the water ahead. The *sbirro* on his right hand emitted an immense yawn. This provided the other to mutter curses on the tediousness of all this affair. Cosmo had been too perplexed to feel bored. Just then as if in antagonism to those offensive manifestations he felt very alert. Moreover, the moment when something would have to be done was approaching, a tension of all his senses accumulating in a sort of all-over impatience. While in that state, staring into the night, he caught sight of the man-of-war's boat.

But was it?—well, it was something dark on the water, and as there was no other boat about . . . It was small—well, far off and probably end on. . . . He had heard no sound of rowing . . . lying on her oars . . . He could see nothing now . . . well, here goes, on the chance.

Without stirring a limb he took a long breath and let out the shout of "Boat ahoy" with all the force of his lungs. The volume of tone astonished himself. It seemed to fill the whole of the harbour so effectually that he felt he needn't shout again and he remained as still as a statue. The effect on his neighbours was that both gave a violent start, which set the boat rolling slightly, and in their bewilderment they bent forward to peer into his face with immense eyes. After a time one of them asked in an awestruck murmur, "What's the matter, signore?" and seized his cloak. The other, Cosmo heard distinctly whisper to himself, "That was a war cry," while he also grabbed the cloak. The clasp being undone, it slipped off Cosmo's shoulders and then they clung to his arms. It struck Cosmo as remarkable that the old boatman, had not ceased his feeble rowing for a moment.

The shout had done Cosmo good. It reestablished his self-respect somehow and it sent the blood moving through his veins as if indeed it had been a war cry. He had shaken their nerves. If they had not remained perfectly motionless holding his arms there would have started a scrimmage in that boat which would certainly have ended in the water. But their grip was feeble. They did nothing, but, bending towards each other in front of Cosmo till their heads almost touched, watched his lips from which such an extraordinary shout had come. Cosmo stared stonily ahead as if unconscious of their existence, and again he had that strange illusion of a dark spot ahead of the boat. He thought, "That's no illusion. What a fool I was. It must be a mooring buoy." A couple of minutes elapsed before he thought again, "That old fellow will be right into it, presently."

He didn't consider it his business to utter a warning because the bump he expected happened almost immediately. He had misjudged the distance. Owing to the slow pace the impact was very slight, slighter even than Cosmo expected against such a heavy body as a mooring buoy would be. It was really more like a feeble hollow sound than a shock. Cosmo, who was prepared for it, was really the one that felt it at once, and the ancient boatman looked sharply over his shoulder. He uttered no sound and did not even attempt to rise from the thwart. He simply, as it seemed to Cosmo, let go the oars. The *sbirri* only became aware of something having happened after the hollow bump was repeated, and Cosmo had become aware that the object on the water was not a buoy but another boat not much bigger than theirs. Then they both exclaimed and in their surprise their grip relaxed. One of them cried in astonishment, "An empty boat." It was indeed a surprising occurrence. With no particular purpose in his mind Cosmo stood up while one of the *sbirri* stood up either to catch hold of the boat or push it away, for the two boats were alongside each other by that time. A strange voice in the dark said very loud: "The man in the hat," and as if by enchantment three figures appeared standing in a row. Cosmo had not even time to feel surprised. The two boats started knocking about considerably, and he felt himself seized by the collar and one arm and dragged away violently from between the two *sbirri* by the power of irresistible arms which as suddenly let him go as if he were an inanimate object, and he fell heavily in the bottom of the second boat almost before his legs were altogether clear of the other. During this violent translation his hat fell off his head without any scheming on his part.

He was not exactly frightened but he was excusably flustered. One is not kidnapped like this without any preliminaries every day. He was painfully aware of being in the way of his new captors. He was kicked in the ribs and his legs were trodden upon. He heard blows being struck against hard substances which he knew were human skulls because of the abortive yells ending in groans. There was a determination and ferocity in this attack combined with the least possible amount of noise. All he could hear were the heavy blows and the hard breathing of the assailants. Then came a sort of helpless splash. "Somebody will get drowned," he thought.

He made haste to pull himself forward from under the feet of the combatants. Luckily for his ribs they were bare, which also added to the quietness of that astonishing development. Once in the bows he sat up, and by that time everything was over. Three shadowy forms were standing in! a row in the boat, motionless, like labourers who had accomplished a notable task. The boat out of which he had been dragged was floating within a yard or two, apparently empty. The whole affair, which could not have lasted more than a minute, seemed to Cosmo to have been absolutely instantaneous. Not a sound came from the shipping along the quays, not even from the brig and the xebec which were the nearest. A sense of final stillness such as follows, for instance, the explosion of a mine and resembles the annihilation of all one's perceptive faculties took possession of Cosmo for a moment. Presently he heard a very earnest but low voice cautioning the silent world: "If you dare make a noise I will come back and kill you." It was perfectly impersonal; it had no direction, no particular destination. Cosmo, who heard the words distinctly, could connect no image of a human being with them. He was roused at last when, dropping his hand on the gunwale, he felt human fingers under it. He snatched his hand away as if burnt and only then looked over. The white hair of the old boatman seemed to rest on the water right against the boat's side. He was holding on silently, even in this position displaying the meek patience of his venerable age—and Cosmo contemplated him in silence. A voice, not at all impersonal this time, said from the stem sheets, "Get out your oars."

"There is a man in the water here," said Cosmo, wondering at his own voice being heard in those fantastic conditions. It produced, however, the desired effect, and almost as soon as he had spoken Cosmo had to help a bearded sailor, who was a complete stranger to him, to haul the old man inside the boat. He was no great weight to get over the gunwale, but they had to handle him as if he had been drowned. He never attempted to help himself. The other men in the boat took an interest in the proceedings.

"Is he dead?" came a subdued inquiry from aft.

"He is very old and feeble," explained Cosmo in an undertone. Somebody swore long but softly, ending with the remark: "Here's a complication."

"That scoundrel Barbone dragged out a dying man," began Cosmo impulsively.

"*Va bene, va bene* . . . Bundle him in and come aft, signore."

Cosmo, obeying this injunction, found himself sitting in the stem sheets by the side of a man whose first act was to put his hand lightly upon his shoulder in a way that conveyed a sort of gentle exultation. The discovery that the man was Attilio was too startling for comment at the first moment. The next it seemed the most natural thing in the world.

"It seems as if nothing could keep us apart," said that extraordinary man in a low voice. He took his hand off Cosmo's shoulder and directed the two rowers—who, Cosmo surmised, were the whisperers of the tower—to pull under the bows of the brig. "We must hide from those custom-house fellows," he said. "I fancy the galley is coming along."

No other word was uttered till one of the men got hold of the brig's cable and the boat came to a rest with her side against the stem of that vessel, when Cosmo, who now could himself hear the faint noise of rowing, asked Attilio in a whisper: "Are they after you?"

"If they are after anything," answered the other coolly, "they are after a very fine voice. What made you give that shout?"

"I had to behave like a frightened mouse before those *sbirri*, on account of those papers you left with me, and I felt that I must assert myself." Cosmo gave this psychological explanation grimly. He changed his tone to add that, fancying he had seen the shape of the English man-of-war's boat, the temptation to hail her had been irresistible.

"Possibly that's what started them. They know nothing of us. Luck was on our side. We slipped in unseen." The sound of rowing meantime had grown loud enough to take away from them all desire for further conversation, for the noise of heavy oars working in their rowlocks has a purposeful relentless character on a still night, and the big twelve-oared galley, pulled with a short quick stroke, seemed to hold an unerring way in its hollow thundering progress. For those in the boat concealed under the bows of the brig the strain of having to listen without being able to see was growing intolerable. Cosmo asked himself anxiously whether he was going to be captured once more before this night of surprises was out, but at the last moment the galley swerved and passed under the stem of the polacca as if bent on taking merely a sweep round the harbour. Everybody in the boat drew a long breath. But almost immediately afterwards the sound of rowing stopped short and everyone in the boat seemed turned again into stone.

At last Attilio breathed into Cosmo's ear, "*Per Dio!* They have found the other boat."

Cosmo was almost ashamed at the swift eagerness of his fearfully whispered inquiry:

"Are the men in her dead?"

"All I know is that if either of them is able to talk we are lost," Attilio whispered back.

"These *sbirri* were going to deliver me to the gendarmes," Cosmo began under his breath, when all at once the noise of the oars burst again on their ears abruptly; but soon all apprehension was at an end, because it became clear that the sound was receding towards the east side of the harbour. In fact the custom-house people who had started to row round because of a vague impression that there had been some shouting in the harbour had to their immense surprise come upon a boat which at first seemed empty but which, they soon discovered, contained two human forms huddled up on the bottom boards, apparently dead, but at any rate insensible if they were still breathing. Attilio's surmise that as the quickest way of dealing with this mystery the custom-house officer had decided to tow the boat at once to the police station on the east side was perfectly right; and also his conviction that now or never was his chance to slip out of that harbour where he and his companions felt themselves in a trap the door of which might snap to at any time. At the best it was a desperate situation, he felt. Cosmo felt it, too, if in a more detached way—like a rather unwilling spectator. Yet his anxiety for the safety of his companions was as great as though he had known them all his life. Though he had in a way lost sight of his personal connection he could not help forming his own view, which he poured into Attilio's ear while the two rowers put all their strength into their work.

Tensely rigid at the tiller, Attilio had listened, keeping his eyes fixed on the gap of dark gleaming water between the black heads of the two breakwaters.

"The signore is right," he assented. "We could not hope to escape from that galley once she caught sight of us. Our only chance is to slip out of the port before she gets back to her station outside the jetties. This affair will be a great puzzle to them. They will lose some time talking it over with the gendarmes. Unless one or another of those *sbirri* comes to himself."

"Yes. Those *sbirri* . . ." murmured Cosmo.

"What would you have? We did our best with the boat-stretchers, I can assure you."

Cosmo had no doubt of that. The sound of crashing blows rained on those wretches' heads had been sickening, but the memory comforted him now. So did the return of the profound stillness after the noise of the galley's oars had died out in the distance. Cosmo took heart till it came upon him suddenly that there never had been a starry sky that gave so much light, no night so amazingly clear, no harbour of such an enormous extent. He felt he must not lose a minute. He jumped up and began to tear off his coat madly. Attilio exclaimed in dismay, "Stay! Don't!" It looked as though his Englishman had made up his mind to swim for it. But Cosmo with a muttered, "I must lend a hand," stepped lightly forward past the rowers, and began to feel under thwarts for a spare oar. Before he found it his hand came in contact with a naked foot. This recalled to him the existence of the ancient boatman. The poor old fellow who had taken no part in the fray had fallen overboard from mere weakness and had had a long soaking in chilly water. He lay curled up in the bows, shivering violently like a dog. For the moment Cosmo was simply vexed at this additional dead weight in the boat. He could think of nothing but of the custom-house galley. He imagined her long, slim, cleaving the glassy water, as if endowed with life, while the clumsy tub in which he sat felt to him a dead thing which had to be tugged along by main force every inch of the way. He set his teeth hard and pulled doggedly as if rowing in a losing race, without turning his head once. Suddenly he became aware of the end of the old Mole gliding past the boat, and that Attilio instead of holding on this way had taken a sweep and was following the outer side of the breakwater towards the shore. Presently, at his word, the oars were taken in, and the boat floated arrested in shallow water amongst the boulders strewn along the base of the Mole. The men panted after their exertions. Not a breath of wind stirred the chilly air. Cosmo returned aft and sat down by Attilio after putting on his coat.

It seemed as though Attilio, while steering with one hand, had managed with the other to go through the pockets of Cosmo's coat, for his first words murmured in an anxious tone were "Signore, where are those papers?"

Cosmo had forgotten all about them. The shock was severe. "The papers," he exclaimed faintly. "In my hat."

"Yes, I put them there. You had it on your head in the boat. I recognized you by it."

"Of course I had it on. Where is it?"

"God knows," said Attilio bitterly. "I was asking you for the papers."

"I only discovered that the packet was in my hat after I put it on," protested Cosmo. "Four were standing over me already."

"Is it possible?" exclaimed Attilio, very low.

"Afterwards I was watched all the time."

While they were exchanging those words in the extremity of their consternation, the man nearest to them went down suddenly on his knees and began to grope under the thwarts industriously. Having heard the word "hat" he had remembered that while battling with the sbirri he had trodden on some round object which had given way under his foot. He assured the signore that it was a thing that could not be helped while he tendered to him apologetically the rim with one hand and the crown with the other. It was crushed flat like an empty bag, but it was seized with avidity and presently Cosmo's feelings were relieved by the discovery that it still contained the parcel of papers. Attilio took possession of it with a low nervous laugh. It was an emotional sound which, coming from that man, gave Cosmo food for wonder during the few moments the silence lasted before Attilio announced in a whisper, "Here she is."

Cosmo, looking seaward, saw on the black and gleaming water, polished like a mirror for the stars, an opaque hummock resembling the head of a rock; and he thought that the race had been won by a very narrow margin. The galley in fact had reached the heads of the jetties a very few minutes only after the boat. On getting back to his station the officer in the galley pulled about fifty yards clear of the end of the old Mole and ordered his men to lay oars in. He had left the solution of the mystery to the police. It was not his concern; and as he knew nothing of the existence of an outside boat, it never occurred to him to investigate along the coast. Attilio's boat lurking close inshore was invisible from seaward. The distance between the two was great enough to cause the considerable clatter which is made when several oars are laid in together at the word of command to reach Cosmo only as a very faint, almost mysterious, sound. It was the last he was to hear for a very long time. He surrendered to the soft and invincible stillness of air and sea and stars enveloping the active desires and the secret fears of men who have the sombre earth for their stage. At every momentary pause in his long and fantastic adventure it returned with its splendid charm and glorious serenity, resembling the power of a great and unfathomable love whose tenderness like a sacred spell lays to rest all the vividities and all the violences of passionate desire.

Dreamily Cosmo had lost control of the trend of his thoughts, as one does on the verge of sleep. He regained it with a slight start and looked up at the round tower looming up, bulky, at the water's edge. He was back again, having completed the cycle of his adventures and not knowing what would happen next. Everybody was silent. The two men at the thwarts had folded their arms and had let their chins sink on their breasts; while Attilio, sitting in the stern sheets, held his head up in an immobility to which his open eyes lent an air of extreme vigilance. The waste of waters seemed to extend from the shores of Italy to the very confines of the universe, with nothing on it but the black spot of the galley which moved no more than the head of a rock. "We can't stay here till daylight," thought Cosmo.

That same thought was in Attilio's mind. The race between his boat and the galley had been very close. It was very probable that had it not been for Cosmo volunteering to pull the third oar it would have resulted in a dead heat, which of course would have meant capture. As it was, Attilio had just escaped being seen by pulling short round the jetty instead of holding on into the open sea. It was a risky thing to do, but then, since he had jeopardized the success of his escape through his desire to get hold of Cosmo again, there was nothing before him but a choice of risks.

Attilio was a native of a tiny white townlet on the eastern shore of the Gulf of Genoa. His people were all small cultivators and fishermen. Their name was Pieschi, from whose blood came the well-known conspirator against the power of the Dorias and in the days of the Republic. Of this fact Attilio had heard only lately (Cantelucci had told him) with a certain satisfaction. In his early youth, spent on the coast of the South American continent, he had heard much talk of a subversive kind and had become familiar with the idea of revolt looked upon as an assertion of manly dignity and the spiritual aim of life. He had come back to his country about six months before and, beholding the aged faces of some of his people in the unchanged surroundings, it seemed to him that it was his own life that had been very long, though he was only about thirty. Being a relation of Cantelucci he found himself very soon in touch with the humbler members of secret societies, survivals of the revolutionary epoch, stirred up by the downfall of the Empire and inspired by grandiose ideas, by the hatred of the Austrian invaders bringing back with them the old tyrannical superstitions of religion and the oppression of privileged classes. Like the polite innkeeper he believed in the absolute equality of all men. He respected all religions but despised the priests who preached submission and perceived nothing extravagant in the formation of an Italian empire (of which he had the first hint from the irritable old cobbler, the uncle of Cecchina) since there was a great man—a great Emperor—to put at its head, very close at hand. The great thing was to keep him safe from the attempts of all these kings and princes now engaged in plotting against his life in Vienna—till the hour of action came. No small task, for the world outside the ranks of the people was full of his enemies.

Attilio, still and silent by Cosmo's side, was not reproaching himself for having gone in the evening to say good-bye to Cecchina. The girl herself had been surprised to see him, for they had said good-bye already in the afternoon. But this love affair was not quite two months old and he could not have been satisfied with a hurried wordless good-bye, snatched behind a half-closed door, with several people drinking at the long table in Cantelucci's kitchen on one side and a crabbed old woman rummaging noisily in a storeroom at the end of the dark passage. Cecchina had, of course, reproached him for coming, but not very much. Neither of them dreamed of there being any danger in it. Then, straight out of her arms, as it were, he had stepped into that ambush! His presence of mind and his agility proved too much for the party of the stupid Barbone. It was only after he had given them the slip in the maze of small garden plots at the back of the houses that he had time, while lying behind a low wall, to think over this unexpected trouble. He knew that the fellows who were after him belonged to the police, because they had called on the soldiers for assistance; but he concluded that he owed this surprise to some jealous admirer of Cecchina. It was easy enough for any base scoundrel to set the police after a man in these troubled times. It may even have been one of Cantelucci's affiliated friends. His suspicions rested on the small employees who took their meals at the inn, and especially on a lanky scribe with a pointed nose like a rat who had the habit of going in and out through the courier's room, only, Attilio believed, in order to make eyes at Cecchina. That the ambush had been laid on the evening fixed for his departure was a mere coincidence.

The real danger of the position was in having the papers on him, but, anxious that his friends at the tower should not give him up, he came out of his hiding-place too soon. The soldiers had gone away, but the *sbirri* were still half-heartedly poking about in dark corners and caught sight of him. Another rush saved him for the moment. The position he felt was growing desperate. He dared not throw away the papers. The discovery of Cosmo sitting amongst the stones was an event so extraordinary in itself that it revolutionized his rational view of life as a whole in the way a miracle might have done. He felt suddenly an awed and confiding love for that marvellous person fate had thrown in his way. The pursuit was close. There was no time to explain. There was no need.

But directly he found himself safe in the boat Attilio began to regret having parted with the papers. It was not much use proceeding on his mission without these documents entrusted to him by Cantelucci, acting on behalf of superior powers.

He asked himself what could have happened to Cosmo? Did the fellows arrest him on suspicion? That was not very likely, and at worst it would not mean more than a short detention. They would not dare to search him, surely. But even if they found the packet Cosmo would declare it his own property and object to its being opened. He had a complete confidence in Cosmo's loyalty and, what was more, in that young Englishman's power to have his own way. He had the manner for that and the face for that. The face and bearing of a man with whom it was lucky to be associated in anything.

The galley being just then at the other end of her beat, Attilio saw his way clear to slip into the harbour. The state of perfect quietness over the whole extent of the harbour encouraged his native audacity. He began by pulling to the east side where the gendarmerie office was near the quay. Everything was quiet there. He made his men lay their oars amongst the shadows of the anchored shipping and waited. Sleep, breathless sleep, reigned on shore and afloat. Attilio began to think that Cosmo could not have been discovered. If so, then he must be nearing Cantelucci's inn by this time. He resolved then to board one of the empty coasters moored to the quay, wait for the morning there, and then go himself to the inn, where he could remain concealed till another departure could be arranged. He told his men to pull gently to the darkest part of the quay. And then he heard Cosmo's mighty shout. He was nearly as confounded by it as the *sbirri* in the boat. That voice bursting out on the profound stillness seemed loud enough to wake up every sleeper in the town, to bring the stones rolling down the hillsides. And almost at once he thought, "What luck!" The luck of the Englishman's amazing impudence; for what other man would have thought of doing that thing? He told his rowers to lay their oars in quietly and get hold of the boat-stretchers. The extremely, feeble pulling of the old boatman gave the time for these preparations. He whispered his instructions: "We've got to get a foreign signore out of that boat. The others in her will be *sbirri*. Hit them hard." Just before the boats came into contact he recognized Cosmo's form standing up. It was then that he pronounced the words, "the man in the hat," which were heard by Cosmo. Attilio ascribed it all to luck that attended those who had anything to do with that Englishman. Even the very escape unseen from the harbour he ascribed, not to Cosmo's extra oar, but to Cosmo's peculiar personality.

Without departing from his immobility he broke silence by a "signore," pronounced in a distinct but restrained voice. Cosmo was glad to learn the story before the moment came for them to part. But the theory of luck which Attilio tacked on to the facts did not seem to him convincing. He remarked that if Attilio had not come for him at all he would have been far on the way in his mysterious affairs, whereas now he was only in another trap.

For all answer the other murmured, "*Si*, but I wonder if it would have been the same. Signore, isn't it strange that we should have been drawn together from the first moment you put foot in Genoa?"

"It is," said Cosmo, with an emphasis that encouraged the other to continue, but with a less assured voice.

"Some people of old believed that stars have something to do with meetings and partings by their disposition and that some if not all men have each a star allotted to them."

"Perhaps," said Cosmo in the same subdued voice. "But I believe there is a man greater than you or I who believes he has a star of his own."

"Napoleon, perhaps."

"So I have heard," said Cosmo, and thought, "Here he is, whenever two men meet he is a third, one can't get rid of him."

"I wonder where it is," said Attilio, as if to himself, looking up at the sky. "Or yours, or mine," he added in a still lower tone. "They must be pretty close together."

Cosmo humoured the superstitious strain absently, for he felt a secret sympathy for that man. "Yes, it looks as if yours and mine had been fated to draw together."

"No, I mean all three together."

"Do you? Then you must know more than I do. Though indeed as a matter of fact he is not very far from us where we sit. But don't you think, my friend, that there are men and women, too, whose stars mark them for loneliness no man can approach?"

"You mean because they are great."

"Because they are incomparable," said Cosmo after a short pause, in which Attilio seemed to ponder.

"I like that what you said," Attilio was heard at last. "Their stars may be lonely. Look how still they are. But men are more like ships that come suddenly upon each other without a warning. And yet they, too, are guided by the stars. I can't get over the wonder of our meeting to-night."

"If you hadn't been so long in saying good-bye we wouldn't have met," said Cosmo, looking at the two men dozing on the thwarts, the whisperers of the tower. They were not at all like what he had imagined them to be.

Attilio gazed at his Englishman for a time closely. He seemed to see a smile on Cosmo's lips. Wonder at his omniscience prevented him from making a reply. He preferred not to ask, and yet he was incapable of forming a guess, for there are certain kinds of obviousness that escape speculation.

"You may be right," he said. "It's the first time in my life that I found it hard to say good-bye. I begin to believe," he went on murmuring, "that there are people it would be better for one not to know. There are women . . ."

"Yes," said Cosmo, very low and as if unconscious of what he was saying. "I have seen your faces very close together."

The other made a slight movement away from Cosmo and then bent towards him. "You have seen," he said slowly and stopped short. He was thinking of something that had happened only two hours before. "Oh well," he said with composure, "you know everything, you see everything that happens. Do you know what will happen to us two?"

"It's very likely that when we part we will never see each other again," Cosmo said, resting his elbows on his knees and taking his head between his hands. He did not look like a man preparing to go ashore.

There were no material difficulties absolutely to prevent him from landing. The foot of the tower with the narrow strip of ground which a boat could approach was not sixty yards off, and all this was in the shadow of its own reflection, the high side of the breakwater, the bulk of the tower, making the glassy water dark in that corner of the shore. And besides, the water in which the boat floated was so shallow that Cosmo could have got to land by wading from where the boat lay without wetting himself much above the knees, should Attilio refuse to come out from under the shelter of the rock. But probably Attilio would not have objected. The difficulty was not there.

Attilio must have been thinking on the same subject, as became evident when he asked Cosmo whether those *sbirri* knew where he lived. After some reflection Cosmo said that he was quite certain they knew nothing about it. The *sbirri* had put no questions to him. They had not, he said, displayed any particular curiosity about what he was. "But why do you ask?"

"Don't you know?" said Attilio, with only half-affected surprise. "There might have been a dozen of them waiting for you in the neighbourhood on the chance of your returning, and you have no other place to go to."

"No, I haven't," said Cosmo in a tone as though he regretted that circumstance. He thought, however, that there might have been some of them out between the port and the town, and he knew only one way and that not very well, he added.

As a matter of fact that danger was altogether imaginary, because Barbone, who certainly was in the pay of the police for work of that sort, was not imaginative enough to do things without orders, and after sending his prisoner off left the rest of the gendarmes and went home to bed, while his young acolyte went about his own affairs. The other two *sbirri* were being medically attended to, one of them especially being very nearly half killed by an unlucky blow on the temple. All the other *sbirro* could say in a feeble voice was that there were four in the boat, that they were attacked by an inexplicable murderous gang, and that he imagined that the other two, the prisoner and the boatman, were now dead and very likely at the bottom of the harbour. The brigadier of the gendarmerie could not get any more out of him, and, knowing absolutely nothing of the affair, thought it would be time to make his report to the superior authorities in the morning. All he did was to go round to the places where the boats were chained, which were under his particular charge, and count the boats. Not one was wanting. His responsibility was not engaged.

Thus there was nothing between Cosmo and Cantelucci's inn except his own distaste. There was a strange tameness in that proceeding, a lack of finality, something almost degrading. He imagined himself slinking like a criminal at the back of the beastly guardhouse, starting at shadows, creeping under the colonnade, getting lost in those dreadful deep lanes between palaces, with the constant dread of having suddenly the paws of those vile fellows laid on him and being dragged to some police post with an absurd tale on his lips and without a hat on his head and what for? Simply to get back to that abominable bedroom. However, he would have to go through it.

"Pity you don't know the town," Attilio's cautious voice was heard again, "or else I could tell you of a place where you could spend the remainder of the night and send word to your servant to-morrow. But you could not find it by yourself. And that's a pity. I assure Your Excellency that she is a real good woman. To have a secret place is not such a bad thing. One never knows what one may need, and she is a creature to be trusted. She has an Italian heart and she is a *giardiniera* too. What more could I tell you?"

Cosmo thought to himself vaguely that the girl he had seen in Cantelucci's kitchen did not look like a woman gardener, though of course if Attilio had a love affair it would be naturally amongst people of that sort. But it occurred to him that perhaps it was some other woman Attilio was talking about. He made no movement. Attilio's murmurs took on a tone of resignation. "Your luck, signore, will depart with you, and perhaps ours will follow after." Cosmo protested against that unreasonable assumption, which was of course an absurdity but nevertheless touched him in one of those sensitive spots which are like a *défaut d'armure* in the battle-harness of various conceits which one wears against one's kind. He considered luck less in a sudden overwhelming conviction of it, in the manner of a man who had crossed the path of a radiating influence, or who had awakened a sleeping and destructive power which would now pursue him to the end of his life. He was young, farouche, mistrustful and austere, not like a stoic, but in the more human way like a man who has been born fastidious. In a sense altogether unworldly. Attilio emitted an audible sigh.

"You won't call it your luck," he pursued. "Well, let us leave it without a name. It is something in you. Your carelessness in following your fantasy, signore, as when you forced your presence on me only two days ago," he insisted, as if carelessness and fantasy were the compelling instruments of success. His voice was at its lowest as he added: "Your genius makes you true to your will."

No human being could have been insensible to such words uttered unexpectedly in a tone of secret earnestness. But Cosmo's inward response was a feeling of profound despondency. He was crushed by their appalling unfitness. For the last twenty-four hours he had been asking himself whether he had a will of his own, and it had seemed to him that he had lost the notion of the real nature of courage. At that very moment while listening to the mysteriously low pitch of Attilio's voice the thought flashed through his mind that there was something within him that made of him a predestined victim of remorse.

"You can't possibly know anything about me, Attilio," he said, "and whatever you like to imagine about me, you will have to put me on shore presently. I can't stay here till the morning, and neither can you," he added. "What are you thinking of doing? What can you do?"

"Is it possible that it is of any interest to the signore? Only the other evening I could not induce you to leave me to myself, and now you are impatient to leave me to my fate. What can I do? I can always take a desperate chance," he paused, and added through his clenched teeth, "and when I think what little I need to make it almost safe . . ." The piously uttered exclamation, "*Ah, Dio!*" was accompanied by a shake of a clenched fist apparently addressed to the universe, but made as it were discreetly, in keeping with the low and forcible tones.

"And what is that?" asked Cosmo, raising his head.

"Two pairs of stout arms, nothing more. With four oars and this boat and using a little judgment in getting away I would defy that fellow there."

He jerked his head towards the galley which in this tideless sea had not shifted her position a yard. "Yes," he went on, "I could even hope to remain unseen on account of a quick dash."

And he explained to Cosmo further that in an hour or so a little nearer the break of day, when men get heavy and sleepy, the watchfulness of those custom-house people would be relaxed and give him a better chance. But if he was seen then he could still hope to out-row them, though he would have preferred it the other way because with a boat making for the open sea they would very soon guess that there must be some vessel waiting for her, and by telling the tale on shore, that government xebec lying in the harbour would soon be out in chase. She was fast, and in twenty-four hours she would soon manage to overhaul all the craft she would sight between this and the place he was going to.

"And where is that?" asked Cosmo, letting his head rest on his hands again.

"In the direction of Livorno," said the other, and checked himself. "But perhaps I had better not tell you, for should you happen to be interrogated by all those magistrates, or perhaps by the Austrians, you would of course want to speak the truth as becomes a gentleman—a *nobilissimo signore*—unless you manage to forget what I have already told you or perchance elect to come with us."

"Come with you," repeated Cosmo, before something peculiar in the tone made him sit up and face Attilio. "I believe you are capable of carrying me off."

"*Dio ne voglio*," was Attilio's answer, "God forbid. The noise you would make would bring no end of trouble. But for that perhaps it would have been better for me," he added reflectively. "Whereas I have made up my mind that there should be nothing but good from our association. Yet, signore, you very nearly went away with us without any question at all, for our head pointed to seaward and you could have had no idea that I was coming in here. Confess, signore, you didn't think of return then. I had only to hold the tiller straight another five minutes and I would have had you in my power."

"You were afraid of the *dogana* galley, my friend," said Cosmo as if arguing a point.

"Signore, this minute," said Attilio with the utmost seriousness. "Wake up there," he said in a raised undertone to his two men. "Take an oar, Pietro, and pull the boat to the foot of the tower."

"There is also that old boatman," said Cosmo.

"Hold," said Attilio. "Him I will not land. They will be at his place in the morning, and then he tells his tale . . . unless he is dead. See forward there."

A very subdued murmur arose in the bows and Attilio muttered, "Pietro would not talk to a dead man."

"He is extremely feeble," said Cosmo.

It appeared on Attilio's enquiry that this encumbrance as he called him was just strong enough to be helped over the thwarts. Presently, sustained under the elbows, he joined Cosmo in the stem sheets, where they made him sit between them. He let his big hands lie in his lap. From time to time he shivered patiently.

"That wretch Barbone knows no pity," observed Cosmo.

"I suppose he was the nearest he could get. What tyranny! The helpless are at the mercy of those fellows. He saved himself the trouble of going three doors farther."

They both looked at the ancient frame that age had not shrivelled.

"A fine man once," said Attilio in a low voice. "Can you hear me, *vecchio?*"

"*Si*, and see you too, but I don't know your voice," was the answer in a voice stronger than either of them expected, but betraying no sort of interest.

"They will certainly throw him into prison." And to Cosmo's indignant exclamation Attilio pointed out that the old man would be the only person they would be able to get hold of and he would have to pay for all the rest.

Cosmo expressed the opinion that he would not stay there long.

"Better for him to die under the open sky than in prison," murmured Attilio in a gloomy voice. "Listen, old man, could you keep the boat straight at a star if I were to point you one?"

"I was at home in a boat before I could speak plainly," was the answer, while the boatman raised his arm and let it rest on the tiller as if to prove that he had strength enough for that at least.

"I have my boat's crew, signore. Let him do something for all Italy if it is with his last breath, that old Genoese. And now if you were only to take that bow oar you have been using so well only a few moments ago, I will pull stroke and we will make this boat fly."

Cosmo felt the subdued vibration of this appeal without having paid any attention to the words. They required no answer. Attilio pressed him as though he had been arguing against objections. Surely he was no friend of tyranny or of Austrian oppressors and he wouldn't refuse to serve a man whom some hidden power had thrown in his way. He, Attilio, had not sought him. He would have been content never to have seen him. He surely had nothing that could call him back on shore this very night, since he had not been more than three days in Genoa. No time for him to have affairs. The words poured out of his lips into Cosmo's ear while the white-headed boatman sat still above the torrent of whispered speech, appearing to listen like a venerable judge. What could stand in the way of him lending his luck and the strength of his arm? Surely it couldn't be love, since he was travelling alone.

"Enough," said Cosmo, as if the word had been extorted from him by pain, but Attilio felt that his cause had been gained, though he hastened to apologize for the impropriety of the argument, and assure the milord Inglese that nothing would be easier than to put him ashore in the course of the next day.

"What do you think. Excellency, there is my own native village not very far from Genoa on the Riviera di Ponente, and you will be amongst friends to carry out such orders as you may give, or pass you from one to another back to Genoa as fast as mules can climb or horses trot. And it would be the same from any point in Italy. They would get you into Genoa in disguise, or without disguise, and into the very home of Cantelucci, so that you could appear there without a soul knowing how you entered or how you came back."

Cosmo, feeling a sudden relief, wondered that he should have found it in the mere resolution to go off secretly with only the clothes he stood up in, absolutely without money or anything of value on him, not even a watch, and without a hat, at the mere bidding of a man bound on some secret work, God knows where and for what object, and who had volunteered to him no statement except that he had cousins in every spot in Italy and a love affair with an *ortolana*. The enormous absurdity of it made him impatient to be doing, and upon his expressed desire to make a start Attilio, with the words, "You command here, signore," told his men it was time to be moving.

In less than half an hour the boat, with all her crew crouching at the bottom and using the oars for poling in the shallow water along the coast with infinite precaution to avoid knocks and bangs as though the boat, the oars, and everything in her were made of glass, had been moved far enough from the tower to have her nose put to the open sea. After the first few strokes Cosmo felt himself draw back again to the receding shore. But it was too late. He seemed to feel profoundly that he was not—perhaps no man was—a free agent. He felt a sort of fear, a faltering of all his limbs, as he swung back to his oar. Then his eyes caught the galley, indeed everybody's eyes in the boat were turned that way except the eyes of the ancient steersman, the white-headed figure in an unexpectedly erect attitude who, with hardly any breath left in his body and a mere helpless victim of other men's will, had a strange appearance of the man in command.

In less than ten minutes the galley became invisible, and even the long shadows of the jetties had sunk to the level of the sea. There was a moment when one of the men observed without excitement, "She's after us," but this remark provoked no answer and turned out to be mistaken, and for an hour longer Attilio, pulling stroke, watched the faint phosphorescent wake, the evanescent fire under the black smoothness of the sea, elusive like the tail of a comet amongst the dim reflections of the stars. Its straightness was the only proof of the silent helmsman with his arm resting along the tiller being still alive. Then he began to look about him, and presently, laying in his oar, relieved the old man at the tiller. He had to take his arm off it. The other never said a word.

The boat moved slowly now. The problem was to discover the awaiting felucca without lights and with her sails lowered. Several times Attilio stood up to have a look without being able to make out anything. He was growing uneasy. He spoke to Cosmo.

"I hope we haven't passed her by. If we once get her between us and the land it will be hopeless to catch sight of her till the day breaks. Better rest on your oars."

He remained standing himself. His eyes roamed to and fro patiently and suddenly he emitted a short laugh.

"Why, there she is."

He steered, still standing, while the others pulled gently. The old man, who had not emitted a sound, had slipped off the seat on to the stem sheets. Attilio said quietly, "Take your oars in," and suddenly Cosmo felt the boat bump against the low side of the felucca, which he had never tinned his head to see. No had or even murmur came from her. She had no lights. Attilio's voice said, "You first, signore," and Cosmo, looking up, saw three motionless heads above the bulwarks. No word was spoken to him. He was not even looked at by those silent and shadowy men. The first sound he heard were the words, "Take care," pronounced by Attilio in connection with getting the old boatman on board. Cosmo, standing aside, saw a group carry him over to the other side of the deck. While the sails were being hoisted he sat on the hatch and came to the very verge of believing himself invisible till suddenly Attilio stood by his side.

"Like this we will catch the very first breath of day-break, and may a breeze follow it to take us out of sight of that town defiled by the Austrians and soon to be the prey of the nobles and the priests." He paused. "So at least Cantelucci says. There are bed places below, if you want to take some rest, signore."

"I am not sleepy," said Cosmo. If no longer invisible, he could still feel disembodied, as it were. He was neither sleepy nor tired, nor hungry, nor even curious, as if altogether freed from the weaknesses of the body, and not indifferent but without apprehensions or speculations of any sort to disturb his composure as if of a fully informed wisdom. He did not seem to himself to weigh more than a feather. He was suffering the reaction of the upheaval of all his feelings and the endless contest of his thoughts and that sort of mental agony which had taken possession of him while he was descending the great staircase of the Palazzo under the eye of the Count of Montevesso. It was as though one of those fevers in which the victim watches his own delirium had left him irresponsible, like a sick man in his bed. Attilio went on:

"Cantelucci's an experienced conspirator. He thinks that the force of the people is such that it would be like an uprising of the ground itself. May be, but where is the man that would know how to use it?"

Cosmo let it go by like a problem that could await solution or as a matter of mere vain words. The night air did not stir, and Attilio changed his tone.

"They had their lines out ever since the calm began. We will have fish to eat in the morning. You will have to be one of ourselves for a time and observe the customs of the common people."

"Tell me, Attilio," Cosmo questioned, not widely but in a quiet, almost confidential tone, and laying his hand for the first time on the shoulder of that man only a little older than himself. "Tell me, what am I doing here?"

Attilio, the wanderer of the seas along the southern shores of the earth and the pupil of the hermit of the plains that lie under the constellation of the southern sky, smiled in the dark, a faint friendly gleam of white teeth in an over-shadowed face. But all the answer he made was:

"Who would dare say now that our stars have not come together? Come to sit at the stem, signore. I can find a rug to throw over a coil of rope for a seat. I am now the padrone of that felucca, but of course barring her appointed work you are entirely the master of her."

These words were said with a marked accent of politeness such as one uses for a courtesy formula. But he stopped for a moment on his way aft to point his finger on the deck.

"We have thrown a bit of canvas over him. Yes, that is the old man whose last bit of work was to steer a boat, and strange to think perhaps it had been done for Italy."

"Where is his star now?" said Cosmo, after looking down in silence for a time.

"Signore, it should be out," said Attilio with studied intonation. "But who will miss it out of the sky?"